MARINE
TERRAN SCOUT FLEET
-BOOK ONE-

©2018
Joshua Dalzelle

First Edition

This is a work of fiction. Any similarities to real persons, events, or places are purely coincidental; any references to actual places, people, or brands are fictitious. All rights reserved.

"New breed? Old breed? There's not a damn bit of difference so long as it's the Marine breed."

—General Chesty Puller, USMC

PROLOGUE

I hadn't even been born yet, the first time they came...the aliens. Even so, my family had been tied up in this shit from the very beginning. It's not something we talked about. In fact, most of my early years were spent trying to hide who we really were, hiding in plain sight under assumed aliases while every three-lettered bureau in the government looked for us.

Perhaps *aliens* is too nonspecific a term given how many species we now know about. Also, the term is now considered xenophobic, or at least that's what we're told in school. So much has changed so fast that the whole world seems to be playing catch-up. All I know is that, a year or so before I was born, a small armada of spaceships arrived over Earth and began making bizarre demands, threatening to destroy our world unless we handed over a single man. Like I mentioned, I wasn't alive yet, but those who were still talk about the whole thing in hushed whispers despite the fact that interstellar spaceflight and even aliens living on Earth is becoming semi-routine. It was easily the most traumatic thing anybody had lived through in generations, at least from a psychological standpoint.

That episode ended when yet *another* spaceship came to our rescue, but that's about the extent of what's known to the public.

There is a lot of speculation on the Internet regarding the strange ship that arrived, far smaller than the invasion ships. Some think it was a top-secret American craft, others think it was stolen by the Americans and that's why the first ships showed up demanding we turn over someone named Jason Burke. It was all very strange, and the governments that were involved are still being tight-lipped about it. The incident soon faded into legend, and from that disaster, humans were eventually able to reverse engineer the wreckage and begin launching their own starships into space. Even then, we weren't ready for the second time they came.

In an incident eerily similar to the first, an alien fleet arrived and held Earth hostage until someone swooped in to our rescue. This time it was a whole fleet belonging to a group who called themselves the Cridal Cooperative. They were able to chase the invaders—a species called the Ull—back out of the Solar System before they could do too much damage. As before, rumors swirled in the alternative media about high-level conspiracies and human collaborators, but nothing was ever substantiated by what I would consider a credible source. After kicking the Ull's ass off our planet the Cridal—who are actually a conglomerate made up of different species—stayed and began helping humanity not only reach for the stars but fix the mess we'd managed to make of our own planet. I was around fourteen years old at this time, so I remember it well.

So, who am I? Nobody special.

My name is Jacob Brown. I was born in Colorado and raised by my grandparents in a small cabin in the Rocky Mountains. My mother died in a car accident when I was very young. My father? Who knows where he is... I only met *that* asshole one time and that was enough. All I know is that he abandoned my mom before I was even born to go pursue his own selfish interests. My grandparents don't like me talking about him like that and say I'm being unfair, so I've made concessions and only talk about him like that when they're not around...if I bother to talk about him at all.

I love my grandparents, but I hated living in such a tiny town with nothing to do and nobody to do it with. As soon as I was old enough, I drove myself to the recruitment station in Colorado Springs and enlisted in the United Earth Armed Services (UEAS), specifically the Navy. I figured as long as I'm leaving Colorado, I might as well leave Earth, too, and see just how far I could go. What surprised me was that when I took the requisite battery of tests, I was approached by someone in a United Earth Navy uniform and asked if I'd like to attend the Academy on Terranovus, Earth's first—and so far, only—colony world.

Would I?!

In as long as it took me to call my grandparents and tell them I was sorry and wasn't coming back home, I was whisked away in a shuttle up to the Aurora Orbital Platform to begin medical testing and processing before being loaded up on a starship bound for Terranovus.

In hindsight, even someone as young and naïve as I'd been should have questioned how a slot at the Academy was just given out to some random guy when people all over the planet were cashing in major political favors and *still* weren't able to get their kids in. It's this lack of introspection that would come back to bite me in the ass but, at the time, I was convinced I was going to be an officer on a capital warship within the United Earth Navy. I wasn't at all concerned with the details.

Granddad told me that my father was a rash man who seldom looked at the consequences of something before acting. Maybe we're more alike than I wanted to admit.

1

"Brown! Move your fucking ass!"

"Yes, sir!"

Jacob Brown huffed and grunted as he scrambled up the hill. It was their second week in the field since being dropped off in the middle of nowhere and the platoon was being whittled down by the enemy a little each day as they pressed towards the objective. Platoon Leader Coulier had picked Jacob and two others to scout ahead and try to get an idea where the enemy might hit them next.

Coulier had been full of swagger and bombast at the beginning of the mission, dead certain that under his leadership 3rd Platoon would meet their objectives quickly and decisively. That was twelve days ago. Now the beleaguered platoon leader had lost a quarter of his people while falling further and further behind schedule. The self-doubt was as plain on his face as his crooked nose, and as his confidence faltered, dissention reared its ugly head. The phrase 'nature abhors a vacuum' is never so apparent as when it's applied to a military unit whose leader has failed to lead. Every failure emboldened the squad leaders, and it was clear to Jacob that Coulier was now on borrowed time. They were going to frag the poor bastard, he could feel it.

Knowing that the two remaining squad leaders were probably going to kill Coulier and assume leadership created quite the quandary for Jacob, doubly so now that he'd been handpicked for this special assignment. When he did the cold calculus, he figured there were really only two options available to him if he wanted to survive the coming coup: alert his platoon leader of the pending attack and help squelch the little rebellion before it started, or he could take Coulier out himself. Given his proximity to Coulier, sitting things out as a bystander wouldn't work. The others would be organizing now, with plans to take out the entire recon team as it returned.

"What do you think we should do?" Coulier asked him once he'd gotten up the hill and lay down beside him.

"You're the one calling the shots here," Jacob countered. "You tell us what to do."

"I-I'm just not sure." Coulier looked down into the valley below, the indecision and fear etched on his features. Jacob looked away in disgust.

"You'd better figure it out soon, sir," he said and pointed down to where a group of red lights could be seen bobbing among the trees. "It looks like they're organizing for another assault tonight."

"We need to get back and warn—"

"I don't think that's wise," Jacob said, his mouth going before his brain could stop it.

"Why?" Coulier asked suspiciously. "Marcos and Guerra?"

"Yeah," Jacob said quietly.

"When?"

"Probably tonight."

"You're not in on it?"

"Would I be telling you if I was?" Jacob silently cursed his carelessness. With one slip of the tongue he'd positioned himself as standing with Coulier. He consoled himself with the fact that he was on the right side of the UCMJ—the Uniform Code of Military Justice—in the matter as it was quite clear on the subject of mutiny. The charter had been adapted from the American military apparatus and modified for use in the United Earth Armed Services, but the basics like respecting the chain of command were still there. Jacob hadn't actually read through all the articles, but he was almost certain there were no provisions for offing your commanding officer when he proved to be an incompetent fool.

"So, I just let these assholes hit my platoon again tonight just to save my own skin?" Coulier asked, a bit of steel creeping back into his voice.

"No, sir," Jacob said. "But I think we might be able to kill two birds with one stone. Judging by the lights down there, it looks like they're sending a sizable force, so we have an advantage right now."

"A rear attack with four people?" Coulier asked. "You're good, Brown, but you're not *that* good."

"You're not tracking with me, sir," Jacob said. "They look like they're bringing most of their troops on this assault. Send Jenkins back to warn the platoon to be ready and then you, me, and Reedy press ahead to where we think their forward base is. It can't be very well guarded right now." A slow grin spread across Coulier's features as he caught on to what Jacob was suggesting.

"If the platoon could hold them off again tonight *and* we achieve our objective—"

"We'd snatch victory from the jaws of defeat," Jacob finished. "It won't be easy, but it's doable."

"You swear you had nothing to do with what Marcos and Guerra were planning?"

"Jesus Christ, Coulier...we need to focus on what we're about to do," Jacob said in exasperation. "Yes, I'd caught wind that they were planning on assuming leadership of the platoon during this deployment, but I had nothing to do with it. They never even approached me."

"But if they had?" Coulier pressed.

"Don't ask questions you don't want the answers to," Jacob said pointedly. "This mission is out in the weeds right now, but if you press ahead tonight, and we're successful, then I'll stand as a witness for you at their tribunal when we get back to base."

"Fair enough," Coulier said. "I'll go back down to brief the others and get Jenkins moving. Your eyesight's better than mine, so you stay here and observe the enemy's movements until I come retrieve you."

"Yes, sir."

Jacob held his position as Coulier shimmied back down off the outcropping. This far north the mountains were breathtakingly beautiful and, for just a moment, he felt a twinge of homesickness for the Rocky Mountains. He stared down at the narrow valley below, watching the enemy troops bumble their way through the darkness. They were so overconfident after the last handful of victories they weren't even trying to be quiet, laughing and joking as they crashed along. After a few more minutes, the sloppy column came to a halt, and Jacob's keen ears could discern the sounds of ration packs being torn open, probably the ones they'd stolen from his platoon two nights ago.

When he checked the mission computer on his wrist for the local time, he saw it was a bit early for a midnight raid, so the enemy commander had likely called a halt well away from their camp for his people to eat and let Jacob's platoon settle in for the night. With eyes that saw better in the dark than those of his peers, Jacob watched as the enemy formation began to relax and become even more careless, if that was even possible.

"Hmm...interesting," he muttered to himself. He looked down the path and didn't see anybody coming back up to relieve him, and he couldn't very well go all the way back to camp to report what he was seeing without risking the enemy moving on. There were some other possibilities, however, that would end this godforsaken mission and get them back to base sooner where there were hot showers, warm meals, and soft bunks.

While Coulier was back down the hill fretting about his own people getting ready to dispose of him, the enemy commander was making increasingly bold moves to eliminate all of them before they could reach the objective. Coulier's platoon was a numerically superior force, but the more agile enemy was quickly evening the odds with their nightly raids. Jacob looked down and counted heads again and realized they must have only left three people guarding their base of operations. Would they ever get an opportunity like this again?

"Screw it," he said, his decision made. He stripped off most of his gear save for his weapons, ammo, and a half-full canteen of water, leaving the rest in an orderly pile and drawing an arrow in the dirt pointing towards the suspected location of the enemy base. Coulier's oblivious ass would probably miss the arrow, but all of Jacob's gear left neatly behind would tell him that his scout hadn't been captured or killed.

Satisfied with his preparations, Jacob stepped off the edge of the outcropping and dropped thirty feet to a ledge below. He hit the rock surface as softly as he could, absorbing the shock with his legs and not uttering a sound. While he froze to see if he'd been detected, he was already scouting out where his next jump would be to. From up top, he'd only been able to see this particular ledge but assumed there would be others. If not, he could make the jump all the way to the ground and not be hurt, but it would kick up a hell of a racket.

Luck was on his side, and he was able to make two shorter hops down before his boots hit the thick carpet of needles that covered the ground. Jacob knelt and held absolutely still where he had landed, barely breathing as he listened for any sign his descent had been detected. Nothing. The troops to the north of him in the trees were still chattering away like they hadn't a care in the world. Their overconfidence and cavalier attitude rankled him. It was one thing to have their ass kicked so thoroughly over the last three days, but it was another for the enemy to show no respect or even a twinge of fear before another attack.

For a moment, he considered revising his plan and attacking the disorganized cluster from the rear. He figured he could take out at least half a dozen, probably more, before they could mount any sort of defense. By that time, he could slip back off into the woods. The only thing that held him in check was knowing that his own forces further up the valley were likely no better prepared. If his strike prompted them to attack early, his whole platoon would probably be wiped out.

"Fuck it," he grunted, moving off to the south towards the enemy encampment. He had a mission, and he couldn't afford to get bogged down indulging himself because of petty insults. Once he felt he was safely out of earshot, he broke into a run. With his keen vision, he flew through the woods, his feet seeming to barely touch the ground as he leapt over and dodged around obstacles. Now alone, he tossed off his normal restraint and pushed himself to his full speed. It was reckless, but he wanted to reach his objective while the enemy was unprepared.

"Halt! Who goes—" That was all the sentry could get out of his mouth before Jacob slammed into him, driving him to the ground and cracking three of his ribs from the impact.

"Sorry! I didn't see you there."

"Ungh! Screw you, Brown!"

"Look at the bright side," Jacob said as he stood up and collected the sentry's weapons. "Once we're out of— What the hell?" A bright floodlight illuminated the section of forest they were in.

"End exercise! End Exercise! End exercise!" an omnipresent voice boomed from the sky. "All cadets will secure their weapons and move to the extraction points indicated *immediately!*" The light went out, and Jacob could see it had been from a recon drone. *Shit! Had it seen him running to the enemy base?*

"I guess this month's pointless torture session has come to an early ending," Cadet Bishop said, rolling to his hands and knees and holding his sides. "I fucking owe you for this, Brown."

"I said I was sorry." Jacob shrugged, barely listening. His mission computer lit up with a new bearing and distance for his extraction point. He looked down at Bishop's wrist and saw that it was the same. Great. A long ride back to base with the enemy.

"Whatever. Help me up," Bishop grumbled. "And after that, help me to the extraction point." Jacob wordlessly reached down and helped the injured man to his feet so they could begin the long walk back to the Jumper.

2

"What the hell is going on?"

"No idea, but it doesn't look good," Jacob said as he helped Bishop down out of the Jumper, the ubiquitous troop carrier used by the UEAS. Across the active ramp, there were seven military police and a gaggle of officers in dress blacks surrounding the ramp of another Jumper that had already touched down. The MPs were armed, of course, but didn't have their weapons trained on anyone and seemed relaxed.

"It was that fuck up, Coulier," someone said from behind them. "Some shit went down last night and now a bunch of idiots will be explaining themselves at captain's mast." Jacob turned and saw it was Cadet Barya. The lanky, quiet Ugandan seemed to have a knack for getting information before everyone else and was more often right than not.

"Shit," Jacob muttered. "It was just a damn exercise. We're two months from graduating and these dumbasses couldn't just go through the motions?"

"You know what went down?" Bishop asked.

"I have a good idea," Jacob said. "Come on, let's get as far away from this bullshit as we can."

Jacob checked in his gear, including the now-deactivated Mk.9 training carbine that fired non-lethal marker rounds, his tactical harness that recorded the hits, and made it back to the barracks just in time to get cleaned up for final formation. While standing at parade rest, he largely ignored the instructor droning on from an elevated platform and tried to locate Cadet Coulier. He couldn't be sure the Jumper the MPs had been boarding had been the one the beleaguered platoon leader had been on, but Coulier's absence was conspicuous.

" ... and that means *all* weekend passes have been suspended."

"Wait, what?!" Jacob hissed. "What did he say about—"

"Shut up, Brown!"

He began listening in earnest, trying to pick up something to clue him in as to why the weekend right after a lengthy field training exercise had been canceled. Could someone have screwed up so badly that the admiral wanted them *all* punished?

"Seriously, what was he talking about?" Jacob asked once they'd been dismissed. He got a few unfriendly looks but was largely ignored. "What the hell?"

"I heard it was your platoon that screwed up and got us locked down, Dipshit," a voice said from behind him. He turned and looked to see who had spoken up. She was a second-year cadet who he'd seen on the grounds before but had never talked to. Her green eyes flashed and her jaw jutted out while she glared up at him. Just as he was about to open his mouth to respond, he saw a few more cadets had drifted over, their posture and focus making it clear they were there to back her up.

Jacob knew most of his fellow cadets were well aware of his reputation with the instructors and supervising officers, and they also knew he was one more major incident away from getting booted from the Academy altogether. Most of what was said about him was bullshit, but it was true he couldn't afford another physical altercation. Not this close to graduation. He'd already shut down most of his other scams, including the underground casino and the distillery.

"You don't know shit," he said, laughing in her face and turning to leave. How the hell was it his fault he'd randomly gotten stuck with Coulier when they divided them up for a training exercise? As he walked through the throng of cadets, he could feel the mood was dark. Probably best to get back to his room before someone started spreading the rumor that weekend passes were canceled because of Jacob Brown, and not for the first time.

The United Earth Naval Academy on Terranovus was a relatively new institution. While they tried to draw much of their traditions and methodology from the United States Naval Academy, the founders had also wanted to forge their own path in preparing generations of officers for service aboard Terran starships. One of the major differences with how the brass ran things on Terranovus is that here, away from the prying eyes of politicians, the kinder, gentler way of training adopted by many Western militaries on Earth was abandoned in favor of the old ways. Even a certain amount of fighting within the cadet ranks was not only overlooked, it was expected.

Jacob sighed to himself as he walked along, staring down anybody who looked like they might be about to say something to him. After his four years at the Academy, he had learned a few truths. First, the quality of people the Navy was finding for their officer corps was impressive. All of them were motivated, intelligent, and tough... both mentally and physically. Second, despite their many admirable qualities, they were still just a bunch of kids in their early twenties. No matter how professional they could be, or how much they wanted to impress their instructors and nab a choice assignment, they couldn't help the little relapses of immaturity. When someone like Coulier began to crack under the pressure, it seemed to Jacob there was a reversion back to schoolyard tactics to isolate and abuse them. He'd found himself on the outside more than a few times during his stay on Terranovus, but normally not because he'd screwed up. His transgressions were making the others look bad from time to time.

Other than a few sideways looks, he made it back to his building without further incident. He went through the entry ceremony with the first-year cadet pulling guard duty and stepped into the cool lobby, the sigh of the door closing behind him mirroring his own of relief.

"Heard you had fun this week."

"Piss up a rope." Jacob tossed his hat at his roommate.

"So, what happened? We heard the Jumpers fly out last night and the scuttlebutt is that they canceled the exercise early for a real-world emergency having to do with y'all's platoon." Spencer was born in Louisiana but later moved to Indiana. Every once in a while, his native accent would slip out.

"I was running as a scout with that moron, Coulier." Jacob flounced on his rack. "Gibson's platoon was gearing up for a final assault to wipe us out before we could find their base and get the flag. They called the whole thing while I was still out in the woods by myself, so I have no idea what happened."

"Lucky you," Spencer said. "Word is, a bunch of folks is gettin' sent home and a few more are heading to the brig."

"No shit?" That last part surprised Jacob. There were so many people fighting for slots into the Academy that the worst punishment meted out was normally a long flight back to Earth in disgrace. If someone was getting cycled through for a judicial punishment, an actual crime would have had to occur. "I'm almost afraid to find out what that pack of idiots did... You know what? Who gives a shit. These exercises are a waste of time anyway. They have us crawling around playing soldier when most of us are going to be commissioned into the Navy and put on a starship."

"Marines."

"Huh?"

"We don't have soldiers, we have Marines aboard ships," Spencer said. "And some of the people here will be going into the United Earth Marine Corps as infantry officers."

"Then let the Corps train the five percent they skim off the bottom to lead their grunts." Jacob sneered. "It's not like we have much infantry training before getting split up into platoons and dropped off in the wilderness to fight it out."

"I don't think that's the actual point of the exercise," Spencer sighed. "I can see there's no talking to you right now. So, what do you want to do tonight since you got us locked down?"

"Please, don't encourage that rumor," Jacob said. "It'd probably be smarter if I—" He never got to finish his sentence because of a hard pounding on their door.

"They startin' this party early," Spencer said, climbing off his rack and stretching his arms out. He had leapt to the same conclusion Jacob had: the scuttlebutt about his involvement had spread and now someone was at their door for a little *non-judicial* punishment.

"Someone picked the wrong door to bang on," Jacob said, his blood boiling. He nodded to Spencer and yanked the door open, his shoulders slumping as he saw who was there.

"You're on your own," Spencer said when he looked over Jacob's shoulder and saw four MPs standing in the hall.

"Cadet Brown, the admiral would like a word with you," the shorter one in front said.

"Give me a minute to put on my service dress?" Jacob asked.

"Thirty seconds, Cadet."

"Thank you." Jacob didn't see any benefit in antagonizing the MPs. The fact that they were there at all to collect him and not a CQ runner meant he was likely in some sort of trouble. *Big* trouble. No point in giving them a reason to slap him in cuffs and march him out of the barracks like a criminal.

The *admiral* was Vice Admiral Wallace Cornett, the superintendent of the Academy. If Jacob was being dragged before him, it was also clear that whatever he'd fucked up this time had nothing to do with academics. Shit. He ran all the current scams he'd had going through his head and tried to determine if any of them would be severe enough to send him all the way to the top. He supposed it didn't matter what he was in trouble for. A visit to see Admiral Cornett meant he was likely being kicked out of the Academy as he'd originally feared. Ain't that a bitch?

"It seems like you've had quite the time here, Mr. Brown," Admiral Cornett finally said, still not looking up from the tablet as he scrolled through Jacob's disciplinary file.

Jacob had been standing at attention for the better part of thirty minutes after he'd been hastily ushered into the admiral's office, the huge doors made from some indigenous wood booming closed behind him. Admiral Cornett wasn't a very imposing man, and Jacob's focus was drawn away from the administrator to the two men lounging on couches in the office. One was a captain in the UEN, but Jacob could tell this was no paper pusher. This man looked sharp, dangerous, and he stared at Jacob with an intensity that made him uncomfortable.

The other man looked like a vagabond. He was in civilian clothes and lounged indolently on a couch, one leg hanging over the armrest. When Jacob's gaze fell across him, the guy answered with a knowing smirk that angered the cadet. Who the hell was this clown?

"Am I boring you, Mr. Brown?"

"No, Admiral," Jacob answered without thinking.

"That's good, Cadet," Cornett said. "Now, what do you want to say about this latest incident?"

"I'm sorry, Admiral?" Jacob asked, genuinely confused. *Should've been paying closer attention, damnit.*

"The field exercise you recently participated in was the last chance for Cadet Coulier to prove he had what it takes to be an officer in the United Earth Navy," Cornett began. Now Jacob was really confused. What the hell did Coulier have to do with him? "Unfortunately, he didn't impress. He allowed a mutiny to fester under his command, and then, when you sent him back alone while scouting an enemy position, he was assaulted by four other cadets, two of whom were squad leaders."

"Yes, sir," Jacob replied out of reflex.

"Shut up. I'll let you know when I want you to speak," Cornett said conversationally. "All five cadets were collected by MPs, stripped of rank and privileges, and will be shipped back to Earth on the next scheduled transport. We've also initiated disciplinary action on nine other cadets who either helped, or failed to stop, said mutiny. Which category do you suppose you fall under?"

"The second, sir," Jacob said. So, this was how they'd get him? Because he let Coulier get his ass kicked—deservedly so in his opinion—he was going to be drummed out and sent back to Earth with his tail between his legs.

"The second," Cornett confirmed, standing and walking to the full-length window. "By itself, it would be nothing more than an embarrassing blemish on your school record but, in your case, there is a cumulative effect. Your dozens of petty violations over the last four years have painted a picture of someone who, while proficient, doesn't take his military career very seriously. You're always careful to tiptoe right up to the line of doing something that would get you expelled but never stepping over. Does that sound about accurate, Cadet?"

"Yes, sir."

"Not even going to defend yourself?" Cornett was incredulous. "A disappointment to the end, I see." The admiral gave the captain standing in the office a meaningful look and rolled his eyes at the scruffy looking man who was now flipping through a magazine.

"As much as I'd like to send you packing if for no other reason to prove a point, you're too well-connected politically and you've almost made it to graduation. You'd already be out in the Fleet by the time the paperwork cleared to terminate your enrollment." Jacob stood silently at that. He was genuinely surprised he was being considered for expulsion based on something he'd had no direct part in. The other thing that confused him was that he no knowledge of any political connections in his family, much less someone pulling strings to get him an Academy slot.

He was also surprised at how knowledgeable the superintendent of the entire school was with his exploits although, in hindsight, he shouldn't have been. The UEAS was so new that Earth had been forced to pull seasoned officers and enlisted personnel from the ranks of existing militaries. The Academy was training up the next generation of officers even as boot camps and tech schools on the planet did the same for the enlisted ranks, but it would be many years before they were ready to be in charge. As such, the size of the Academy classes was still relatively small for what they were tasked to do since there weren't many instructors to go around yet.

"You had dreams of serving on a capital ship, didn't you, Brown?" Cornett asked. "Standing on the bridge of a mighty warship in your dress blacks, traveling to new and exotic places with a front row seat to the action?"

"I did, sir," Jacob said. In fact, it was that dream that had made the tedium of the Academy bearable. He saw himself standing on the bridge of his own destroyer, protecting Earth—and his family—from any threats that may come from the stars. He'd be the stalwart protector his father wasn't, wherever the hell that loser even was these days.

The admiral turned to look out the window, gazing over the manicured azure lawn of the Terranovus Naval Academy. He looked lost in thought, as if he'd forgotten there was anyone else in the office with him. When he turned back to Jacob, there was a malicious glint in his eye, and he wore a half-smirk that turned the cadet's stomach. *What now?*

"I'm not sending you home, Cadet Brown, but don't think it's because I wouldn't like to. I resent people like you taking up spots that could be given to *quality* candidates who actually want to be here," Cornett said. "But it's not up to me...apparently. In fact, you could say you're getting an early graduation."

"So, I'll still have the chance to serve aboard a starship, Admiral?" Jacob asked, scarcely believing his luck.

"Not exactly." This time, Cornett favored him with a predatory smile. "This is where I'll hand you over to Captain Marcus Webb, the man in uniform standing to your left. Dismissed, Cadet."

3

"The fucking Marine Corps!?"

"Watch your fucking mouth, *Cadet!*"

Within the span of time it had taken for him to follow Captain Webb and the civilian down the hall to an empty side office, Jacob's world had crumbled down around him. It turned out Webb was actually *that* Captain Webb, the man in charge of Naval Special Operations Command, or NAVSOC. All of the black ops the Fleet ran outside of human controlled space did so with this man's knowledge. Jacob had been dutifully impressed when Webb had introduced himself, although he'd been worried he'd be asked to serve aboard some intelligence trawler instead of one of the big, shiny capital ships he could see in orbit on a clear night. As it turned out, the reality was much worse.

Cornett had been honest about the early graduation, at least. What the old bastard hadn't mentioned was that it was predicated on Jacob accepting a commission into the United Earth Marine Corps, *not* the Navy. In an instant, Jacob's dreams turned to ash and blew away. Marines didn't stand on starship bridges except as sentries, and they sure as hell didn't command main line ships.

"Of course, sir. Sorry, sir."

"This is a take it or leave it offer, Brown," Webb said, sitting back in the chair behind the desk and putting his feet up.

"A question, sir?"

"Why you?" Webb guessed. "Why single you out when there were undoubtedly cadets with worse academic or disciplinary records? You feel like you're being discriminated against? Well, you are, but not for the reason you may think."

"That sums it up, Captain," Jacob said.

"Take a look at this video and tell me what you think," Webb said and flicked at a screen on his com unit. It was the name everyone on Terranovus used, but everyone on Earth would recognize the device as a smartphone, although the type carried by UEAS personnel had little in common with its terrestrial cousin.

The window behind Webb darkened, and then a grainy clip of a nighttime scene began playing. Jacob recognized the scene immediately as he watched himself jump thirty foot off a ledge where Cadet Coulier had just been.

"And then this one," Webb said and changed the scene. It was an aerial view of Jacob sprinting through the forest. "The analysts already looked at this and said you were running at around twenty-five miles per hour. That's faster than Earth's best sprinters can manage, and you did it in combat gear, at night, over rough terrain, and for at least three kilometers. Care to explain?"

"Obviously there was some issue with the drone footage, sir," Jacob said. His gut clenched up in fear, and he berated himself for being so stupidly careless. Years and years his grandfather had beaten it into his head: don't let them find out what you really are. And here he was, looking at high resolution video footage of him doing something no other human could do.

"A reasonable explanation," Webb said, his smile making it obvious he didn't buy it. "But we both know that's bullshit."

"Come on, sir," Jacob decided to go on the offensive. "You know the simplest answer is often the correct one. What are the odds that this is *actually* footage of me running faster than any other human ever has? Almost none, right?"

"Point of clarity, this isn't even the fastest that *I've* seen," Webb said. "There's a man I know who can beat your speed by around ten miles per hour, which brings up point number two: is there a particular reason you go by your mother's maiden name, Brown?"

"It's the only name I've ever known," Jacob said. "I never knew my father. He dipped out on my mom before I was born."

"Now, now, Cadet we both know that's not exactly true," Webb said. "You see, I know your father, and so do you. So, I'll ask again, is there a particular reason you're not using your father's name?"

"That name means less than nothing to me...sir." Jacob could feel his blood burning, and his ears were ringing just by the mere mention of the scumbag who happened to have sired him. It wasn't only because the guy had knocked up his mom and then split... Jason Burke was the reason that he was a freak who had to constantly worry about hiding how fast and strong he was.

"I see," Webb said noncommittally. "While I normally couldn't give two shits about some snot-nosed cadet's family drama, how about you fill me in?" And Jacob did. At length. Through the entire tirade Webb was a statue, making no comments and asking no questions.

"I'm not sure why this is even relevant, sir," Jacob finished his story. "Isn't Jason Burke an enemy of Earth? I'd heard as much on the news after the last time he disappeared." Webb didn't answer. The captain just continued to stare at him with that same unreadable expression.

"You still want him?" Webb finally asked.

"Sure," the shabby looking man in civilian clothes said, still not looking up from his com unit. "He's a whiny, self-absorbed little shit, but the Corps will burn that out of him. I don't need him for his winning personality."

"This is Lieutenant Commander Ezra Mosler," Captain Webb said before Jacob could open his mouth and ask. "He's the executive officer of 3rd Scout Corps and runs Team Obsidian. Once you complete the requisite training, you'll be reporting to him for your first assignment. You've heard of Scout Fleet, Cadet?"

"I have not, sir," Jacob said, his head swimming. *What the hell was happening?*

"Scout Fleet is the umbrella name for the composite, clandestine force that provides real-time intelligence to Fleet Operations," Mosler spoke up, walking around and sitting on the edge of Webb's desk. "We also handle discreet interdictions and tactical strikes when necessary. We're the ones who gather the intel Fleet requires before they send a taskforce into an area we've never been. Scout Fleet operates in small teams made up of sailors and Marines flying nonregistered ships we've either purchased from our alien allies or had purpose-built here on Terranovus."

"How much did you pay attention in class, Brown?" Webb asked. "Specifically, what do you know of the political make-up of the galactic quadrant?"

"I know that Earth is a full member in the Cridal Cooperative, a loose trading confederacy made up of a couple dozen systems, but the only true superpower in the region is the ConFed," Jacob said, not sure how deep he was supposed to drill down with his answer. "There's also the Eshquarian Empire and the Saabror Protectorate to round out the top four players. Would you like me to list all of the smaller nations and independent systems, sir?"

"Unnecessary." Mosler shook his head. "I can already tell you don't know shit."

"Sir?"

"What I'm about to tell you is highly classified," the Scout Corps commander said. "I'm not talking slap-on-the-wrist classified, I'm talking we-fake-your-death-in-a-training-accident-if-you-talk classified. Understood?" When Jacob nodded, he continued. "I'm only telling you this because I believe in giving you all the information you'll need in order to make your choice."

"What choice would that be, sir?"

"This is still a volunteer service, Dipshit," Mosler said. "You're not being shanghaied. If you don't want to be a Marine, you can still opt out and go back home to Colorado. You want me to continue?"

"Yes, sir."

"There is no more Eshquarian Empire," Mosler said. He said it with such dramatic flair that Jacob knew the right response would be to act shocked even if he wasn't sure why. "Three months ago, the ConFed hit them hard, took the capital system, and moved quickly to install their own regional government. Do you know why this is important?"

"Other than the fact a major power launched a preemptive attack on another? Aren't the Eshquarians major arms suppliers in the region?"

"They are *the* arms supplier for all the major militaries," Webb said. "They supplied weapons and small ships to the ConFed while retaining their own capacity for building capital ships. The big ships were only for their own fleet and were never offered to anybody who might use them against the Empire."

"If they were already trading partners, why would the ConFed risk such an overly-aggressive move?" Jacob wondered aloud. "They'll receive a negligible advantage in owning the small-arms and light craft production facilities outright, but they'll have announced to the entire region they're now willing to use their military to force concessions from their neighbors." When he looked up both officers were just watching him, Mosler with a bemused smile. "Sorry, sirs, just thinking aloud."

"And now you know why we exist," Mosler said. "Scout Fleet will be deploying throughout the quadrant to begin pulling in intel so Earth has all the information we can give them when the conflicts of the galactic core inevitably reach our shores."

"Is Earth at risk, sir?" Jacob asked.

"We're a two-planet, emerging power signed onto a binding protection treaty with the weakest of the three remaining major powers," Webb said. "While the ConFed might not be fully aware of us specifically, we have to assume the risk level is certainly elevated. I obviously can't tell you any more than we already have until you're cleared."

"Why me? Why the Marines?" Jacob tried one more time to get his life back on the track he thought he wanted. "Why can't I serve in Scout Fleet as a Naval officer? I just don't—"

"Why? Why? Why? Why? *Why?*" Mosler mocked him in a singsong falsetto. "What part of *service* was unclear to you when you signed up? The offer is for the Marine Corps because that's where the UEAS needs you the most. Your test scores and grades show you'd be a mediocre bridge officer, at best, but your psychological profile and aptitude for small unit tactics suggests that serving as a detachment officer aboard a Scout Fleet ship would suit you just fine. And, of course, there's also your physical gifts. Not too many jarheads can run over thirty miles per hour or have to hide the fact they can bench press over six hundred pounds."

And there it was. He was being asked to throw away his dream and join the Corps for no other reason than his freakish, alien traits that made him useful as a weapon. It was the precise reason he'd tried so hard to hide them. He wasn't standing there because of any discipline issues at the Academy, it had been a convenient con to get him to where they wanted him. What the hell had he been thinking?! Of *course*, they'd be monitoring the exercise area! *If that fucking Coulier had kept it together, I wouldn't have—*

"Yes or no, Cadet?" Webb said. "I'm sorry, son, but I need an answer now. For the record, I don't like doing this to you. I'm breaking my word to a close friend by pulling you out like this, but desperate times and all that. My loyalty to that friend takes a backseat to my loyalty to Earth. It would be irresponsible of me to not recognize the potential I see in you and have it wasted as you wrote efficiency reports and fetched coffee for flag officers."

Jacob thought hard for a moment, his first instinct being to tell these two to shove it up their asses and put him on the first ship back to Earth. If he'd been in a better frame of mind, he would have been more suspicious about who Captain Webb's *friend* was and what the promise was involving him, but he was too busy wallowing in self-pity to analyze it that closely.

The thought of his grandparents back on Earth stopped him cold before he could tell Webb to piss off. If the alien attacks on his home world had taught him anything—other than that his father was an asshole and possibly a traitor to his species—it was that Earth was vulnerable. Even now, with their shipyards cranking out warships as fast as they could be assembled, he still felt that vulnerability as if it were a tangible thing he could reach out and touch. He'd come to the Academy to serve and protect the ones he loved the best he could. Maybe this path wasn't what he'd chosen, but it was still fulfilling that obligation.

"I'll do it...sir," he said finally. He hadn't meant for it to come out sounding like an admission of defeat like it had. "What's next?"

"I've already looked over your transcripts, and you've satisfied the requirements to graduate with your class without any special exemptions being filed that might draw undue attention," Webb said, now all business. "We'll swear you in tonight, right now. After that, you'll be turned over Lieutenant Commander Mosler."

"The voluntary training you took at the Academy helps...a lot," Mosler said as he flipped through the hardcopy of Jacob's file. "Survival school, both phases, the aforementioned small unit tactics, and your major was in astronautical engineering, so you'll be easy to train up on ship operations. To be honest, other than SERE school here on Terranovus and a two-week stint on Restaria, I think he's ready to be tossed into the deep end. The best way to learn is to get into it."

"Restaria?" Jacob asked, alarmed. "You can't mean the same Restaria that's in the Galvetic Empire?"

"Oh yes, I do." Mosler smiled evilly. "We have a sort of informal training exchange program going on with them. You're going to absolutely *love* hand-to-hand combat training with the Galvetic Legions." Jacob returned the smile, but where Mosler's was full of malicious enthusiasm, his own was a little sickly. While most had only heard of the famed Galvetic warriors through their course work and had seen the images the instructors used, Jacob had actually been face to face with one when he was fourteen years old. It had been one of the single most terrifying events of his life. It was also one of those things nobody was supposed to know about, so he kept his mouth shut.

"You'll be fine," Webb said distractedly. "I believe Mazer Reddix is still running the school, and he'll take a special interest in making sure you survive the training."

"That doesn't make me feel any better, sir," Jacob said.

"That's a shame," Webb deadpanned. "Because *I* feel completely fine about things."

4

Jacob was whisked out of the office Captain Webb had commandeered and into a small briefing room where Admiral Cornett was waiting. The superintendent looked less than thrilled that he was being inconvenienced by a mere captain, a cadet, and someone who could have been mistaken for a shiftless bum.

"Let's get this over with," he growled, gesturing for Jacob to take his place in front of the red backdrop. The cadet did as instructed, flanked on either side by the United Earth and Terranovus flags. The former was a blue background with a green circle in the middle representing the unified Earth governments, while the latter looked like the Polish flag with the red and white inverted. Jacob thought both designs showed a shocking lack of imagination...but nobody had asked him.

The normal tradition for a graduating class was to fly back to Earth and hold the ceremony there so that families could be in attendance so that Fleet PR could really sell the idea of a spaceborne military to a public still having a hard time adjusting to their new reality. Instead of standing tall, resplendent in his service dress with his grandparents watching on, Jacob would be sworn in by a reluctant

Admiral, into a branch he didn't really want to be in, and handed over to a commanding officer who made him extremely nervous.

As Admiral Cornett droned on, reciting the ceremony with all the enthusiasm of someone watching paint dry—he actually paused twice to yawn—Jacob's thoughts drifted to his current predicament. He hadn't completely given up on the idea of being a Naval officer and serving aboard mainline warships, he just had to figure out how one would transition from the Marine Corps to the Navy. The problem was that the UEAS was such a new organization that they were still ironing out all the procedures and policies for mundane personnel issues like some junior officer wanting to switch branches.

"Now, raise your right hand and repeat after me," Cornett yawned. Jacob went through his Oath of Office, feeling humiliated and cheated as he stood there alone. The universe had once again decided to shit on Jacob Brown. It just wasn't fair, damnit.

"Congratulations, Lieutenant Brown," Cornett said, managing some enthusiasm finally. "I have no doubt you will do the Marine Corps, this Academy, and your home planet proud. Serve with honor." The shift in the Admiral's demeanor from when he'd berated Jacob in his office to now congratulating him didn't escape the new lieutenant's notice and he suspected that the scene had been an act the whole time.

"Now what, sir?" Jacob asked Mosler once Cornett and Webb had said their congratulations and left the room.

"Now that you're a lieutenant, you can take it easy with the *sirs*," Mosler said. "And as to your question, you belong to me for now. We'll head back to base, and I'll get you checked into billeting. You'll start your medical procedures for off-world service tomorrow, and then we'll see about getting you a ride to Restaria."

"Wonderful," Jacob said.

"This may not be what you think you want, but believe me, if you want to make a difference—*really* make a difference—you want to be in Scout Fleet," Mosler said.

"I can't refute what you're saying, but I can't help but feel I'm being boxed in by this forced commission into the Marines," Jacob said. "My options were just limited to detachment duty on a starship, a dirtside assignment, or NAVSOC."

"Kid, life isn't fair," Mosler said and nodded towards the door. Jacob rolled his eyes at the comment and followed his new CO out into the hallway. "It's especially not fair for someone who, through no fault of his own, was given special abilities that made him too damn valuable to waste on the bridge of a cruiser out shadowing one of the Cridal ships."

"Fucking alien blood in me," Jacob muttered. The revulsion he felt about why he was so different wasn't as sharp as it had once been, but he was far from making peace with it.

"Alien? What the hell are you blathering about, Lieutenant?"

"You know why I'm so fast, right?" Jacob asked as they got into the elevator.

"I know exactly why." Mosler nodded and hit the button for the roof. "I've not only been briefed but I've met the source, in a manner of speaking. You think you have alien blood in your veins?"

"You're saying I don't?" Jacob frowned. "Wait! You've met my... The man who—"

"Yes, I've met your father...sort of." Mosler cut off Jacob's stammering. "Our paths crossed very briefly on a shithole planet called Nott."

"I've never heard of it."

"I'm not surprised. It's in a region of space called the Kaspian Reaches," Mosler said. "It's a lawless, wild bit of space no government has been able to subdue enough to lay claim to. Your pop's crew was working on something of their own when Team Obsidian got in a bit over our heads. He took the heat off us enough that we could get airborne and escape."

"You're saying I'm going to run into that son of a bitch out there?" Jacob asked, unable to keep the venom from his voice.

"Unlikely." Mosler shrugged. "It's a very, *very* big galaxy and your old man tries to keep off of the radar as much as he can. Anyway, everything you have comes from him. There's no alien DNA anywhere in your makeup."

"I don't underst—"

"That's between you and him." They arrived at the roof level, and Mosler led Jacob out to where a small intra-atmospheric runabout was parked on the landing pad. "Your family drama isn't my concern. You do your job, and do it well, and I'll make sure to make it worth your while. That's your ride. The pilot knows where to take you, and one of my NCOs will meet you at the base."

"You're not coming?"

"I have to talk to Captain Webb about some...stuff," Mosler said darkly. "I'll be there before you undergo the neural implant procedure and all the nasty immunizations you'll get pumped full of."

"Lovely."

The flight out to the remote base NAVSOC called home was uneventful. Jacob had been met at the landing pad by a bored looking Marine noncom who was dressed much like Mosler had been, so determining his exact rank was impossible. Like most NCOs, he looked at the fresh new lieutenant as nothing more than an unwelcome burden. He was shown to his spartan quarters and told to dump his gear and change out of his service dress and into utilities. Later, he was led over to medical to begin the preliminary workups and baselines before they installed the neural implant.

"I thought we weren't going to start this until Commander Mosler got here sometime tomorrow," Jacob had said after being brusquely pushed into an exam room.

"You got anything better to do right now?" the noncom had asked before walking off. Jacob had never gotten his name.

The Mercury Mk.2 neural implant, named for the Roman god of communication—among other things—was the latest and greatest in Terran nanotech. It was largely copied from alien tech provided by the Cridal Cooperative as part of the treaty deal, but human engineers had adapted this version for use specifically with specialized military units, Scout Fleet being one of them.

The unit was made up of millions of specialized nanobots that, when injected into the victim—er, *subject*—would travel up to the base of the brainstem and assemble themselves into the implant's processing center. Nanobot chains would then form to access specific parts of the brain directly. The whole unit only had the total mass of around one- and three-quarter grams, but the way it was described to Jacob, it sounded like they were going to be driving railroad spikes into his cerebral cortex. When assembled and functioning correctly, the implant would allow Jacob to understand any alien dialect that was spoken to him as long as it was loaded into the translation matrix. The implants were one of the most common devices in the quadrant and, aside from faster-than-light ships themselves, were the main reason such a vast interstellar community could even exist.

"Good evening, Lieutenant. My name is Commander Ellis, and I'll be overseeing your procedure." Jacob looked when Commander Ellis walked in. She was flanked by two more enlisted nurses from the Medical Corps, both of whom immediately went to work prepping the machines for the implant procedure.

"Will this hurt?"

"I won't feel a thing," Ellis said. "Go ahead and strip down and hop up on the table. While it's not necessary, we typically administer a general anesthesia for this procedure. There can be some...discomfort...in some patients. Once the implant has formed and integrated, we'll wake you up."

"How long does that take?" Jacob asked.

"Depends on the person," Ellis said. "Count on being out for at least a twelve-hour period."

Jacob just shrugged and began peeling off his uniform despite two females still standing there. The Academy was a fully gender-integrated institution; any modesty he'd once harbored about being nude in front of the opposite sex had been burned away within the first six months. The school, due to its daunting task of prepping personnel for the rigors of service in space, was part U.S. Naval Academy, part Army boot camp, and as much emphasis was placed on practical skills as on the usual coursework needed to become an officer.

After neatly folding his uniform on top of his boots, he hopped up on the table and let the nurses begin to strap him down. The restraints would keep him from hurting himself from any involuntary twitches or jerks he may experience while the implant wormed its way through his brain.

"Is your will and power of attorney up to date?" Ellis asked.

"Wait! What? I thought this was a routine procedure!"

"It is, but so is a carotid stent and that has a mortality rate of forty percent. But I'm sure you'll be fine," she said. "Are we ready?"

"Nanobots are responding and the scanners are all ready, Doctor," the male nurse said, his name tape read *Brenton*.

"What's the mortality rate for these implants?" Jacob asked. "Doctor?"

"Proceed," Commander Ellis said, smiling down at Jacob as the other nurse pressed the green button on the machine that would administer the anesthesia and monitor his vitals while he was under. "It'll all be over before you know it." Her voice floated down to him as if through a long tunnel as his vision closed in around him. He tried to offer up one more complaint about the lack of bedside manner and professionalism, but he had already lost control of his voluntary muscles.

He never felt the large-bore needle inserted into his femoral artery where a suspension fluid, loaded with nanobots, was fed into his bloodstream.

"How do you feel?"

"Whaaaa?"

"That's completely normal," Commander Mosler assured him.

"How long was I out?" Jacob asked.

"You actually just set a new record for fastest recovery," Mosler said. "Less than five hours from the time the implant assembled and gave a good status to the time the machine said you were ready to open your eyes. That's good. Now get off the table, get dressed, and meet me in the ready room in twenty minutes."

"Where's the ready room?"

"I guess you'll need to figure that out, huh?" Mosler smiled humorlessly. "You're Scout Fleet now, Lieutenant. If I can't trust you to find the fucking ready room, how can I trust you when I drop you on an alien planet I need intel on?"

Before Jacob could answer, his CO was already gone. He rushed to the door, still naked, so he could at least see which direction Mosler had gone and saw the commander's retreating just round a turn to the left.

"The fun and games begin already," he grumbled as he quickly dressed and ran out the door.

As it turned out, finding the ready room for Team Obsidian was even easier than pestering people he passed in the hall for directions. No sooner had he subvocalized in his head the name of the place he wanted to go then a green arrow appeared in his vision, seeming to be on the floor, and a number appeared in the upper, left corner of his field of view. After a moment, he realized it was a countdown timer displaying an ETA to his destination...and it was now at twenty-eight minutes.

"Shit!" He took off at a quick shuffle/jog down the corridor, following the arrow and watching the timer closely. Other displays kept popping up in his vision, put there by the neural implant by injecting the data directly into his visual cortex. The arrow on the floor led him down a few more corridors before it began flashing by an exit. Damnit. The place he needed to be was apparently not in this building and it was a sprawling base. If it was on the other side of the flightline, he'd be in trouble without access to a vehicle.

Sure enough, when he kicked open the door from the medical center, he saw that the arrow appeared again in the distance, this time vertically and pointing to a building well on the other side of the tarmac. He couldn't cut straight across either since it was an active ramp and ships were coming and going with enough regularity to make it dangerous.

He started to jog around the perimeter until he came to a marked walkway that would allow him to bisect the flightline, the area apparently the delineation zone between the maintenance area to the south and the active ramp to the north. The good news was that it was a straight shot. The bad news was the timer still read over twenty minutes. *How the hell have I lost time?!*

"Fuck it," he said and spurred himself into a sprint. The whole reason he was wearing Marine fatigues and playing these games on a NAVSOC base was because of his goddamn *talents* anyway. May as well put them to use since it seemed pointless to keep it a secret any longer.

His boots slammed against the concrete as he accelerated to his top speed, something he hadn't been able to do since living in rural Colorado. He actually had no idea what he was even capable of now after the physical rigors of training, but judging from the rushing of the wind in his ears and the tears streaming down his face, he'd picked up an MPH or two.

As he crossed to the far end, his endurance holding as his body processed the lactic acid as quickly as his muscles produced it, he approached a group of maintainers working on removing an outboard engine from a Jumper. When he blew by the group, Jacob could see out of the corner of his eye the slack jaws and dropped tools as all heads turned to follow him. *What the hell, they probably will think I'm an alien in a Marine uniform.*

The soles of his boots were heating up from the abuse enough that he could feel it in his feet by the time he had to begin slowing down, so he didn't overshoot the sidewalk and hit the hangar in front of him. The timer in the corner of his eye now said he would arrive in less than three minutes, well ahead of when Mosler told him to be there. All he had to do was follow the helpful green arrow the rest of the way.

Once he was inside the building, the sign telling him it was the operations center for 3rd Scout Corps, he walked past the ready rooms for Team Titanium and Team Diamond before reaching the wide double doors for Team Obsidian.

"Son of a *bitch!!*"

The shouted obscenity was how he was greeted when he opened the door and walked in.

"Pay up, Asshole!" came another call.

"All you idiots shut up!" Mosler shouted, walking over to Jacob from where he'd been lounging in a padded chair.

"I take it I was the subject of a friendly wager?" Jacob asked.

"Bingo," Mosler said. "You made it across the base in under twenty minutes. So, how'd you do it? Hitch a ride? Steal a Jumper?"

"I ran." Jacob shrugged.

"Bullshit!" someone else shouted. "What the hell, Skipper? You going to let the new LT get away with lying like that?"

"Shut up, Wilkins," Mosler sighed. "Everyone get back to work. Lieutenant, I'll see you in the hall. Afterwards, we'll make the formal introductions."

"Did I do something wrong, sir?" Jacob asked when they were in the hallway alone.

"I thought you were trying to hide the fact that you're...different."

"There didn't seem to be a point anymore," Jacob said. "Isn't that sort of the whole reason I'm here?"

"It's partially that," Mosler admitted. "There were also aptitude batteries, intelligence tests, and psychological profiling during your time at the school that let us know you were especially suited for this type of work. Your genetic quirks aside, you'd already been marked for this job well before you let the cat out of the bag."

"I see," Jacob said noncommittally. "So, you think I should still keep certain things under wraps?"

"It's up to you, Lieutenant. We operate in small teams and stay deployed for extended periods of time. You're going to have to learn to trust them and they you," Mosler said. "Come on back in and we'll make the formal introductions before setting you up with your permanent billet."

"Just out of curiosity, sir, did you bet for or against me making it in time?"

"I always bet on my men," Mosler said, suddenly serious. "Always."

"Good to know, sir," Jacob said, unsure what to say in the face of his CO's abrupt mood change.

"Come on." Mosler yanked the door open, the lopsided grin back. "I'll introduce you to the rest of the team."

When they walked back into the ready room, Jacob counted twelve people, fourteen including him and Mosler. Some were dressed in a mishmash of non-uniform attire like the skipper, others were in UEN fatigues worn by the enlisted ranks. All those in uniform had patches on their left breast pocket that he recognized as the NAVSOC crest.

"This is our newest jarhead," Mosler announced loudly, cutting off all conversation. "You animals say hello to fresh butter bar, Lieutenant Jacob Brown. Assuming he isn't killed by the Galvetics on Restaria during training, he'll be taking command of the ground team." There was a chorus of jeers and insults that apparently passed as a greeting. Jacob noted the enlisted weren't shy about insulting him despite the gold bars on his collar.

"Jake, your teammates are the mangy looking ones in civvy attire. The ones in uniform are the Terranovus support crew specifically assigned to Obsidian. They keep the *Corsair* flying and procure anything and everything we may need before deploying. The tall guy on the left is our pilot, Lieutenant Ryan Sullivan, and the Chief Petty Officer seated next to him is our engineer, Michael Scarponi. The three of us make up the Naval personnel on the team, the other four are all your filthy Marine brethren. I'll let you introduce yourself to them and vice versa. Just remember, in Scout Fleet, rank and branch mean next to nothing once we're out there. We cross-train to make sure we can fill a critical role no matter who falls."

"Understood, sir," Jacob said. When Mosler just stared at him expectantly he went on. "I'm...happy...to be here."

"Bullshit," Sullivan snorted. "Nobody is happy to be here."

"I—"

"Let's try to keep our butter bar pure and positive for as long as possible," Mosler said. "I don't want you cretins burning away his new-guy enthusiasm until at least the second cruise." He elbowed Jacob and nodded towards the door. "Let's go and link your com unit to this base's automated services. You'll be able to call for a ground car or grab food at the mess hall after that, so you'll have a little more independence."

"So, I'm officially going to be attached to Team Obsidian?" Jacob asked.

"Assuming you survive training and perform as I expect you will, yeah. You'll be assigned to my crew. Once you're back from Restaria, you'll have a few more months of specialized technical training here on Terranovus, and then you'll begin working with your own people. All your Marines have been on at least two deployments, so you won't be saddled with a bunch of FNGs. They know their shit. Just make sure you do, too, because they won't put up with a new lieutenant who's a liability for very long."

Jacob new that FNG stood for *fucking new guy*, and that's exactly what he was. He was breaking into an established team with its own internal dynamics and, being honest with himself, he knew he wasn't always the easiest person to get along with. He'd been so fixated on the fact that he didn't want to be a Marine at all that he hadn't realized just how difficult it was going to be for him, stepping into a close-knit unit of badass operators. This was going to a disaster.

He made it back to his room by way of the mess hall, where he gorged himself on some of the best food he'd eaten in his life. Apparently, no expense was spared for NAVSOC when it came to keeping its people happy. He called for a pickup and saw he was now tied into the network of automated ground cars that patrolled the base and stopped when summoned. Convenient. For a moment, he debated having it drop him of at the Officer's Club but decided the most prudent thing would be to go back to billeting and start studying the pile of material Commander Mosler had dumped on him before leaving, making it quite clear he would be expected to know it backwards and forwards before he shipped out for training.

The last thing he thought as he drifted off to sleep was how different the firsthand accounts of ConFed space were compared to the sanitized version they learned in the classroom. The mission briefs Mosler had given him were loaded with some truly terrifying details. What the hell had he gotten himself into?

5

"Brown...wake up."

"How did you get in—"

"No time for that." Mosler loomed over Jacob, and it took the lieutenant a moment to realize he was still in his bed on the NAVSOC base. "Grab your gear and be at the operations center as fast as you can get there. Don't talk to anyone and stay off the net. From the time I leave to the instant you step into the ops center, I want you thinking OPSEC every step of the way, you read me?"

"Y-yes, sir," Jacob managed to get out. He was about to ask what the hell was going on but bit his tongue. His room was unsecured, and Mosler was already walking back through the door anyhow. He checked his com unit and saw that it was 0340 local time. Terranovus had a twenty-two-hour day thanks to a faster rotational speed than Earth despite the two being of similar mass and orbital paths around their respective stars.

"If this is another *new guy* hazing thing, I'm going to be so pissed," he grumbled as he pulled on his uniform and grabbed his go-bag that was inside the first wall locker. He was out the door and waiting for his summoned ground car in three minutes.

The NAVSOC base, named Taurus Station, was sparsely populated to begin with, a secret installation on a planet with a population of barely six million people, but at this time of night, it was a veritable ghost town. It wasn't until he approached the well-lit flightline that he saw signs of life as maintenance vehicles scurried about dropping technicians and parts off to the ships parked back beyond the maintenance line. He saw a few Jumpers, a couple smaller ships he couldn't identify, and a *Peregrine*-class fast assault ship that dwarfed the others on the ramp. This piqued his interest since that class of ship would normally not make landfall for something as mundane as maintenance. It would be serviced on one of Fleet's orbital facilities that could be seen with the naked eye streaking across the night sky.

The closer he looked at the *Peregrine*, he could see that the discoloration he noticed on the hull was obviously from energy weapon fire. Interesting. It was doubtful his middle-of-the-night muster and a warship that had signs of battle being parked on the ramp were unrelated. Soon, the car was beyond the view of the flightline and moving between the massive hangars towards the 3rd Scout Corps Ops Center. Jacob put his head back against the rest, now satisfied this wasn't just some hazing ritual but a real-world situation. He was probably being summoned just to make him feel like part of the team. It wasn't like a lieutenant that was so new he squeaked when he turned too fast would have much input to give.

"This is a bad idea, Skipper. He ain't ready to be in the shit. He just graduated all of ten minutes ago."

"I think the kid may surprise you. He's already had more training that most U.S. Special Forces go through during his time in the Academy, and all of it voluntary. There's also his...special skills to consider."

"Being fast isn't the same as being well-trained and experienced, damnit! What happens when—"

"My decision on this has been made, Murph. Unless you have something more that isn't about my command decisions on personnel, this conversation is over."

Jacob heard some more grumbling from where he'd stopped just outside the ready room door. He knew *Murph* was actually Alonzo Murphy, one of the Marines on his ground team, and the other voice unmistakably belonged to Commander Mosler. It was also painfully obvious who they were talking about. *Shit, making friends already.* He waited for a five count, and then strode quickly into the room as if he'd just arrived.

"Brown, go sit with your guys," Mosler said without looking up from his tablet. "We'll be starting our initial brief in a minute, and I'll get you spun up on everything else once we're aboard the *Corsair* and on our way. Once we leave this room, make sure you talk to Petty Officer Owens about some appropriate attire. We don't wear uniforms, in case you hadn't noticed."

"Yes, sir." A million questions flitted through Jacob's head, but he did as he was told and went to sit with his team. "Gentlemen." He nodded to them before slouching into the padded chair. There was a chorus of greetings ranging from, "Hey, LT," to a simple nod, but thankfully nothing like, "What the hell are you doing here?" as he'd almost expected.

"Everyone, shut up." Mosler walked to the lectern, his usual bored, sarcastic demeanor replaced with a razor-sharp alertness and an urgency that alarmed Jacob for some reason. "This is Captain Wilford, she's from Fleet Intelligence and is here to brief us on our next assignment. I know I told you we'd have a couple months of downtime, but the situation is critical and we're the only crew with the needed experience for the mission. Captain?"

"Thank you, Commander Mosler." Captain Wilford was a tall, willowy woman who looked to be in her early forties. "I apologize for pulling Obsidian back into the rotation before your turn, but you're the only crew that has operated in the region of space germane to this mission."

"Which area would that be, ma'am?" Sullivan, the pilot, spoke up.

"The Kaspian Reaches," Wilford said.

"Fuck me."

"Goddamnit."

"I wish I'd never enlisted."

"Are we about finished?" Captain Wilford had waited patiently for the mumbled complaints to die down before continuing.

"I apologize, Captain," Mosler said as he looked his crew over, his glare promising violence upon the next person who opened their mouth.

"There's an intelligence asset within the Reaches who is now in danger, someone critical to our continued operations as we push outward into ConFed space," Wilford continued. "This...person... operates within the Reaches and has contacted us requesting help."

"So, this is a simple extraction mission?" Mosler asked.

"If it was, we certainly wouldn't need you." Her tone of voice made it clear she didn't appreciate all the interruptions. "The asset is no longer responding to queries through any of the normal channels. We fear she may have gone underground and is being actively pursued. As you can assume from the fact that she operates within the Kaspian Reaches, she's not affiliated with any government and, given the level of information she's sold us, would be a tempting target for any intelligence service, either to use her or silence her. The other critical component to this is that the asset isn't human, she's Veran. The government on Ver long ago disavowed her from pressure by the ConFed Council, so don't expect any help from their security patrols if you get into a tight spot."

"Anything else we'll need to know that you can think of? Anything that might not be in the mission packet?" Mosler waited this time until he was sure she was done talking.

"One point of interest, something she let us know before going dark, was that she'd recently helped out a mercenary crew that had a human with them. I think you know who that would be."

"We do," Mosler confirmed. "They were there the same time we were. Helped us escape a sticky situation on Nott."

"So I read," Wilford said. "Just so we're clear on this, Jason Burke is still officially considered a criminal and a rogue element by Earth. Do you understand what I mean by that, Commander?"

"Understood," Mosler said stiffly.

Jacob tuned out the rest of the briefing, his ears ringing at the mention of Burke. So, his new team had had more than just casual contact with his estranged father or, at the very least, felt like they owed him a favor. Was that why he was here? He hadn't missed the hardening of the eyes on Mosler when Wilford proclaimed his father a criminal.

The fact that Jacob was now being forced to drag out his feelings for a man he'd only met once and reexamine them irked him. Who seriously gave a shit about Jason Burke? These NAVSOC clowns spoke of him in hushed, reverent tones, but from what Jacob understood, he'd been responsible—at least indirectly—for not one but *two* attacks by alien armadas on his own home planet. Then, like a coward, he hopped on his stolen ship and blasted off before he could be apprehended to stand trial for his crimes. All of that didn't even begin to touch on his feelings regarding Burke, about the questionable genetic makeup he passed on and ditching his mom after getting her pregnant.

In high school, when they'd learned about the two attacks in history class, he'd been forced to watch the videos from when one of the aliens hijacked the world's broadcast systems and actually demanded that his father be turned over along with the ship he'd stolen. It was beyond humiliating despite the fact nobody knew they were related.

He'd met his father once at the insistence of his grandparents. The man had landed his ship in a field in the middle of the night and had come sauntering down the ramp with his crew of alien mercenaries in tow. Jacob had been fourteen and had been especially terrified of the hulking alien he now knew was a Galvetic warrior and a being that was actually a sentient machine he always thought of as an android, though that wasn't what they called themselves. The other three aliens had been weird, but appeared harmless. He never could figure out why they would follow Burke, a human who had admitted to bumbling into possession of a powerful ship and had nearly gotten his own people wiped out twice.

"Hey! Pay attention, Brown!"

"Yes, sir," Jacob barked out of reflex, acknowledging that he'd been spoken to by a superior yet not actually admitting he hadn't been paying attention. He'd been half-listening to Wilford and knew she'd been droning on about logistics and the guts of their mission brief would be sent to their ship via a secure link for security reasons. Now, Commander Mosler was back up at the lectern and had been going over maintenance issues with his support crew. Jacob had heard the doors open and close behind him but hadn't turned to look and see how had entered.

"As a professional courtesy, we'll be taking Captain Webb with us on the *Corsair* when we depart," Mosler was saying, gesturing to the head of NAVSOC as he walked into the ready room. "We'll fly out of here fast and link up with the *Pathfinder*-class starship, *Endurance*, and drop him off before pushing ahead with our own mission. Put your fucking hand down, Sullivan. I'm not taking any questions until we get our official orders and mission brief." The team's pilot lowered his hand and shrugged.

"Murph, you take Brown to logistics and get him geared up before hitting the armory and letting him pick out any personal weaponry he may want that we don't have on the *Corsair*. Lieutenant, just make sure anything you grab you're actually qualified to use."

"Yes, sir," Jacob and Murph said in unison.

"You're dismissed, but you are *not* to leave the Ops Center," Mosler said. "You can grab chow in the flight kitchen and piss away the time in the rec room, but I catch any of you leaving and I'll keelhaul you myself. That's a serious punishment on an interstellar ship." There were some dutiful chuckles at the joke and everyone climbed out of their seats to file out of the ready room.

"Let's go get you some spaceman clothes, LT," Murph said with a friendly slap on the back. "You comin', Fisk?" The question had been to Staff Sergeant Brian Fisk, one of Jacob's two support noncoms.

"Nope. You two have fun playing dress-up."

"So, I hear you don't want me along for this one, Sergeant?" Jacob asked after they'd cleared out of earshot. He hadn't meant for it to sound so confrontational.

"No offense intended, LT." Murph shrugged, not at all looking embarrassed or contrite. "I'm not exaggerating when I say it's a fuckin' jungle out there, and until you experience it firsthand, no amount of training can prepare you for it. The Reaches are an especially shitty part of an already shitty region of the quadrant."

"Fair enough," Jacob said, appreciating the straightforward answer. Despite having heard Murph talking behind his back, he couldn't help but like the guy. The tall African-American had a powerful build and seemed to glide across the ground when he walked and possessed an easy-going demeanor that belied the fact that he was a highly trained operator in a UEAS Special Forces unit. "Just do me a favor?"

"If I can," Murph said.

"I take criticism fairly well. If you see me about to step into a huge pile of shit, feel free to nudge me out of the way." Murph laughed at that.

"Hell, I'd have done that without you asking," he said before growing serious again. "Getting down there on these planets, interacting with aliens even though you can understand them, it takes some getting used to. Even people who pass the psych eval sometimes crack up the first time something that looks like a potato with eyeballs asks them where the nearest bathroom is. We all have to depend on each other, so if you feel like you can't handle it, just be honest with us. Ain't no shame in admitting you're freaked out by freaky shit."

"Will do," Jacob said, thinking back to the time he'd met his father's crew. If the aliens they'd meet weren't too much more exotic than that group, he should do okay.

"You like our ride?"

"She's a beauty," Jacob said, and he meant it. The ship before him looked both graceful and menacing.

"Captain named her the *Corsair*," Murph continued. "No class designation, she's one of one, no other boats like her in the fleet. She's also the only ship currently assigned to Scout Fleet that was designed and built entirely by humans. The others have all been bought off our alien friends and modified."

"A lot bigger than I thought it'd—she'd—be." Jacob hurriedly corrected himself. Murph may have been a jarhead, but he seemed to view his ship with the same reverence any spacer would who was worth their pay.

"Three decks, seventy-three meters in length and a wingspan of fifty-eight meters and some change. I forget her gross weight," Murph said as the automated open-air car pulled to a stop before the ship. The support crews were scrambling all over her, and Jacob could see half a dozen cables and hoses still attached.

The *Corsair* had a pure delta wing configuration, her main hull blending seamlessly into the wings. There were no visible weapons or even portholes. The ship appeared a single, monolithic construct. Even the gaps for the access panels were all invisible.

"Now you look more like you belong," Mosler shouted over the noise as he walked up. "A few more scars and a bit less clean and you'll be ready for the Reaches...mostly."

"When do we leave?" Jacob asked.

"We're topping off our fuel now and Munitions has already been out to arm her, so as soon as our VIP gets here, we'll be clearing out. Murph get you squared away with gear?" Mosler asked.

"Yes, sir," Jacob said, jerking a thumb over his shoulder at the three hard cases that contained the rest of his clothes, equipment, and the personal weapons assigned to him. Murph had told him to just take whatever they offered and lock it up in his stateroom since the *Corsair's* armory was fully loaded with alien armament that

Command wasn't even aware they had. Jacob had raised an eyebrow at the NCO casually admitting to about half a dozen regulatory violations and one outright crime right in front of an officer but said nothing.

"Come over here for a minute so I don't have to keep shouting," Mosler grabbed him by the shoulder and led him over to a small security shack near the landing pad. "One more thing we haven't talked about... I know you're beyond green, and we're throwing you into the shit well before you're probably ready for it, but you're technically second in command on this mission."

"What about Sullivan?" Jacob asked. "He outranks me." Although they were both lieutenants, Sullivan was in the Navy, which meant he was an O-3 while Jacob, a Marine second Lieutenant, was an O-1.

"True, but Scout Fleet crews are organized so that the Marine detachment commander is higher up the chain than the pilot regardless of rank," Mosler said. "Sullivan is a competent officer and a good leader, but he'll have his hands full most of the time navigating and piloting. This isn't a debate. I'm asking you if you can handle taking command if something happens to me."

"Yes, sir," Jacob answered with a confidence he didn't feel. What's the worst that could happen? If Mosler was taken out of action for some reason, Terranovus would order the *Corsair* back to human space immediately rather than turn the mission over to some rookie second lieutenant.

"Good," Mosler said. "Go get your shit and put it in your stateroom. You'll be on the command deck across from me If you go up the— You know what? Just have Murph show you where it is, and then go up on the bridge and wait for me. Don't touch anything."

Murph had helped Jacob get his gear secured in his quarters and pointed him in the right direction for the bridge. The bridge itself was situated at the prow of the ship and sandwiched in between deck two and the command deck. When he walked onto it, he sucked in a breath at the stunning view. It appeared that he was just standing on a platform overlooking the flightline since the main display began at the rear bulkhead and encompassed the entire bridge.

"Real windows and portholes are fairly useless on a starship," Ryan Sullivan said, startling Jacob. He was seated at the pilot's station that was near the front of the bridge and sunk into the deck in a sort of pit, for lack of a better term. "There's nothing to see outside once we're in space, and I don't even look out while flying within an atmosphere anymore. They're just a needless vulnerability. This wrap-around display is also holographic so it can project images in front of you or highlight details outside in three dimensions. There are also displays mounted in the external bulkheads throughout the ship. Psychologists seem to think it helps even though, like I said, there's nothing to see. Pretty cool shit either way."

"Definitely," Jacob said. "I took a few classes in naval starship design and never heard of this technology."

"It won't make it to the rest of the Fleet for another ten years or so. Fleet brass doesn't like to put untested systems onto their capital ships," Sullivan said, climbing out of the pit and extending his hand. "Welcome aboard. None of us go by our names or rank in this outfit. Just call me Ryan or Sully."

"Thanks," Jacob shook the proffered hand. "So, the *Corsair* is that far out on the cutting edge?"

"In most ways, yes," Sully said. "What's not widely known is that some of our systems were adapted from alien technology we procured on our own without the help of our Cridal allies. That's definitely something you don't want to talk about to an outsider. The common misconception about the new generation of scout ships entering service is that they're designed and built totally in-house and, for the most part, that's true, but Scout Fleet crews are always on the lookout for anything that can give us an edge."

"It's one of Scout Fleet's standing secondary directives," a new voice from the bridge entrance said. Both Sully and Jacob turned to see Captain Webb leaning against the hatchway. "The terms of our binding agreements within the Cridal Cooperative dictate what we're allowed to receive from our trading partners and make sure that Cridal oversight knows who's sending what, where. But Earth was careful to negotiate the explicit right to develop our own technology as well as purchase and scavenge as needed. It's a thin gray line we're walking in that we're not entering into new trade agreements with outsiders when we simply buy or...*acquire*...something from an outside source. With that in mind, it only makes sense to have our most forward units keep their eyes open for anything useful. The main fleet has no such standing order."

"I see, sir," Jacob said carefully. It seemed a risky game that NAVSOC was playing, but he had to take it on faith that Fleet brass and the civilian oversight on Terranovus knew what Captain Webb and his operators were up to. He couldn't even fathom that a lowly captain would be rolling the dice with the safety of their home world by executing unsanctioned trades and, if he was reading between the lines right, theft of sensitive technology.

"I doubt that," Webb said, "but you've never been out of Terran space and graduated from the Academy all of ten minutes ago. You'll learn. How long until we're ready to push off, Lieutenant?"

"The *Corsair* is ready, sir," Sully answered. "Reactor is nominal, engines are ready, and the ground crew is standing by to unhook the umbilicals at our order."

"Very good," Webb said. He looked like he had something more to say but, instead, turned and walked back through the hatch.

"Webb doesn't leave Terranovus much anymore, not even to go back home," Sully said quietly. "I wonder what the hell is so important he'd hitch a ride with us out to a *Pathfinder*-class ship."

"Isn't the *Endurance* the ship that was involved in the attack that led to the collapse of the central banking system within the ConFed?" Jacob asked, digging deep to try and remember any of the scuttlebutt he'd heard floating around about human involvement in the incident.

"*Involved* might be too strong a term, but she was there in-system when the shit hit the fan. Word has it— Captain on the bridge!" Sully snapped to attention, and Jacob followed suit out of instinct as Mosler strode through the hatchway.

"As you were," he said. "Are either of you two dipshits even paying attention to what's happening outside the ship?"

"I—"

"Shut up," Mosler cut Jacob off. "We have visitors, very distinguished visitors who want to talk to you."

"Me?" Jacob asked.

"This is going to be a long cruise if you continue to act confused and question everything I tell you, Lieutenant," Mosler sighed. "Get your ass outside, now. Was that clear enough?" Jacob wisely clamped his mouth shut and followed Mosler back through the ship to the rear loading ramp.

"I don't know what they want with you. They don't really talk to anyone except Webb," Mosler said. "In fact, this is the first time I've seen them outside of their own compound since they arrived here."

"Who are *they*, sir?"

"Political refugees, and not human ones, either. It may have something to do with your unusual family makeup, or they may have just seen your face and don't like you. They're quite enigmatic, and also unimaginably powerful. A single one of these guys could kill us all within the span of seconds."

That last bit of description gave Jacob an inkling of who he was going to see...and why. As he jogged down the ramp—with Mosler staying conspicuously in the ship—he saw that he was correct: battlesynths. Three of them.

The species was a subset within a race of intelligent beings that had been created on a planet called Khepri. They were actually machines, designed at first to do menial tasks for their masters and then, if the legend is to be believed, an accident in their development led to full sentience. The species that made them, the pru, named them something that roughly translated to *synthetic*, or *synth* for short. Most synths were average sized bipedals that, while strong, weren't necessarily dangerous. Their cousins, dubbed "battlesynths" were a different story. They were hulking, powerful machines that had onboard weaponry, armor plates covering vital parts of their body, and were known to have a lack of humor and general distrust for anyone not of their kind. Jacob knew more about them than most humans. He'd actually met one in person when he was a child.

Jacob knew that a regular synth had been behind the attack on

Earth that happened before he was born, its picture still all over the Nexus if anyone wanted to search for it. But one of the secrets he carried with him from his childhood was that when his father had come to visit after the second attack on Earth, when Jacob had told him that his mother was dead and that he never wanted to see him again, one of the members of his alien crew had been a battlesynth named Lucky.

"Greetings, Jacob Brown," the baritone voice boomed from the lead battlesynth. "Or should I say, *Lieutenant* Brown. Congratulations on successfully completing your training at the Academy."

"Thanks?" Jacob said hesitantly. It took all his willpower to not flinch or retreat as it closed in on him, leaning down to look him in the eye.

"We are friends of your father, although we have heard you do not wish to be associated with him," the battlesynth said. "Perhaps a wise decision. He is an honorable, though erratic man. That is not the purpose of my visit, however. My designation is Combat Unit 707. I am in command of what remains of Lot 700 here on Terranovus."

"Is Lucky one of you?" Jacob blurted out before he could silence himself. He didn't know enough about these beings to know what might be an insult or not.

"Combat Unit 777, or *Lucky,* as he was known, was killed while trying to save our comrades as well as the life of your father," 707 said. "But yes, he was a member of Lot 700."

"I see," Jacob said. So, it looked like Lucky was another casualty of his father's blundering ways.

"We owe your father and his crew a great debt," 707 continued. "He negotiated with your government to allow us a home here and risked his own life for ours on more than one occasion. In return, we offer our services to you, if they are ever needed." He handed Jacob a small cylindrical device. "This is a slip-com homing beacon. If you activate it near an active slip-com node, it will be able to get a signal back to us. I will assume it is a dire emergency and take necessary steps. I understand you will be assigned to Marcus Webb's command and can only assume you will find yourself in grave peril at some point in the future. I urge you not to use this frivolously, however, for all our sakes." Jacob almost refused the device, looked up at the unreadable mask of the machine's facial armor, and simply nodded. He pocketed the device and figured it'd be simpler to just destroy it later than argue with this strange being.

"I'm sorry about your friend," he said. "I met him once. He seemed...nice."

"He was the best of us," 707 said. "Far too great a mind for a simple soldier. Good luck, Lieutenant Brown." With that, he turned and rejoined the two other battlesynths, speaking shortly to Captain Webb before walking back towards an exotic looking transport with an open cabin design. Jacob supposed when you were constructed of impervious metal, there was little need for a sealed passenger space.

"I can never figure out where they're getting their intel from," Webb said as he walked up to Jacob. "They knew who you were—who you *really* are—before I could even try to deny it. The fact they knew you were assigned here and that you were about to deploy means their information is in real-time. What'd they want, anyway?"

"Just to tell me that someone I'd met a long time ago had died," Jacob said.

"Lucky." Webb nodded. "We'd heard about that. Come on, they're waiting on us to depart. We'll talk more once we're underway."

"Yes, sir," Jacob said, not at all looking forward to the prospect. All of these people, even the aliens on this planet, seemed to revere his father and hold him up on a pedestal. At first it had angered Jacob, but now it just left him confused. The more people he met who admired the man who sired him left him less and less sure that his anger wasn't misplaced somehow.

6

The launch from Taurus Station was uneventful given the low volume of air traffic. Sully smoothly fed power to the gravimetric main engines, and the *Corsair* lifted off the tarmac vertically before accelerating along the course Terranovus Orbital Control had given them so they could enter into the pattern of outbound ships near the planet's equator.

Gravimetric drives, or "grav-drives," as the engineers called them, were one of the first bit of serious tech to come from their alien alliances. The seemingly miraculous devices could create gravitational distortions that allowed the ship to move in three dimensions through space. Jacob had been told in one of his Introduction to Engineering classes that the only thing limiting what a grav-drive could do was the universal constant—the speed of light in a vacuum—and the power source feeding it. Intellectually, he understood the principles that made the engines work, but as the *Corsair* effortlessly lifted her bulk into the muggy Terranovus night sky, Jacob couldn't help but be impressed.

"We've been released from Orbital Control. Setting course for our mesh-out point and prepping the slip-drive," Sully said, referring to the *Corsair's* second drive system that would push the ship out of normal space and into slip-space, the name for the faster-than-light propulsion method used by nearly every spacefaring species in the galactic quadrant. Jacob had little understanding of how the system circumvented Newtonian physics. All he knew was that he was never fully settled when a ship made the transition out of normal space.

"You're cleared to engage the slip-drive at your discretion, Sully," Mosler said. The commander—*captain* while aboard his ship—was sitting at a station to the right of the pilot pit. On the *Corsair*, he would control the ship's weaponry and communications while the pilot flew the ship and handled navigation. Jacob looked around and saw that there were several other auxiliary stations, but he had no idea what they were for. When Mosler spoke up again, it was like he'd been reading Jacob's mind.

"We have a crash course prepared for you to get you up to speed on the *Corsair* and her systems, Jake— Do you go by Jacob or Jake, Lieutenant?"

"Jacob, sir."

"Okay, Jake, like I was saying, you'll need to get with the program pretty fast. I don't expect you to be able to take her apart and put her back together, but as XO on this cruise, you'll need to at least have a passing familiarity."

"I'll be like a sponge, sir," Jacob said, deciding not to make an issue of the captain calling him by the wrong name. As with most things in the military—especially for FNGs—this was a test. The crew would poke and prod him to see what sort of reactions they'd get, what kind of team player he was, and how far they could push him before they'd allow him to settle into any sort of normal routine.

"Outstanding. No time like the present for a little on the job training," Mosler said. "Take the tactical station and make sure Sully doesn't run her into a moon. I'm going back to sleep."

"That was one time, sir, and I didn't actually hit it," Sully spoke up. Mosler let out a sound that was half-grunt, half-growl and stomped off the bridge.

"You hit a moon?" Jacob asked as he slid into the still-warm seat that Mosler had just vacated.

"No. Well...the thing is— Look, there were a lot of bugs to work out on this ship, and we were rushed through trials and activated before we were ready," Sully said. "One of the things that didn't work so great was the master warning system that *should* have let me know that the landing gear wasn't deployed before I tried to land."

"I see," Jacob said, not sure what to make of the story or how much of it he should believe. "So, technically—"

"Technically it was an unintentional belly landing, but still a landing. I didn't *hit* the moon, merely brushed up against it."

Jacob chose not to pursue the matter further. Instead, he began inspecting the tactical station the ship's commanding officer sat at, realizing again how unprepared he was for this assignment. When he touched the screen to his right, it went dark for a moment before it came back up with a new menu, his name and rank correctly displayed at the top. He was impressed with how seamlessly it was able to read his biometric data by the light touch and asked Sully about it.

"It's actually reading your neural implant," the pilot said. "The ship can monitor all the unique signatures our wetware puts out and determine where we are, what we might need, if we're under duress... that sort of thing. It's far less vulnerable to hacking than simply reading your DNA, and fingerprints won't work since not all the species that work with Scout Fleet even have those."

"There are aliens actually serving in the Navy? Not just in an advisory capacity?" Jacob asked, surprised.

"Yep," Sully said. "That battlesynth you were talking to earlier is actually a full colonel in the Marines. That's a formality, of course, since command can't actually order them around. It's just convenient when they do happen to help out with training or advising Fleet on certain areas of space if they have a rank and clearance. There are also a handful of refugees who have come to Terranovus through the Cooperative and have been placed in service on NAVSOC ships."

"Interesting." Jacob wasn't sure how he felt about that. He liked to think of himself as evolved past the simple xenophobia most on Earth had about aliens, but letting them into the military? There was so much they didn't know about the universe they were stepping into, and it made him nervous to think about how much blind faith they had to place in beings that might look at them as no more than vermin.

"If you're bored, go into the menu marked 'Crew Resource Management' and scroll through the training programs," Sully said. "The computer has your full profile and will shuffle coursework so that the most critical modules are at the top."

"Why not," Jacob said and began drilling down through the training tabs to see what was available. He began with an overview of the *Corsair*, and then queued up two more modules on the practical applications of slip-space drives and the standing rules of engagement for Scout Fleet personnel when deployed outside of Terran space.

The hours ticked by as he immersed himself in the material. He attacked it with a seriousness he lacked in school now that his status had been switched from student to operational. He'd been so engrossed he completely missed the slight shudder through the deck as the *Corsair* meshed-out of the Terranovus system and sent him streaking away from home faster than the light of its star.

"You still salty about being forced into the Corps?"

Jacob looked up from his tablet to see that Captain Webb had walked over and was standing on the opposite side of the table he was seated at. He was between shifts and had come down to the galley to grab a quick bite and do some reading that didn't involve technical specifications of a Terran starship.

"I'm not thrilled about how it was done, if that's what you're really asking, sir." Jacob moved his own tray out of the way and Webb correctly took that as an invitation to sit across from him.

"Explain."

"I'm not as stupid as people seem to think, sir." Jacob closed his book file and shut the tablet off. "I'm not here because I'm uniquely qualified for this duty, I'm here because someone found out about the...*gifts*...I inherited. I realized that as soon as I was being railroaded onto a career path I didn't want and, if we're being honest, it's probably the only reason I was even at the Academy to begin with.

"Now here I am, lightyears from home and in well over my head. I can't imagine what you and Commander Mosler were thinking putting me on this ship before I had even been through the first bit of post-Academy training."

"Are you finished?" Webb asked, sounding bored. "In the spirit of full disclosure yes, your appointment to the Academy was a favor, but we weren't sure what, if any, traits from your father you might have inherited until your little display in the woods on Terranovus."

"My father." Jacob sneered. "If that loser hadn't been so—" that was as far as he got before Webb leaned across the table and punched him in the face with enough force to knock him back in his seat.

"I think I've had about enough of your mouth regarding that subject," Webb said conversationally while Jacob spit blood onto the table, utterly shocked. He forced himself to remain still and had to fight the instinct to grab Webb and throttle him. The captain may have been a Navy SEAL before transferring over to the UEAS, but Jacob knew just how fast and strong he really was and didn't fear the over-the-hill ex-operator.

"Your father was a victim of circumstance when he was taken aboard an alien ship. Jason Burke has sacrificed more for Earth than any one man should ever have to, and what did he get for his troubles? A planet that thinks he's a traitor to his species thanks to the politics of it. Oh! And a sniveling little shit of a son who spits on his name despite the fact he saved the planet from alien invasion not once but twice. He never asked to be ripped from his home and forced to fight for his life, but he made the best of it with what he had.

"So, yes, your Academy slot was all but guaranteed. It was a backchannel favor from the United Earth Council to your father in acknowledgement of his sacrifices on behalf of Earth. Despite what you've heard, there's a standing order for any human ships deployed that Omega Force is to be considered an ally." Jacob sat stunned for a moment, the blood dripping from his busted lip hitting the table unnoticed.

"Omega Force?" he finally asked.

"It's the name he and his crew call themselves," Webb said and tossed a napkin at him. "I don't expect you to change your mind about your father just because I told you so. You'll have to settle that for yourself. Just know that he's *not* a criminal or a traitor and the reasons why he's been listed as such are classified far above your level. Shit, the only reason I even know is that I was there."

"You've actually met him, sir?"

"I was sent to try and kill him...once." Webb's eyes lost focus, and he shuddered before looking back to Jacob. "I can't say anything more about that. It was in the early days when Terranovus was little more than a forward base." Jacob did the math in his head and realized it must have been about the time the second alien attack hit Earth.

"There are other things," Jacob said. "He may have taken the rap for something he didn't do, but that doesn't change things between him and I."

"That's *your* problem." Webb shrugged. "And it's pretty far off-topic of what you asked. To answer your question: yes, your physical gifts you received from Jason Burke make you unique, but the results of your psychological evaluation and aptitude batteries locked you into this role. Very few people are suited for the challenges of serving on Scout Fleet ships, fewer still are able to deploy to the surface of alien worlds and function. Your test results indicate you can, though that's yet to be proven. There are things happening in the quadrant right now that have our allies scared, but they're being tight-lipped about it. In a perfect world, I would have been able to let you serve out your time on the bridge of a starship like you wanted, but our intelligence services think something big is on the horizon, and they've tasked us with finding out what it is. I'm shorthanded, and I just couldn't leave an asset like you off the board. Was there anything else?"

"There is one more thing that you might be able to answer," Jacob said, hesitant to bring up his next concern. "I've always assumed my speed and strength were the result of alien DNA, that maybe my father was some sort of hybrid and passed them on to me. Mosler said that's not true."

"I'm not hearing a question in there."

"Is there any—"

"Alien DNA in your blood?" Webb finished. "Of course not. What I'm about to tell you is *highly* classified, but I figure you have a right to know. One of the members of your father's crew had been a talented geneticist in his previous life. He, with the help of some former colleagues, have modified Burke's genetic structure over the years to maximize his potential. His speed, strength, and endurance make you look like you're stuck in molasses. He also has a few other enhancements like a reinforced skeleton and these cool ocular implants we've not been able to obtain for ourselves yet. As best we can tell, you were conceived just after his second round of upgrades. Some of what Doc—that's the geneticist—did to Jason was passed down to you."

"How many rounds of upgrades has he had?" Jacob asked.

"Four that we know of, but we're unable to track his status or position with any sort of accuracy" Webb said, standing up. "That's all I'm willing to say. I like you, kid, but I'm not going to risk my career for you. Chances are good you'll never cross paths with your father out here...it's a very big galaxy...but if you ever want to talk to him, it can probably be arranged."

"I'll keep that in mind," Jacob said to the captain's retreating back. He didn't bother picking his tablet back up, now completely disinterested in any recreational reading. His hatred for his father had been one of the things that had defined his life, and he sure as hell didn't appreciate Webb punching holes in it.

He looked at the clock on the bulkhead and decided to try and get a few hours' sleep before he had to be back on duty. Mosler wanted him down on the engineering deck shadowing Scarponi for the entire watch to get hands on with the machinery that made the *Corsair* work. At least it would be something to break up the monotony of the extended slip-space flight.

7

Once the manic energy and excitement of departure had passed, and the novelty of traveling on a ship going faster than light faded, Jacob was faced with the hard reality of interstellar travel: it was boring as shit. Days and days on end, staring at the same bulkheads and passing the same assholes in the corridors, he could feel his sanity slowly slipping away.

The problem, he concluded, was that the *Corsair* was tiny. Unbelievably so. Even with only eight crew and one VIP on a three-deck ship, it seemed there was nowhere to go where he wasn't being loomed over or breathed on by someone else. Even with the distraction of the near-constant training regimen that Mosler had imposed on him and his Marines, there still seemed to be too many hours in the day with too little to do.

"Today's the day, LT," Sergeant Jeff Mettler said. Jeff was a former U.S. Marine who had transferred over to the U.E. Marines when the initial call went out. Like Jacob, his psych profile had identified him early on as being suitable for Scout Fleet service, so he was rolled into NAVSOC almost immediately. Unlike Jacob, he was enlisted so he was never given the option of turning down the assignment and going back home. Now, he was one of four Marines directly under his command. When they were deployed, he also served as Team Obsidian's medic.

"Day for what?"

"We meet up with the *Endurance*," Murph said. "Then it's another three *long* weeks back out to the Kaspian Reaches."

"At least it's a break from the normal tedium. I try to be a glass half-full kinda guy," Jeff said.

"Half-full, half-empty...in the Corps, it's still just half a glass of piss they expect you to take a swig of and say thank you," Corporal Angel Marcos said. Angel was the squad's weaponeer—an infantry designation specific to the new branch—and had been given the nickname "Machine Gun Marcos" after Obsidian's second mission. That had been shortened so that everyone now just called him "MG."

"Is Taylor still on the bridge?" Jacob asked, referring to his tech specialist, Taylor Levin. They'd been in the *Corsair's* main cargo hold training on EVA operations for Jacob's benefit. Although unable to go outside the ship while in slip-space, at least in the large area they were able to disable the artificial gravity and let the new lieutenant practice basic maneuvers in a weightless environment. Jacob was comfortable and competent with the equipment, but the gut-wrenching sensation of freefall was still a distraction for him while his own men zipped about like they were born in zero-g.

"Cap has him up there going through all the intel we have available on the target and the planet we're going to," Jeff said. "We've been through there once before. It seems nice at first but you get a strange vibe right as soon as you walk out of the starport."

"It looks and feels like any other ConFed city, right up until you notice everyone seems to be really well armed." MG drifted by on his way to the main hatch. "Gravity is coming back up so, unless you want to fall, I'd get your asses to the floor."

"Apparently, the gangster who runs the faction controlling the planet has some strange ideas about making it look and feel like a respectable, normal world," Jeff said. "Not sure if there's a logical reason for it or if the guy is just a little nuts."

"Niceen-3—that's the planet—is the gateway to the Reaches,"

Murph said. "Everyone who wants in has to go through that system. I'm not sure where I was going with that, it just seemed like it might be related."

"Good story, Murph." MG rolled his eyes. A moment later, they were all slammed into the deck as the gravity came back up well beyond the normal limits. It was another second before a grinning MG turned it back down to 1-g.

"Fucking dickhead," Jeff moaned from where he'd come down on the corner of a transit case.

"I told you to get clear and on the floor."

"*You idiots stop fucking around in there before you break something,*" Mosler's voice broke in over the intercom. "*Stow your gear and get to your stations, we're coming up on mesh-in in a few hours.*"

"You're certain about this?" Captain Webb demanded, jabbing a finger at the holographic display in front of him.

"Yes, sir," Mosler said. "That's the *Endurance*, or what's left of her."

They'd meshed-in without incident at the prescribed coordinates and found the *Pathfinder*-class ship, *Endurance*, sitting close to where they expected her, but the ship was adrift and the aft section of the hull looked like it had been shredded. The melted edges indicated it had likely been hit with plasma weapons.

"Power signature is non-existent, and she looks dark on thermal optics. Whatever happened, it happened a while before we got here," Mosler said. "Sully, go ahead and move us in closer so the sensors can get a better look at the damage."

Jacob's stomach was churning from where he sat at an auxiliary sensor station on the left side of the bridge. He'd been in the military for nearly five years, had seen people die, and on an intellectual level knew there were no *safe* jobs in space, but all of that was in training, on the ground of Terranovus. As he stared at the spinning hulk of the derelict starship, all the bravado and swagger he'd displayed, bragging about how ready he was for the Fleet, came crashing down around him. Hundreds of humans had lost their lives on that ship, a ship that had been attacked by an alien species. It was so surreal he could almost convince himself it was a dream.

"Hey! Brown? You okay over there? You look a little green around the gills."

"Good to go, sir."

"Keep an eye on the long-range active scanners in case whoever did this is still in the area," Mosler ordered. "Sully will have his hands full avoiding anything big in this debris field, and I'll be focused on the ship itself."

"I'll be in the SCIF," Webb said. "Command needs to know about this ASAP."

A SCIF—pronounced *skiff*—stood for Sensitive Compartmented Information Facility. It was a lot of military jargon that meant it was an isolated room with secure communication and data network access people could discuss sensitive information in. An apparent ambush attack on a Terran warship would most certainly qualify as something sensitive they wouldn't want to broadcast over their standard com array.

"These are the coordinates for our rendezvous. Someone knew the *Endurance* would be here," Sully said. "Inside job? Another traitor?"

"*Another?*" Jacob asked.

"Likely she was tracked back from the inner systems by raiders." Mosler shot Sully a warning glare. "How about we focus on not hitting any big chunks of debris and leave the speculation for later?"

"You got it, boss," Sully said.

The bridge fell into an uncomfortable silence as the three of them went about their respective tasks. Jacob quickly reconfigured the *Corsair's* long-range array to continually scan for anything that could possibly be an enemy ship, something he'd only just learned how to do thanks to Captain Mosler's brutal training schedule. As he watched his own terminal, he'd occasionally sneak a peek up at the main display as the wreckage of the *Endurance* came into better view. The computers automatically took the incoming data from the multispectral imagers and created an enhanced image that showed the ship as it would appear if there were a natural light source nearby.

"It looks like we've found the point of impact," Mosler said. "If you look at the rippling on the hull here, and here"—red indicators lit up on the display pointing to what he was referring to—"you can see this is the point where the shields buckled. The attacker concentrated fire here until they got through."

"What's in that area on a *Pathfinder*-class ship?" Jacob asked.

"Let's see... It looks like a maintenance access corridor runs up against the inner hull, and then behind that are some engineering spaces that have something to do with main power distribution," Mosler read off his display. "Huh. It looks like they knew exactly where to hit. Once main power was down, it would be easy to board her, destroy the ship, grapple onto it for salvage...anything you wanted."

"This isn't giving me a great feeling," Sully said. "*Pathfinder*-class ships were some of the first anti-matter powered ships we've sent outside Terran space, but they're still pretty damn new for the specs to be floating around for any random pirate to find."

"Command is sending a ship out here at full burn," Webb said as he walked back onto the bridge. "Our orders are to maintain position and look over the derelict, but we're not to engage anybody who may come back for it."

"That's good since anything that would make short work of the *Endurance*, as appears to be the case, would destroy the *Corsair* within seconds," Mosler said. "This is not a ship designed to slug it out toe to toe with a capital ship."

"Command understands that—after I explained it twice—and if we see anybody coming that isn't flying a Terran flag, we're to withdraw and observe, nothing more," Webb assured him.

Jacob wasn't sure how to feel about Mosler's revelation that the *Corsair* wasn't really much of a fighter. That didn't bode well for him given that the mission was to fly her into some of the most seedy, dangerous parts of the galaxy. Maybe he'd misunderstood and what

Mosler had meant was that the *Endurance* was an especially tough ship.

"Jake, call down to your team and let them know to be ready for a possible boarding action," Mosler said. "If we're going to be here for days waiting on a salvage ship, then it might not be a bad idea to poke around over there and see if anything sensitive was taken. At your discretion, of course, sir."

"That might not be a bad idea at that," Webb mused. "If nothing else, we can have them rig up charges so we can scuttle her completely if someone else comes sniffing around. Brown, I'll take over here. Go down and prep your team."

"Aye-aye, sir," Jacob said. His orders were a little too vague to know exactly what he was prepping them for, but he'd be damned if he stood there with his thumb in his ass whining about needing direction. Though it had been against his wishes, he was an officer in the Marine Corps, and it wouldn't do to mill about like a lost puppy waiting for someone to point him in the right direction.

8

"We're ready when you are, sir."

Jacob's stomach felt like it couldn't make up its mind. It either wanted to climb up into his throat and crowd his larynx or it wanted to escape out his ass and go back into the ship where it was safe and warm. At this point, he was fine with either one, he just wished it would make up its mind. This was no simulator or training exercise. He was standing on the hull of an interstellar starship with four of his men, staring across a gap that, on the sensors, seemed close enough to touch but, in reality, was so far away he couldn't even see the *Endurance* with his naked eye. The best Sully had been able to do was get them within five kilometers before running into debris large enough that they'd had to raise the combat shields.

"Copy, EVA Team," Mosler said over the channel. "You're clear to depart. The shields will allow you to pass through on the way out, but you're going to feel a bit...disoriented."

"Can't wait," Jacob ground out. His squad had filed through the *Corsair's* dorsal hatch until they were all milling about on the hull while Mosler and Webb argued about the best way to get the information they wanted with the relatively short time the Marines had to work with. The air rebreathers would keep them supplied with enough oxygen for days, but the powerpacks on their specialized combat EVA suits would wear down quickly with the long, unassisted flight out and back, as well as the power they would need once they were in the *Endurance*.

"The suit's guidance system is slaved to the sensor feed from the *Corsair*," Murph's voice came in over the team channel. His voice had a definite condescending tone that Jacob didn't appreciate. Jacob was well aware of how the damn suit propulsion worked. "Just execute the formation as you want and our suits will automatically form up around yours."

"Thanks, Sergeant," Jacob bit off his initial sarcastic response. He was the outsider here *and* an untested and newly minted second lieutenant. His team was right to be skeptical, and nothing Murph said had been openly disrespectful or a challenge to his authority. Instead of making an ass of himself, Jacob used his neural implants to scroll through the different formations he could use for the five-man flight and picked the one that had him on point and the rest of the team tucked in and sheltered behind him.

"Everybody ready?" he asked. "In three...two...one...launching."

He gave the command through the neural implant and felt his suit's thrusters light off, pushing him off the hull and towards the spot the sensors said the *Endurance* was. After a quick check that the others were tucking in behind him as they were supposed to, he concentrated on the tumbling chunks of debris the sensors said were along their flightpath.

They were able to cover the first three kilometers without encountering any obstacles before the suit reversed thrust and began decelerating him and veering him over towards the aft section of the derelict. It was once they were locked onto their intended landing site that the first major issue came up. While Jacob was concentrating on the spot near the largest hull breach where they'd make entry, he wasn't monitoring the erratically tumbling debris surrounding the cruiser.

Two of the larger chunks of alloy collided with one another, sending the smaller of the two spinning towards the incoming formation of Marines. As soon as the computer on the *Corsair* recalculated the new trajectories it sounded an alert in their helmets and highlighted the danger on their visor's projected display. Jacob couldn't quite make out the new threat but the new course and speed numbers didn't lie: it was going to intercept them before they would get to the ship if he didn't do something fast. He fought down his panic as he looked at the jagged piece of the *Endurance's* hull on the sensor feed. His men had the same information available and there wasn't a peep on the open channel as they waited for Jacob to do something. Their discipline in the face of something this dangerous was intimidating to the recent Academy grad.

"Break formation!" he ordered, unable to think of anything else to do. "Murph and Jeff go above, Taylor and MG follow me under. Do whatever it takes to dodge the debris, and then land on the hull wherever you can." There was a relieved chorus of affirmatives, and on his display, he could see the squad break up as they all fired their thrusters and accelerated off their flightpath to get clear of the debris. Jacob went to follow, but his suit was still locked onto the same course, slowing him down so that he'd be on a direct collision course with the tumbling chunk of hull plating.

"*Brown, you need to change course immediately!*" Mosler's voice broke in over the com.

"LT, hit the red spot on the left side of your breastplate," MG said over the squad channel. "You're still slaved to the automated guidance." Jacob didn't answer, just started slapping at his chest trying to find the button that would cut his connection to the pre-programmed flightpath that was about to kill him.

"What a stupid fucking system," he griped as he saw the icon for the telemetry feed to the *Corsair* wink out and he had full control of his suit's thrusters again. He saw that the delay had screwed him out of going under it as he'd originally planned as it was angling down and quartering towards him. He didn't have time to try and angle away smoothly as the rest of the squad had done, so he rotated his body perpendicular to his flightpath and commanded the forward thrusters to maximum.

It felt like he shot up and away like a bullet, but his momentum was still carrying him forward towards the *Endurance* and the obstacle as he tried to get up above it. Up and down were relative and not technically accurate when talking about moving in space, but it helped the novice visualize what he wanted to do so he could send the proper commands to his suit.

The suit's computer updated his trajectory, and he could see the green line of his predicted flightpath shift upward...and still put him on course for hitting the obstacle. There was no time left. He subvocalized the command string to override the suit's safeties and pushed the thrusters to their maximum output, ignoring the power draw and nozzle temperature warnings scrolling across the bottom of his display. The blast from his thrusters was so powerful, he was slammed down into his harness and his breath came in short, shallow gasps from the g-loading. He vaguely heard someone shouting at him over the com but the audio was distorted and weak.

"Just a bit more," he grunted, watching the course plot change and was just about to kill his thrusters when everything went dark in his helmet. "Oh, shit."

Now, *really* fighting down the panic, Jacob took a second to do absolutely nothing, afraid that yet another rash move on his part would be the last he made. Without power, the faceplate began to fog up, and he could feel the cold trying to get in now that the heaters were off. He was also now on an uncontrolled, ballistic trajectory without any way to call back to the *Corsair* to let them know he needed rescue.

The deep, calming breaths he took in those few seconds cleared his head a bit, and he was able to focus and remember his training. He reached up to his chest plate, found the recessed switch he was looking for, and twisted it all the way clockwise. When it hit the end of its rotation, he was greeted with a blast of air from the helmet vents, and he could immediately tell his heaters were back on now that emergency power had been activated. He now had air and heat for the next ninety minutes, and he could feel his anxiety ebb away as he began troubleshooting his problems in order of importance.

He booted up the computer off the emergency battery and began a diagnostic. It told him that his main power cell had been knocked offline due to a *thermal event* that caused it to shut down for safety reasons. It prompted him to do a power system reset, which he did, and then told him that main power would be available in thirty seconds. As he waited, he tried to do the math as to how much time had elapsed before he shut his suit down. The chunk of starship hull that had been about to pancake him had to have passed by already, right?

"*—respond! Lieutenant Brown, this is the Corsair...do you require assistance?*"

The shouted words blaring through his headset suddenly startled him. Before he could answer the frantic call, the rest of his systems came online and his holographic display popped up, showing just how far off course he'd drifted.

"This is Brown, I'm fine," he keyed the open channel. "Had a main power failure while trying to dodge the errant obstacle, but it looks like everything is coming back up okay. I have one forward thrust nozzle that is inoperable, and my power is down to forty-six percent, but suit integrity is one hundred and my sensors and guidance are all green."

"Are you still mission capable?"

Jacob couldn't tell who was talking to him but assumed it was Mosler. He checked his position, power levels, and where the *Endurance* was relative to his current course and did the math. He was exhausted after the adrenaline shock of the near-miss and suit failure, but throwing in the towel and asking for a pickup wouldn't do much to earn the respect of the four Marines he was expected to lead.

"I'm good to go, *Corsair*," he answered, putting as much confidence into his voice as he could muster. "I'm heading back to the *Endurance* now."

"We're on the hull and waiting by the breach, LT. You want us to go ahead and make entry?" Murph asked over the team channel.

"Negative, Sergeant. Wait for me."

"Copy, sir."

The flight back to the *Endurance* took longer than he expected, but within forty minutes he saw the cruiser's hull looming out of the darkness. When approaching something like a starship while wearing only a pressure suit, one was almost dumbstruck at just how massive they were. The *Endurance* wasn't considered a large ship by the Navy, but her bulk made him feel small and insignificant as he bent his knees and flared for a landing.

The moment his feet touched, the mag-locks in his boots activated, holding him fast while he shut down his thrusters. He wasn't even inside the damn ship yet and he already felt like he'd been put through the wringer.

"Brown is on the hull," he checked in on the open channel. "Making way to the entry point now. Standby."

"This is creepy," MG said. "None of the lifeboats were launched, but I don't see any bodies."

"There's no evidence of weapons fire either," Murph said. "I don't think they were boarded. If they were, they didn't put up much of a fight."

Jacob had relinquished point duties and put MG in the lead since he said he was familiar with the *Pathfinder*-class layout. They were looking for any signs that might explain what happened to the *Endurance*, but their primary mission was to get to the engineering spaces and make sure her CO, Captain Swank, had activated the failsafes before they lost the ship. It was a critical enough task that the ill-equipped Scout Fleet squad had been sent over in case someone came back for the cruiser before the Fleet's salvage ships arrived.

The going was slow since most of the emergency pressure hatches were still closed and locked. It required that MG get into an access panel beside the hatch and manually decouple the locking mechanism before they could shove the hatch back into the recess. Every time they'd stop to open one, the team would brace themselves in preparation for the explosive decompression of a still-sealed chamber, but halfway into the ship, they'd not found a single compartment that still had atmosphere. They'd also still not found a single crewmember or any evidence of a fight between the crew and boarders.

"Got something up ahead," MG said calmly. "Looks like an appendage in a pressure suit. Not human." The term *'not human'* made the hair stand up on Jacob's neck. The *Endurance had* been boarded by a hostile alien force, and they'd left some of their own behind.

"LT?" Murph prompted.

"Proceed," Jacob said once he realized they were waiting on him. "MG still on point. Murph, you back him up."

"Moving," MG said. Jacob watched as the pair moved off quickly and confidently. MG moved along the right bulkhead while Murph hugged the left and stayed a few meters behind so he could cover his partner. The offending appendage was sticking out of a hatchway on the right so the alien would see Murph first, but MG would be in position to take action if it was hostile...or even still alive.

Jacob could swear he saw the—leg?—twitch as MG approached and leveled his weapon. Even though there wasn't any sound in the vacuum of the dead ship the alien would still be able to detect the vibrations of the suited Marines walking over the deck. Was this an elaborate trap? He forced himself to calm down, well aware that his vitals were being transmitted back to the *Corsair*, and Captain Mosler was likely monitoring them all.

"Looks like we have a second body," Murph said. "Another pressure suit is laying across the first. SHIT! Second target is alive!"

"Converge! Converge!" Jacob shouted and ran forward as MG and Murph rounded the hatchway, weapons trained and yelling at the second figure.

The alien was unmistakable from his coursework: Korkaran. They were a bipedal, saurian species that had retained their long, muscular tails throughout their evolution. The first Korkaran had a huge hole blown through its chest, but the second was alive, though it wasn't making any move to get up or reach for a weapon.

"*Report!*" Mosler's voice came over the com. Jacob nodded to Murph to make the report back.

"Two Korkarans, sir, one still alive," Murph said. "Appears to be injured since it's just staring at us, not moving."

"Scans show extensive bionic upgrades," Taylor said. "Both arms and one leg are cybernetic but appear to be powered down."

"Must be damaged to the point it can't move," Murph said. "LT, you may want to hang back. You haven't gotten the full set of shots yet, and these things carry some nasty shit. It'd be a shame if you picked up something deadly on your first trip."

"Agreed," Jacob said and backed away. There wasn't any pressure within the ship, but there was still some air, and anything coming out of the hole in the first Korkaran might land on his suit. They would go through a decontamination cycle when they went back to the *Corsair*, but why take the chance?

"*Brown, we need to know if Swank was able to hit the failsafes*," Mosler said, subtly coaxing Jacob towards the needed course of action.

"Copy, sir," he replied. "MG, restrain and secure the living Korkaran. Murph, you and I will push forward towards the bridge. Everyone else will go to Engineering and check to make sure everything down there was purged."

"This way, sir," Murph said and continued up the corridor they'd been following.

The rest of the way to the bridge was as boring as Jacob secretly hoped it would be. He kept track of the rest of his team on the holographic display in his helmet and saw they had made it to Engineering before he and Murph actually stepped onto the bridge.

The bridge of the *Endurance* gave Jacob a pang as he looked around, realizing his dream of serving aboard such a vessel as a bridge officer was well and truly dashed. As with the rest of the ship, there were no signs of a struggle, nor were there any bodies of the crew.

"The bridge failsafe was triggered," Murph said, pointing to the captain's key hanging from the armrest of command chair. A small access panel had slid open when that key was turned, then whoever was on bridge watch would have hit the button to destroy the servers that were in a secure room one deck down. The button had to be punched with enough force to break the thin glass rods that were in place to ensure it was never accidentally pressed, but once it was, explosive charges would decimate the hardware below them that contained any classified information Earth wouldn't want to fall into unfriendly hands.

There was an identical system down in Engineering that would ensure all the computers that controlled the *Endurance's* slip-drive and weaponry were destroyed so that reverse-engineering the *Pathfinder*-class ship would be impossible. The hardware could be copied, but without knowing the drive field equations and look-up tables the Terran engineers and scientists had used, it wouldn't even be worth the effort.

"Engineering failsafe was also triggered," MG said over the team channel after Jacob had checked in with them and told them what he and Murph had found. "We're also near the hull breach so we're recording all the data we can to take back to the *Corsair*."

"Copy," Jacob said. "We'll work our way down to you now as soon as we gain access to the server vault and ensure the charges did their job."

"*Belay that, Lieutenant,*" Mosler broke in. "*Secure your prisoner for the recovery crews and get your asses back here, double-time. We have company...and it isn't one of ours.*"

9

"It's been sitting just at the edge of our detection range for the last hour or so, but now it's moving towards us." Mosler pointed to the unknown ship's signature on the main display when Jacob walked back onto the bridge. "Good job getting your people out of the way when that bit of debris came in on you, by the way."

"Yes, sir," Jacob said. He'd gotten out of his pressure suit and back into regular clothes as quickly as he could. "You'd think the guidance system would be smart enough to automatically steer us around obstacles like that." Mosler and Sully exchanged a glance that didn't go unnoticed, but neither said anything.

"No transmission from the newcomer so far?" Webb asked.

"None yet," Mosler said. "It may be just another scavenger and thinks we're the same. How would you like this handled, sir?"

"I'm just a hitchhiker, not even here as an advisor." Webb put his hands up and shook his head. "This is your show, Captain."

Jacob tried to follow the action as Mosler and Sully went back and forth on strategy while the ship on sensors got close enough to begin making out some detail. The system they'd met the *Endurance* in wasn't populated. It was an unremarkable yellow dwarf star with a system of three uninhabitable planets. There weren't any significant resources that would make it attractive to a mining operation, and it wasn't close to any of the well-used interstellar lanes the larger ships in the quadrant tended to stick to. It was picked because it was a conveniently located navigational point. The fact that a ship had shown up here after the attack on the *Endurance* was beyond coincidence. Whoever it was skulking out near the edge of detection range had something to do with it.

"It's moving again," Sully said. "Coming straight for us."

"They've been painting us with active sensors since they arrived," Mosler said. "Now that they know how small we are, and that we don't fit any know military vessel classification, they'll probably get a lot bolder in trying to chase us off."

"We're able to get a bit more resolution on the target now that she's closer," Sully said. "Standby."

"We'll have to back off if they keep coming," Mosler explained to Jake. "From her size, that looks like a cruiser-class ship. The *Corsair* is quick and stealthy but no real match for it in an actual gunfight. What we'll try to—"

"Holy shit," Sully cut off his captain. "You're not going to believe this, Cap. The computer found a type-match for it. That's a *Columbia*-class starship coming towards us."

"That's impossible! Run it again." Mosler turned back to his station to look at the data coming in from the sensor array.

"Already did. Three times," Sully said. "The computer is sure within a ninety-six percent probability."

"*Columbia*-class?" Jacob asked. "I've never heard of—"

"It's a human-built ship," Webb said tightly. "They were in service back before the UEN existed, back when Terranovus was just a top-secret outpost and before Earth began adopting the unification treaties."

"Sir, that doesn't—"

"I'll explain later," Mosler said. "It's classified *far* above your level right now, but we can't exactly just tell you to forget you saw it. The real question is what the hell is it doing here? The only remaining *Columbia*-class ships were scrapped a long time ago."

"The only remaining ships *we* owned were scrapped," Webb said. "There were some that escaped."

"I'm so confused," Jacob said to himself. Pre-United Earth Navy starships? Who the hell did they belong to? The United States maybe?

"You won't be any less confused once it's explained to you...trust me," Sully said. "This does change things a bit, though. That old ship isn't much of a threat to us."

"You're assuming that it hasn't been upgraded," Mosler said. "But looking at these low power signatures, I'm inclined to agree with you. Let's just stay parked here for now and see what it does."

They monitored the ship for another five hours as it continued to hang back around the system boundary. The monotony of the job was so mind-numbing that Jacob found it difficult to maintain focus. He was still worn out from near-disastrous EVA mission to the *Endurance* and now he was staring at a dot on the display that seemed perfectly content to do nothing but sit there.

"Lieutenant, go grab something to eat a couple hours of rack time," Mosler ordered after watching Jacob fighting to keep his head up. "We'll sound the general alarm if you're needed."

"Yes, sir." Jacob didn't argue. He didn't even pull his boots off once he made it back to his quarters, sleep overtaking him the instant his head hit the pillow. So much about the day's events were bothering him, but it was so jumbled and chaotic in his mind that he couldn't see it clearly enough to know exactly why.

Jacob awoke four hours later on his own, feeling surprisingly refreshed. He tapped the screen on the bulkhead and saw there were no alarms and that everything on the *Corsair* was green across the board. He rubbed a hand across the three days' worth of beard, remembered what Mosler said about him looking too clean, and decided to leave it. After four years at the Academy, it felt decidedly strange to not be impeccably groomed and dressed while on duty.

He decided to grab something to eat before heading back up to the bridge since he'd skipped that in lieu of more sleep. While he was in the galley rummaging around, he saw movement out of the corner of his eye. When he turned to look down the main corridor, he caught sight of Murph quietly slipping down the stairwell to the engineering deck. There was something about the way the man was moving that told Jacob he was trying to not be seen. His curiosity piqued, he decided to follow him.

The *Corsair* was not a big ship, so it took Jacob less than a minute to locate Murph and see what he was up to. The sergeant had gone into an avionics service bay, something that, as far as Jacob knew, he wasn't qualified to be messing around on.

"Lose something, Sergeant?"

"Shit! Damnit, LT. You scared the—"

"What are you doing down here?" Jacob asked. By the time he'd gotten to the service bay, Murph had already opened up one of the *Corsair's* avionics boxes and was poking about with a flashlight between his teeth.

"Just checking on something. What are you doing down here?"

"I saw one of my noncoms going into an area that didn't concern him and decided to investigate," Jacob said. "I've read your jacket, Murph. While impressive, it didn't include any training that you may have taken that explains why you'd be down here poking around in the guts of the ship."

"Look, LT, there are some things goin' on that you're not aware of," Murph said, apparently deciding that bluster was his best strategy. The odd thing was Jacob hadn't really suspected Murph of any wrongdoing until he couldn't come up with a good answer as to why he was down in Engineering. For all the fresh lieutenant knew, there was some extra duty that had been assigned to the cagey NCO that Mosler had neglected to tell him about.

"There's a *lot* going on I'm not aware of," Jacob snorted. "That'll happen when you're yanked out of training early and put in an operational unit. That still doesn't explain why—" The general alarm blaring cut him off, and the lighting along the walkways switched from soft blue to red, indicating there was a critical situation.

"*Everyone, get to your stations,*" Mosler's voice came over the intercom. "*Our visitors are making a move.*"

"We'll finish this later," Jacob said, waiting until Murph had closed the black box he'd been poking around in and exited the service bay before following him up to the main deck.

"That cruiser is on a direct intercept now," Mosler said as he walked onto the bridge. Jacob felt a pang of guilt as it was obvious his CO hadn't had a wink of sleep while he'd luxuriated in hours of rack time. "She's still taking her time, but this doesn't look like another half-assed feint."

"What's the ETA on our salvage fleet?" Jacob asked.

"Thirty-nine hours, but we just got word from Fleet Ops that they've dispatched an actual warship to help secure our position," Webb answered. "No word on which ship it is or how quickly it can make it here."

The next few hours were tense. The *Columbia*-class ship kept at its interminable crawl towards where the wreckage of the *Endurance* hung in a heliocentric orbit, trailing behind the second planet. Fatigue had finally overcome Mosler, and he'd left Jacob in charge with *very* explicit instructions to wake him if anything changed. The captain ordered Sully to sleep at the pilot's station in case they needed to retreat quickly.

Soon, all Jacob had for company was the soft hiss of the air handlers, the beeps from the bridge stations, and the not-so-soft snoring from the *Corsair's* pilot. He watched the sensor feed at the captain's station with great interest, wondering about a ship that, according to everything he'd been taught, shouldn't exist. The public knew very little about Earth's first foray into space as possessors of slip-drive technology, but what they'd been told unequivocally was that there had been no space-borne military fielded by humanity until they'd reached a partnership with the Cridal Cooperative. Looking at the sensor data on his display refuted that. How much more was out here that the civilians on his home world were totally in the dark about?

"What the fuck?" Jacob shot up in his seat as the incoming ship did something completely unexpected. "Sully! Wake up!"

"No, sir! I'm sober!" Sully exclaimed as he bolted upright in his seat.

"What?" Jacob asked

"What?"

"Never mind. Look at what our friend is doing."

"Interesting," Sully mused, rubbing at his face. The cruiser had come about hard onto a reciprocal course and was pushing back towards the system boundary at what appeared to be full burn for the aging starship. "She's pushing for mesh-out. The older ships needed a little bit of forward relative velocity this close to a star before the slip-drive could stabilize the fields. Why are they retreating? What did you do?"

"I didn't do shit," Jacob said, reaching over and sending an alert to Mosler's stateroom.

"Something has spooked them, but I don't see anything else on sensors, and ours are a lot better than theirs," Sully said. "This probably isn't great news for us."

"Report!" Mosler barked, looking refreshed and energized after only two hours of sleep. Jacob filled in his captain on what he'd seen, and then replayed the sensor logs so that Mosler could look for himself. "They've gotten new information about something. They're not running from anything in this system."

"Could they have gotten close enough for their sensors to detect what weaponry we have aboard?" Jacob asked.

"Virtually impossible," Mosler said. "Our armament is so well shielded that even the newer ConFed battlecruisers can't detect anything when we've passed within ten thousand klicks. Twice they've let us land without incident on ConFed worlds that explicitly prohibit unregistered warships, which we technically are since we're not flying a Terran flag."

"So now, the real question is, did the new information or orders they received even have anything to do with us?"

"Very good, Lieutenant." Mosler nodded. "For now, we'll assume nothing. Maintain position and posture. Keep an eye out for anyone trying to sneak in on different vectors while we're staring at the tailpipes of a fleeing ship."

"Should we at least—" Sully was cut off by an alarm from the captain's station indicating a priority message was coming in over the slip-com node. Everyone on the bridge remained silent as Mosler read through the plain-text message

"That was a follow-up from Fleet Ops. The ship they dispatched ahead of the salvage fleet is the *Defender*-class destroyer, *UES Sunder*," Mosler said. Sully whistled softly.

"One of the new ones," he said. "I'd heard that most of the Defenders we built were being pressed into service with Cridal units."

"Keep your wild speculation to yourself," Mosler said. "We'll maintain watch here until the *Sunder* shows up, likely dump Captain Webb off on them, and then get the fuck on with our own mission. We've wasted far too much time here as it is."

"A word in private, sir?" Jacob asked softly when Mosler went to leave the bridge. The captain just looked at him for a moment before shrugging.

"Sure," he said. "Sully, you're in charge for a minute. Don't do anything stupid."

"No stupid shit, aye!"

"That may not actually stop him," Mosler said as he led Jacob into the room across the corridor from the SCIF, just aft of the bridge. It was a multi-purpose room dominated by a large table display, complete with holographic generators. Mosler used it as an office/ready room when it wasn't being used for mission planning. "What's on your mind?"

"I'm not sure how to bring this up without making it seem like—"

"Just spit it out, Lieutenant," Mosler sighed. "If it's serious enough to pull me aside then just tell me in a straight-forward manner. This unit doesn't operate any other way."

"I saw Sergeant Murphy down in one of the avionics service bays on the engineering deck poking around inside one of the black boxes," Jacob said. "He seemed high-strung and was extremely evasive when I asked him what he was doing."

"Murph?" Mosler seemed genuinely surprised. "He's not qualified to be fucking around with any of the avionics boxes. You said he was *inside* of one?"

"Yes, sir," Jacob said. "He'd pulled it out of the rack enough to pop off the top inspection panel."

"You remember which box it was?"

"Yes."

"Let's go. Show me."

Jacob was inexplicably nervous on the way down to Engineering. Maybe he should have tracked down Scarponi, the ship's engineer, before going straight to the captain. Even on a ship as small as the *Corsair*, there were still proper protocols for these sorts of things. Mosler was visibly angry as they walked down the main corridor to the ladder well, and Jacob couldn't tell if it was with him for bringing his petty issues directly to the top of the chain of command or with Murph for digging around in areas he wasn't qualified for.

"It was this box, sir," Jacob said, pointing to the avionics module he'd seen his NCO messing with.

"This one? You're *sure* about that?" Mosler pressed. When Jacob nodded, the captain swore and began pulling the connectors off the box. "Shut that emergency hatch. I don't want Scarponi walking in on this."

Jacob did as he was told and watched as Mosler pulled the box out of the rack and laid it gently on the deck. He pulled a multi-tool from his hip pocket and quickly undid all the quarter-turn fasteners to give him access to the box's innards. Muttering to himself, Mosler quickly went through everything until he found a particular circuit board that seemed to offend him, judging by the scrunched-up face he was making, and pulled it out.

"See this?" he asked. Jacob looked over the board in a glance, trying to see something amiss. Even to his untrained eye—or at least barely-trained eye—he could see something that stood out.

"One of the chips on this board doesn't have any conformal coating on it," he said. "So, either it's been repaired or—"

"Or someone has modified it," Mosler finished. He tapped his finger against his chin for a moment before putting the box back together and reinstalling it in the rack. "Follow me. Not a word until I say so."

Jacob, now thoroughly confused, followed his captain back up to the command deck and into the SCIF. Once the hatch closed, and the light turned green to indicate the anti-eavesdropping measures were active, Mosler turned to him.

"That board was not only modified, it was done so with a part that isn't approved for use by Fleet. The part number on the top of that chip was still legible," he said.

"Which means it didn't come from our supply system," Jacob said.

"Another sharp guess, Lieutenant Brown. I guess they didn't send me a dud this time after all," Mosler said. "You're absolutely correct. Furthermore, that box is part of the DataLink Routing and Management Subsystem. Remember when you mentioned that you were surprised the ship's guidance didn't move you around that obstacle automatically? It was supposed to. One of the jobs that box does is relay the commands from the computer to the com system for things like EVA and docking procedures."

"You're suggesting sabotage."

"I'm suggesting nothing, just stating a list of disassociated facts," Mosler corrected, turning to one of the terminals and logging in. "We don't know what that unauthorized part is doing in that box. For all we know, it could have been mistakenly installed by a backshop long before it made it to the *Corsair*, but the fact your whole team almost bites it, and then Murph is down there messing around? A little too coincidental for my liking."

"So, what do we do about it, sir?"

"I'm checking to see... Yep, it's like I thought. We don't have spare DataLink router aboard," Mosler said. "But...the *Sunder* will be here shortly, and that part is common enough they may be carrying one."

"Okay," Jacob said, following the train of thought. "So, we swap out the suspect box for a new, good one. Then what?"

"Then the *Sunder* takes the suspect box and tests it for us," Mosler said. "If we find out that the modification was responsible for almost getting your guys killed, we'll take further steps. That box does a lot more than just sent telemetry to suit guidance during EVA operations, so let's just keep this between us for now."

"Yes, sir," Jacob said, still trying to wrap his head around the fact that the ship might have been sabotaged. "Oh, on an unrelated note, why did you look so pissed when you found out the *Sunder* was inbound?"

"Actually, it's not so unrelated," Mosler said. "We got the call that the *Sunder* was coming just after the inbound cruiser turned tail and ran. I think it's safe to assume that they got the same call." When Jacob just looked confused, he went on. "I know you're well aware of the official story about the second alien attack on Earth."

"Of course," Jacob almost spat out, the anger making his face flush. "A species called the Ull attacked us with the help of—"

"That's not actually what happened." Mosler held up a hand, stopping Jacob before he could launch into another hate-filled tirade about his father. "The Ull were actually partners of Earth, unbeknownst to the general population. They're actually the species we got our initial slip-drive technology from, and they gave us Terranovus, a planet suitable for us that they had colonization rights to.

"The *other* part you don't know is that the administrator for the Terranovus colony that the U.S. government put there had bigger plans for herself. She made a backdoor deal with the Ull and came to Earth with most of the Terranovus fleet. Your old man was the one who helped stop her by bringing his friends from the Cridal Cooperative along with their big capital ships. Most of the fleet surrendered when the Ull abandoned them, but the Terranovus administrator escaped along with about a third of our *Columbia*-class starships. It's almost certain the ship we saw was one of hers."

"And equally certain she still has sympathizers within Earth's military command apparatus," Jacob said, compartmentalizing all the information he'd been given for the moment and focusing on the immediate problem. "You think someone let them know that a destroyer was on its way and they needed to clear out."

"You're quick on your feet." Mosler nodded with approval. "What's not well known is that a lot of officers from the old Terranovus fleet ended up in the UEN when we were trying to cobble together an entire armed service with a few ships and a group of people with no experience serving in space. It's fairly common knowledge within the intel and special operations communities that there are still some loyalists among us."

"This is...distressing," Jacob said, searching for the right word. "You think Murph may be one of them?"

"I'm really hoping not," Mosler said. "He's too young to have served in the original Terranovus fleet, so that would mean the loyalists are turning new recruits."

"I... Thanks for telling me this, sir."

"You won't believe how highly this is classified, so keep your fucking trap *shut* about this," Mosler said. "Don't even talk about it with Webb. I told you not only because eventually you'd be cleared to know about it when I approve your permanent transfer to my crew, but because that chip on your shoulder about what you think your old man did—or didn't do—is heavy enough to cause you trouble. We're not having a Dr. Phil moment here, and I'm not your shoulder to cry on about your daddy issues, I'm just letting you know that you don't know as much as you think you do."

"Thank you anyway, sir," Jacob said stiffly.

"Now get out of here," Mosler said. "I have some people to get in touch with and you have bridge watch until the *Sunder* shows up."

10

"The shuttle is on the way over," Mosler said. "I'll keep Scarponi up here and you grab that new box, get down there, and swap it, and make sure the suspect one is on the shuttle back to the *Sunder* with Captain Webb."

"On it, sir."

As soon as the *Sunder* had appeared in the system, Mosler had requested a secure channel to her captain and made his unusual request for an avionics box out of their spares kit. Once he'd made it clear to the other captain that things needed to be done as discreetly as possible, he'd sent Jacob to get prepped on their side to make sure he could swap out the modules without anybody noticing.

It'd been necessary to bring in Captain Webb, but they both figured if the NAVSOC commander had been compromised, they were more or less screwed anyway. When they'd briefed Webb about what they suspected and now wanted to prove, the ex-SEAL took it with his usual stoicism. He made it clear he didn't want Sergeant Murphy accused of treason without solid evidence since there was only one punishment for it on Terranovus, and there was no way to reverse it should they be mistaken. While he couldn't explain why a Marine NCO would be poking around in Engineering, he seemed to firmly believe that, if the box had been tampered with, it had happened on the ground and installed in the ship during routine maintenance.

"The shuttle is docking now, sir," Sully said.

"I want you to grab some rack time while the *Sunder* is here watching local space," Mosler told his pilot. "Call down and have Scarponi come up and babysit the bridge while we go down and greet our guests."

"Yes, sir!" Sully said enthusiastically, the idea of sleeping in his bed rather than the pilot's seat overriding any questions he might have about the unusual order.

"You ready?" Mosler asked Jacob.

"Ready, sir."

"Let's go."

The ceremony for allowing the crew of the *Sunder's* shuttle aboard the *Corsair* took less than a minute and the three enlisted crewmembers that came over began unloading cargo onto the deck while the officers talked. A tall, Asian petty officer gently set a padded case slightly away from the rest of the cargo and looked Jacob right in the eye, pointing at it for a split second before going on about his task.

Jacob made some show of shifting the transit cases around to organize them before hefting the soft case and walking out of the airlock antechamber. He didn't see anyone as he hauled ass down to Engineering and entered the security override code Mosler had given him on one of the bulkhead displays to disable any warnings to the bridge when he began pulling off connectors. Once he was in the right avionics bay, he verified that the part number on the box the *Sunder* has sent over matched the one they had in their rack and quickly swapped them out. When all the status lights on the new box switched from amber to green, he packed up the suspect module, reset the ship's monitoring and reporting system, and made his way back to the airlock.

The Asian petty officer saw him coming and, without making eye contact, pointed at a spot near the hatch while the *Sunder's* crew finished stacking the cases. While most of it was an elaborate ruse to cover the exchange, it didn't hurt to take on extra provisions from the bigger ship since they were now going to press ahead with their mission.

"A word, Lieutenant?" Captain Webb asked, having snuck up without Jacob noticing him.

"Of course, sir," Jacob answered and followed Webb back to the ready room.

"Mosler told me he'd partially briefed you on matters *well* above your clearance level," Webb continued. "For the record, I think you have a right to know if for no other reason to provide you some context for your...family...issues. Just be smart and keep what you've learned to yourself. It's fairly common knowledge within NAVSOC that there is a rogue human faction out here, but the regular Navy is more or less kept in the dark until we can manage to do anything about it. Even some of our mainline ship captains don't know about the Terranovus coup attempt, and we need to keep it that way for now."

"Understood, Captain," Jacob said. He felt like he was walking a tightrope all of the sudden. Webb often presented himself as a mentor to Jacob, but he had no doubt if the captain perceived him as a security risk, he'd be spending some time in a holding facility.

"You're doing good so far." Webb nodded. "Keep asking questions and keep those eyes open. Trust Mosler. He's one of the absolute best I have, and I can't think of anyone else I'd rather have training a brand-new butter bar lieutenant that I have a vested interest in. I know this isn't the career track you wanted, but there's a lot of reward to go along with the risk I'm asking you to take." Jacob's eyes narrowed at that, but he held his tongue.

"I won't let you down, sir."

Webb stared at him for a moment, looked like he wanted to say more, then turned and left the room. Jacob just shrugged and trailed along after him, taking a peek onto the bridge and seeing Scarponi lounging in the captain's seat, feet up on the console and looking completely bored.

After Webb's lackluster pep talk, he, Mosler, and a full commander from the *Sunder* locked themselves in the SCIF for the next thirty minutes while Jacob supervised his Marines stowing all the cargo the shuttle had brought over. As far as he could tell, there was no difference in Murph's demeanor as he went about his menial task, joking with his teammates and altogether looking as if he didn't have a care in the galaxy. Of course, a trained espionage agent probably wouldn't be standing there sweating and stuttering, and it's not like Jacob was trained in counterintelligence.

"Good luck, gentlemen," Webb said as the trio of officers walked back into the airlock antechamber. "This mission is still of critical importance regardless of the tragedy we've encountered here. Press on."

"Thanks, Captain," Murph said with a wave before yawning and walking back to berthing. "I'm gonna catch a few more hours of sleep if you don't mind, LT."

"Go ahead," Jacob said. "Everyone, get back on your regular watch hours and we'll pick training back up tomorrow. Police the galley and the common area before dispersing." There were a chorus of affirmatives before his team went about cleaning up the main deck and breaking off to find whatever distractions they could. All of them except Taylor Levin, his tech specialist.

"You needed something, Corporal?"

"When were we going to debrief from the *Endurance* op?" Taylor asked.

"Tomorrow," Jacob said.

"As a group or individually?" Taylor asked. The question caught Jacob off-guard, and he had to take a moment to think about it. If Taylor was asking about debriefing individually, he had to assume the young man had something he wanted to tell him in private about the mission but didn't want to have to ask for a private meeting.

"I'll pull you each off one at a time in the coming days," Jacob said finally. "Write down a brief, bullet point synopsis so you don't forget any key details. Tell the others to do the same."

"You got it, LT." Taylor walked off, and Jacob could see on his face that he was relieved by the answer he'd gotten. What the hell could be going on now? For such a small team of elite Marines, there sure seemed to be an overabundance of drama and intrigue.

"*Brown! Get your ass to the bridge*," Mosler's voice came over the intercom. "*We're shoving off, and I need you to man a station.*"

"On my way, sir."

When he walked onto the bridge, he saw that Mosler had taken the pilot's seat and was pointing to the captain's station.

"I'm not waking Sully just to pilot us to the mesh-out point," he explained. "I'm a fully qualified pilot, but Fleet regs are pretty strict about there being an officer in the captain's seat while a ship is underway."

"What should I do?"

"Don't touch anything. I've got our course locked in and the slip-drive is primed. Once Scarponi clears us for slip-space, we'll be out of this system. We've wasted far too much time here as it is."

It was less than twenty minutes later and the *Corsair* was streaking through the uninhabited system on her way to a mesh-out point. The points were really just arbitrary locations in space, the slip-drives could be engaged anywhere outside of a star's immediate vicinity, but they were the navigational points that were agreed upon by nearly all of the spacefaring species flying slip-space capable ships in the quadrant.

"Next stop, the Kaspian Reaches," Mosler said as he engaged the slip-drive. "Also known as the galaxy's anus. You're gonna love it."

"I can't wait," Jacob muttered as the *Corsair* disappeared from real-space.

For the next two weeks, the training Jacob was able to accomplish was minimal thanks to the second round of what Captain Mosler had called *immunizations*. What the injections actually were was a cocktail of engineered viruses, programmed nanobots, and a whole host of other microorganisms that would modify the symbiotic microbiota within him so that he could survive on most alien worlds. It was one of the first things humans had been forced to learn about when the initial group of explorers that went to Terranovus died shortly after they arrived from exposure to the alien atmosphere. Other than the slip-drive itself, the method developed to quickly adapt the human body to alien environs was the most critical component when it came to becoming a spacefaring species.

Jacob knew all of this on an intellectual level, had been warned that the full work-up was much more intense than what cadets got before going to Terranovus, but still he was unprepared for the level of agony he was enduring. In addition to the near-crippling muscle cramps and the wild swings between raging fever and dropping body temperature, it seemed as if all the individual fluids in his body had made some sort of pact to leave...and they were finding whichever exit was most convenient when they made a break for it.

"It looks like the worst has passed, LT," Taylor said one day when he stopped by Jacob's quarters to check on him.

"I feel like it's toying with me at this point," Jacob groaned, leaning back in his chair. He'd been trying to at least get on the terminal in his quarters to go through some of the computer-based training on the *Corsair* that Mosler had sent him, as well as a daily regimen of exercises with his neural implant to master his control over the device. "But if it does decide to kick back in full force—just a fair warning—I will be cycling myself out the airlock."

"Explosive decompression is a nasty way to die."

"I doubt I'd even notice right now. So, what's on your mind, Corporal?"

"You read my filed report of what I saw on the *Endurance*?" Taylor asked. *Shit.* Jacob had forgotten all about the fact he was supposed to do follow-up debriefs with his team.

"To be honest, Taylor, the way you've been dying to tell me what you saw your report was a little...light," he said.

"I don't think the *Endurance* was attacked by an alien ship," Taylor said.

"I'm listening."

"The hull rupture we came in through? The one that just happened to be near a critical power junction that took out the whole shipboard grid? The damage and blast discolorations tell me that it was caused by an explosion from *inside* the ship," Taylor said. "At first, I thought it might have been some sort of critical failure that caused the blowout, but there was nothing in that area that could have ripped the outer hull apart like that. Someone planted a high-power explosive on the inside of the hull."

"This doesn't explain why the crew is missing," Jacob pointed out.

"I didn't claim it did," Taylor countered. "I'm just telling you the facts that I *am* sure of. I'm not qualified to speculate past that."

"Okay, so why the big secret?" Jacob asked. "I feel like this is something that you should have just mentioned right away without the big dramatic buildup."

"I would have, but I wanted to talk to you in private...away from Murph," Taylor said. Now *that* perked Jacob right up.

"Murph?"

"Yeah. I had mentioned what we found to him and he cornered me and MG." Taylor was obviously uncomfortable tattling on his NCO, but he apparently felt strongly enough about what he'd found to skip it up the chain. "He got real intense, told us we didn't know what the fuck we were talking about and, if we were smart, we'd not mention anything to you or Captain Mosler about it. When you asked everyone for a written debrief, he made sure we filtered those through him first."

"Interesting," Jacob said, struggling to stay neutral. "Well, you did the right thing. The chain of command exists for a reason, but in a unit this small, I'm running an open-door policy. Don't worry about Murph. He'll never know you came to talk to me about this."

"Thanks, sir." Taylor seemed to sag in relief. "So, what do you think? About the explosion, I mean?"

"I believe you," Jacob said. "And I think you found a critical clue as to what happened aboard that ship. Just as soon as I think I can make it to the bridge without shitting blood, I'll talk to Captain Mosler about it and see what he thinks."

"Yeah, if they'd have told me about this part I would have never enlisted," Taylor said, sounding genuinely sympathetic. "The good news is that once you shake off all the diseases they pumped into you, and the nanobots finish nesting in your digestive tract, you'll never get food poisoning again when you go back home. Roadkill, actual garbage, Cincinnati-style chili, doesn't matter. Whatever you swallow, they'll kill it."

"Good to know," Jacob said. "Now get out of here and let me die in peace."

Once Taylor was gone and the hatch had slid closed, Jacob reached over to the bulkhead panel and locked it. The fact that he'd caught Murph tampering with the *Corsair's* avionics *and* the sergeant had tried to intimidate his subordinates into suppressing critical information could not be mere coincidence. Mosler had wanted to keep an eye on him just in case he hadn't actually been doing anything wrong in the avionics bay, but now Jacob felt Murph was too big a risk to allow him to roam free on the ship.

It was something he would have to take up with his CO again and try to convince him that Murph needed to at least be confined to quarters pending an investigation. Unfortunately, he hadn't been joking with Taylor. Any trip to the bridge to discuss anything with his boss would have to wait until he was feeling a little more chipper. As he drifted off to sleep again, he was comforted by the hope that Murph wasn't the suicidal type of fanatic who would sabotage an interstellar ship in slip-space while he was still on it.

11

"So, we're about to drop out of slip-space in the Niceen system and you haven't figured out a damn thing...in the last fifteen days?"

"No, sir," Jacob ground out, the words tasting like ash as he was forced to admit complete failure to his commanding officer. "I've questioned Sergeant Murphy twice regarding the incident in the avionics bay but he's got this...*odd*...way of being able to either turn the conversation around so that I feel like *I'm* being questioned, or he slips out of it altogether without actually answering a question."

"I'm hearing a lot of fucking excuses here, Lieutenant." Mosler glared at him. "If you don't get control of your team and exert your authority, one of your NCOs will do it for you. They already probably don't think much of you because you're a brand-new lieutenant, you've never actually gone through special forces indoc training, and you've been pretty vocal with your whining about not wanting to be in the Corps. Now you have one of your sergeants going behind your back and running your team and you don't seem to have any answers."

"Yes, sir." Jacob had more to say, he just wasn't sure how to say it without it coming across like another excuse. It also burned him that his captain was right: he didn't have control of his tiny little four-man team. His two NCOs were *handling* him while Murph was the one actually calling the shots.

"That doesn't necessarily make you any different than any other butter bar that's ever had to come in and manage a bunch of grunts, but this job is different...and *you* were supposed to be different." Mosler continued to grind his heel on Jacob's ego. "When Webb yanked you out of the Academy early and sold me on taking you on because of your...talents, he assured me you would be able to hit the ground running. Damnit, Jake, this job isn't just about how much you can bench or how fast you can run, you need to be a leader."

"You've got me over a barrel here, sir," Jacob said finally. "I'm not sure what you want me to do about our immediate situation." Mosler seemed to deflate a bit as he contemplated Jacob's words.

"Sergeant Murphy is a highly decorated Marine who has been on my crew for over a year without so much as being late for a shift," he said. "You've brought some serious accusations against him. It's up to you to prove that there's enough there for me to make it official and begin an inquiry that—even if we're wrong—will ruin his career. NAVSOC is supposed to be above those types of petty considerations, but the reality is that if I went around bringing up my operators on espionage charges without solid evidence, they'll run me right out the door as well.

"I guess I may as well tell you now that there's nothing actionable from the avionics box you pulled off the *Corsair*. When the *Sunder's* backshop began to probe around, it triggered a failsafe and the suspect part destroyed itself. Webb has people backtracking the components through the supply chain, but that's not likely to be much of a help."

"So, without something more solid on why Murph was digging around in that box we don't have anything actionable," Jacob said.

"Right," Mosler said. "Sure, I could drag Murph in here and try to make him talk, but your team would then know you ran to me and that I was coming down on one of them, because of you. If you think they don't respect you now, wait until something like that and see how it goes. They may frag your ass for it." Jacob gulped but said nothing. He was aware of *fragging*, but it was always more of an urban legend among cadets than anything else. What it meant was that if Jacob's team felt he was putting their lives or their mission at risk, they'd kill him and call it an accident.

"I'd like to avoid that if possible," Jacob said.

"Glad to hear it. We land on Niceen-3 in two days. I'd appreciate it if you could either give me some sort of evidence that Murph is tampering with my ship or, barring that, clear him completely so I can tell the computer to stop monitoring his every movement. I've also had Scarponi working sixteen hours a day going over every square inch of this tub to make sure there aren't any other questionable parts on her. I'm sure he'd appreciate the chance to get some sleep." Jacob was surprised to learn that Mosler had at least taken some steps to mitigate any risk Murph may pose. He'd been under the impression the captain was just letting him flounder on his own. "How's your mission planning coming?"

"Good, sir. The fact this team has already been to Niceen-3 and has some familiarity with the planet has helped." Jacob had gotten used to the abrupt subject changes when talking to Mosler. "We're keeping this as straightforward as possible. We'll go through immigration control using the same documents they used the last time to avoid any issues with secondary security protocols like biometric scanners or facial recognition. Humans are still rare enough in this part of the quadrant that there won't be many on record."

"Sensible," Mosler said. "They didn't make too much trouble here last time so you shouldn't be detained."

"If that doesn't work, we'll bribe our way in." Jacob shrugged. Scout Fleet's intel on Niceen-3 was complete enough that he'd even been able to determine how large a bribe he should offer so that it was accepted without haggling, but not so large that they'd have him jumped outside the starport for more. Team Obsidian had been through this region twice before, and MG assured him that getting through the checkpoints was just a formality.

"Just because this seems like a straightforward grab, don't get complacent," Mosler warned. "I've met the target before. She doesn't spook easily, and if she's reaching out for help, there's a damn good reason for it."

"That brings up something that's been bothering me," Jacob admitted. "Why would she reach out to us at all? No offense, sir, but as relative newcomers on the scene, I would think she'd have called someone a little more established than us."

"Like I said: she has a good reason for everything she does," Mosler said. "I couldn't guess why she reached out to us, nor am I particularly interested. Once we turn her over on Terranovus, she's someone else's problem."

"Yes, sir." Jacob stood when Mosler did, assuming the briefing was over.

"*Stand by for mesh-in,*" Sully's voice came over the intercom. "*Welcome back to the Kaspian Reaches, everyone. I hope your wills are updated.*"

"You ready for this, LT?" MG asked with a huge, wide smile.

"Good to go," Jacob said, trying to inject as much confidence into his voice as he could muster. The *Corsair* had been cleared to land almost as soon as they'd hit their holding orbit, and Sully wasted no time bringing the ship down for a smooth landing on their assigned pad. As soon as the landing gear touched the tarmac, Jacob's anxiety had spiked. No more training, no more lectures, no more talking. He was about to set foot on an alien planet as a member of a military special operations unit, and he couldn't have felt more unqualified for the job he was now being asked to do.

Before they'd landed, Mosler ordered Mettler to give Jacob one more scan in the infirmary to make sure he could safely operate in an alien biosphere. When that had checked out, he'd greenlit the operation and told Jacob he had seventy-two hours to grab the target and get back to the *Corsair*. After the final mission brief and equipment check, they were now standing just inside the pressure doors and waiting for Mosler to lower the cargo ramp.

"*Ground Team, you're clear to disembark,*" Mosler's voice came over their coms. "*Good luck and don't drag this out. We want to be gone as quickly as possible. Corsair Actual, out.*" Due to security concerns and the practicality of trying to maintain a constant com link, once the team left the *Corsair*, they'd be out of contact with Captain Mosler unless there was an emergency.

Jacob jumped slightly as the cargo ramp lurched and yawned open with a whine of hydraulic actuators. When the pressure doors cracked open and the cool, dry air of Niceen-3 rolled in, Jacob tamped down his panic reflex and allowed it to be pulled into his lungs, and then promptly began gagging and coughing.

The smell. Oh, holy shit...the horrible, God-awful, mind-altering smell.

While the others laughed and high-fived each other, Jacob had to concentrate on taking shallow breaths through his mouth so he didn't pass out. Eventually, his sense of smell began to attenuate the stench wafting in and he was able to breathe normally without gagging.

"Just a little initiation, LT," Murph said. "All these planets have their own unique stench about them. Niceen-3's just happens to be a little worse than most."

"Good times," Jacob said hoarsely. "Any other surprises?"

"The oxygen content is a bit low on this planet," Murph said seriously. "It's not much, but you'll feel it if you have to exert yourself for any length of time."

"I can handle that," Jacob said. "Alright, enough fucking around. Let's get this job started so we can get it finished."

Niceen-3 wasn't what Jacob expected when he'd been told about how lawless and dirty the Kaspian Reaches were by Mosler and Murph. He figured it would be dirty, rundown, and something like a scene from the American Wild West but with aliens instead of cowboys. What he saw was a bustling modern city that was breathtaking, if somewhat sterile. The spires of the buildings near the urban center reached hundreds of meters into the sky, and Jacob could see the tracks of the public transport mag-lev trains flowing into the epicenter like veins.

Once they cleared through the immigration control checkpoint with shocking ease, Jacob could begin to sense something...off... about the city. He realized the sterility he'd felt at first glance was probably due to the fact that *everything* appeared to be new. The decorative pavers on the walking paths, the glass partitions that separated the passenger platform from the mag-lev tracks, signs that directed pedestrians where to go, all of it looked like it had been installed at the same time, and recently.

"Is the whole planet like this city?" Jacob asked, noticing that a group of aliens they'd just passed were scarred up and appeared to be hiding weapons under their clothing.

"You mean full of aliens?" Murph asked.

"What? No, I sort of assumed an alien planet would come populated with aliens. I'm talking about how clean and...new...everything is," Jacob said.

"So, you're fine being stuck in the middle of all these strange looking beings?" MG asked. "Not feeling panicky or overwhelmed?"

"What is this? You guys fucking with me right now?" Jacob asked, noticing the look exchanged between his two noncoms.

"Just asking," Murph said. "This is your first time out in the wild. Having your psych battery say you're fit for off-world duty is one thing, actually being out here is totally different."

"If I didn't have the neural implant running real-time translation it would probably be a bit scary, but this isn't so bad." Jacob shrugged. "Actually, none of the aliens here look as exotic as I assumed they would."

"Apex beings that evolve on Earth-type worlds tend to conform to a few general types, bilateral symmetry with two legs being one of the most common," Mettler said. "There are some wild looking ones out there, but they'll usually stick together. Apparently, there are a ton of planets with intelligent insectoid life, but their planets usually have an atmosphere that makes them undesirable, so they're left alone."

"Is anyone going to answer my damn question?" Jacob asked.

"Huh? Oh... No, this city is unique," MG said. "The Reaches are controlled by overlapping syndicates, each run by its own kingpin. The boss that runs Niceen likes to fancy himself a legitimate businessman and has spent an unbelievable amount of money building this city and making sure everyone plays nice within it, but make no mistake, this place is dangerous."

The team left street level and made their way up the wide stairs to the mag-lev platform to wait for the next train that would take them into the city proper. The ubiquitous mag-levs were far and away the most common form of mass transit within ConFed controlled space. They were cheap to build, reliable, safe, and lasted forever since the train never actually touched the track. Some of the lines on the older Core Worlds had been in service for hundreds of years with only general maintenance. Jacob had read that the same systems were already replacing traditional trains back on Earth in some of the larger cities.

"Standard spread?" Taylor asked.

"Two groups, same train, different cars," Jacob said. Standard operating procedure for Obsidian would have been to split up into singles or pairs and take two different trains. It helped them detect and shake off anybody that might be tailing them and made sure that nobody saw them together, thus making it impossible to associate them with each other. Jacob decided against that given his status as a rookie and the fact that the humans were already getting enough curious looks as it was. He assumed that was because there just weren't that many humans outside of the Solar System just yet and most of those were serving aboard capital starships, not skulking around in the Kaspian Reaches.

"We'll go to the forward part of the platform," Murph said, grabbing Taylor and Mettler. Jacob had noticed the look between him and MG again and decided not to make an issue about it unless one of them actually started questioning his orders.

"This is going fairly smooth," MG said quietly once the train set off towards the city.

"It also seems like it would be the easiest part," Jacob said. "If anybody were going to intercept us, I doubt it would be so close to the main starport."

"True," MG conceded. "You ever see a Veran before?" Jacob's head snapped up before he remembered that their objective was a Veran female. The fact was that he *had* seen one before, the same place and time he'd seen his first battlesynth when his father had stopped by for a visit, but there's no way MG could know about that. Hell, even Captain Webb didn't know about the brief, late-night visit. He thought it was an odd coincidence that within the span of weeks he had met members from two very different alien species, both of which were also represented on his father's tiny crew.

"Four arms, pale green skin?" Jacob asked. "I've read about them."

"They're an odd species," MG went on. "When they—"

"I don't think it's a good idea to be discussing this particular subject in public," Jacob cut him off. "Given how few of this species are likely here, it would sort of narrow down what we're here to do, wouldn't it?"

"I...uh...yeah, I guess it would, LT," MG stammered. At first, he looked pissed at being reprimanded by the rookie, then looked away. The pair continued to casually scan their fellow passengers and the city they were approaching in uncomfortable silence.

"You pick up on anything?" Murph asked once they'd disembarked at their desired stop and had regrouped.

"Nothing," MG said, seeming to be over his pique at being reprimanded.

"Let's keep the same separation for now," Jacob said. "Murph, your team will take point. We'll follow around fifty meters behind you. Actually, on second thought, I'll take Taylor and Mettler, you and MG have point. Don't break com silence unless absolutely necessary."

"You got it," Murph said, waving for MG to follow him.

They reconfigured into two groups and made their way down off the platform and into the neighborhood that was just on the outskirts of what would be considered the metro area. The buildings were still that same light-gray color, but the tallest in the area only rose to a height of twenty stories. The one they were heading to was five blocks away from the mag-lev platform.

"So, what were you guys doing the last time you were on this planet?" Jacob asked.

"You'd have to ask Captain Mosler about that," Mettler said evasively. "We're not cleared to talk about it."

"Even though you were there? And I'm now in charge of this team?"

"I don't make the rules, LT."

Jacob saw Murph and MG stop in front of the building their objective was supposed to be in and picked up the pace to catch them. Both looked apprehensive when he got to them.

"What's up?" he asked.

"She's not answering the building's page system." Murph gestured to the glass panel near the door he'd been using. "It's not a secure building so we can still get in, but she's not known for liking unexpected visitors."

Jacob thought back to the intel package he'd read on their objective. Weef Zadra, who went by just "Zadra," was a natural born Veran who still held citizenship on her home world of Ver, though she rarely visited. It was unknown where she'd received her training in intelligence and counterintelligence, but she was widely regarded as one of the best at what she did. In other words, she would always see you coming. She was also rumored to be more than capable of defending herself should the need arise, which explained why a lone Veran had thrived for so long on a rough planet like Niceen-3.

"I assume you tried the dead drop com addresses she gave us?" Jacob asked.

"Of course. I tried those as soon as we were off the mag-lev," Murph said.

"No choice but to go up," Jacob sighed. "Let's hope she doesn't have an itchy trigger finger before we can identify ourselves."

The team piled into two different lift cars that whisked them up to the tenth floor of the building where Zadra's office was located. Once the doors opened up, everyone on his team pulled their primary weapons out of concealment, so Jacob followed their lead and unslung the plasma carbine from where it hung inside his long coat. They advanced with Murph in the lead, followed by Jacob, and then MG with the others trailing slightly behind. A few doors slid open up along the hallway and, after one look at the heavily armed humans marching by, closed just as quickly.

"It's not locked," Jacob said when they reached Zadra's door. The touch panel on the frame was ringed in white, not the customary blue that said the door was locked.

"We going in?" Murph asked.

"We're going in," Jacob confirmed, raising his weapon and waiting until his team was in position. A simple breach was one of the things they'd trained on in the *Corsair's* cargo bay, so no verbal commands were needed. Once he saw they were ready, he pressed and held the "Open" icon on the wall panel and moved aside as the door whisked open silently. MG and Taylor rushed inside while Murph cleared immediately to their right. Jacob and Mettler stayed outside to cover the hallway and as a reserve force should the entry team hit resistance.

"Clear."

"Clear!"

"All clear, LT!"

Jacob motioned Mettler in before moving into the office/residence himself and closing the door. It wouldn't obey his command to lock, so he left it unsecured and stuck a motion sensor on the wall. The device would at least give them warning of anyone approaching, as well as how many individual targets.

When he entered the residence, he was struck by how normal the place would have appeared had it been on Earth. The first two rooms of the apartment looked like any typical small office with a door separating it from the living quarters beyond. What wasn't typical, however, was that the place had obviously been ransacked.

"Someone got here before us."

"No shit, MG," Mettler fired back. "Any other nuggets of wisdom to offer?"

"Just this one; your mom is the best I've—"

"Let's focus on the job so we can exfil and let Captain Mosler know we don't have the objective," Jacob interrupted. "Murph, where the hell do we even start with this mess? Murph? *Murph!*"

"Huh? Oh, sorry, LT." Murph shook off his distraction.

"What is it?"

"This looks...staged," Murph said. "Whoever trashed this place would know she wouldn't be keeping anything of value out here, especially in hardcopy or on an unsecure tablet. I don't see any signs of a struggle. No weapons fire, no blood, none of the other furniture fucked up, just a mess right here near the desk."

"That seems to be good news for us," MG said. "Maybe we can assume she's still alive."

"I think you're missing the point, MG," Jacob said, his eyes never leaving Murph. "If this is staged, who was it done by? More importantly, who was it done *for?*"

"That's the question, isn't it?" Murph asked. A split second later, the motion sensor Jacob had planted sent an alarm to the mission computers they all wore on their wrists letting them know that ten beings were quickly converging on their position.

"I guess that answers *that* question," Jacob sighed. "This is an ambush."

12

"Smooth move with the motion sensor, LT." Murph clapped Jacob on the back as the team took up defensive positions in the apartment. "Do you remember what the other function of that particular device is?"

"Uh..." Jacob's mind had gone completely blank. He stared at Murph in disbelief as he could now hear the assault team outside the door. "Maybe this isn't the best time for a training session, Sergeant."

"The Mk.4 Spider is a multi-spectral scanner that can monitor an area of sixty square meters and has a maximum transmitting range of two kilometers," Murph lectured as the first sounds of someone messing around just outside the door became apparent. "What most people forget is that the device is also an anti-personnel mine that can be set to detonate on proximity or"—Murph gave a predatory smile and poised his finger over the screen of his combat computer —"remote signal." He pressed the green icon, and there was a hard *whump* that shook the door in the frame.

"Yeah, but it's not that powerful," MG said. "That probably took out the two closest to the door but that's about it."

"Better than nothing," Murph said. "Taylor, get the door."

Jacob could feel his heartbeat in his ears and his mouth had gone completely dry. This was happening, and nothing could stop it. When the door opened, a group of aliens were going to come in shooting, trying to kill them, and he'd have to shoot back. All of his training at the Academy seemed to evaporate, and when Taylor hit the door control and scuttled back into a defensive position, he just stood there, rooted to the floor. Even when the first shots were exchanged it seemed to be happening in slow motion through a haze.

"Goddamnit, LT!" Murph shoved him so hard his feet left the floor, and he landed behind the oversized desk. "Get in the fucking fight or get out of the way!"

Jacob's paralysis was snapped as soon as he hit the floor and everything seemed to speed up again around him. He heard the snarl of plasma weapons and the acrid stench of burning building material and upholstery where wild shots scorched whatever they hit. He grabbed his own weapon, flicked the safety off, and came up from behind the desk to see what was happening.

The enemy—he had no idea what species they were—had hit the chokepoint created by the doorway while his own team, having had the luxury of a warning, had picked their positions smartly and were able to overlap their fields of fire to turn the entry into a kill box. Jacob looked as two dead aliens were dragged away and a third appeared, this one wearing a bulky pack with thick power cables that ran to a device it was holding.

"This asshole has a shield generator!" Mettler yelled. "Falling back!" Mettler had to give ground from the enemy's advance since he was the closest to the door. Jacob could now see that what he first thought was a weapon was actually a portable shield generator, a miniature version of the type that protected the *Corsair*. The Marines' fire slammed into the energy barrier and was dissipated. Jacob knew the weapons they carried weren't powerful enough to overwhelm the shield, even if they concentrated all of their fire on it, and that the enemy would soon be able to get past the doorway and into the relative open area of the office where they could use their numerical advantage.

"Everybody, clear out of the doorway!" Jacob shouted, letting his plasma carbine fall and hand by its sling. The massive L-shaped desk he'd been behind was actually two pieces and made of some sort of smooth synthetic material that had some real heft to it. He grabbed the shorter of the two sections and, pivoting on the ball of his right foot, flung it at the alien carrying the shield generator. The energy shield could absorb and dissipate blasts from energy weapons, but when it deflected a ballistic projectile, it transferred the energy back to the source. In this case, it was the emitter strapped to the alien's forearm.

The desk slammed into the shield and the room lit up like the sun from the arcing and flaring, forcing everyone to shield their eyes. Jacob had been expecting that and had been focused on the floor in front of him when the desk knocked the alien into the door frame with a warbling cry. It also raised its arms up to keep from being knocked down completely, exposing its feet and shins. Jacob drew his sidearm and snap fired a dozen shots, scoring nine hits on both the alien's unprotected feet. The warbling cry of surprise turned into a piercing shriek of agony, and it collapsed backwards, the edge of the energy shield cutting into the chest of its comrade that had been standing too close at the time.

"Light 'em up!" Murph barked and the Marines started hammering into the three remaining aliens, putting them down in short order.

"Cease fire!" Jacob shouted. "Mettler, check the ones we killed outside. Is anybody hurt?"

"I got a flash burn from a near miss, but I'll live," MG said, holding his side.

"Anybody else?"

"We're good, LT," Murph said, looking at Jacob oddly. He went over and helped Mettler move the desk out of the way so they could go out and assess the damage in the hallway.

"So, what the hell are these things?" Jacob asked.

"They're a species called the Ull," Taylor said quietly. Before Jacob could ask if they were the same Ull that Mosler had been telling him about some days prior, he was called out into the hall by Murph.

"We have a real problem here," the sergeant said, gesturing down to two dead bodies. The anti-personnel mine had made a mess of things, but when Murph rolled the one over, it was unmistakable that it was human.

"What the fuck?" Jacob asked. "Did we just frag our own?"

"Not likely," Murph said carefully, seeming to hold back. "These may have been...contractors...working with the Ull here."

"Mercenaries?"

"Sure, why not? Let's say they're mercs."

"What would you say they were?" Jacob asked.

"Fucking traitors," Mettler said with enough venom to make Jacob take a step back. The corporal spit on the corpse and walked back into the room to help the other.

"That *would* be more accurate," Murph said. "We'll fill you in later. Right now, we need to get the hell out of here. Niceen-3 is pretty lax on gunplay if it's well contained, but setting off the explosive in the hallway may get their security force's attention."

The team scrambled to drag the rest of the bodies into the ruined apartment to at least clear the hallway. During the firefight, the automated fire suppressant system had triggered, which forced them to blow out one of the floor-to-ceiling picture windows so they didn't asphyxiate from the gas that was being pumped in. Apparently, the building designers were far more concerned about the structure than the survival of the occupants in the event of a fire.

"*Standby.*"

Everyone froze. The voice was obviously computer generated and had come from the overhead speakers. The Marines all just looked at each other, unsure what was going on. A moment later a holographic projector hidden in the wall sputtered to life and the image of a Veran female resolved itself into an impressively solid looking likeness. At a glance, Jacob would swear she was standing in the room with them.

"Humans," she sighed. "I suppose it was too much to hope for that you wouldn't demolish my Niceen home looking for clues. Is all your species this directly savage or have I just been unlucky in the ones I've met so far?"

"Weef Zadra, I presume," Jacob said, taking the lead when nobody else made any move to speak.

"You look familiar," Zadra said. "Have we met before?"

"I guarantee we haven't. My name is Lieutenant Jacob Brown of the United Earth Navy," Jacob said. "We've come all this way to…rescue…you. Any chance you're hiding out in a panic room within this apartment?"

"Not a chance," Zadra laughed. "I left Niceen-3 after the second ConFed hit squad came into that neighborhood looking for me. I've been remotely observing over a secure slip-com link until one of the contractors I'd reached out to showed up to extract me. I have to say I'm somewhat surprised it was Marcus Webb's group. I assumed it would be one of Saditava Mok's teams."

"I don't know who that is," Jacob said, though he caught Murph blanch out of the corner of his eye. "Zadra, time is a little critical right now—"

"Yes, of course, now that you've demolished half the floor of my building, Niceen's pitiful excuse for a police force will be arriving to shake down the perpetrators for money," Zadra said. "I'm not on that planet, Young Lieutenant. The location of where I'm hiding is there"—a red line shot from Zadra's extended finger and pointed to a spot on the far wall—"and you better be quick about it. The authorities are on their way even now."

Before Jacob could ask her to clarify, the hologram disappeared just before Murph took the butt of his weapon and bashed it into the wall right where the line had pointed to. It took a few hits to make it all the way through the fibrous material they used for walls on Niceen-3, and then two people to tear the cladding back so Jacob could look inside. There, in a small shelf built into the metal wall supports, was a case containing two standard data cards.

"Smart," Murph said. "She can't guarantee that her slip-com transmissions aren't being intercepted so she didn't say her location over the link. Hopefully, these aren't encrypted or, if they are, she used a routine she knows we'll be able to unlock."

"Let's get out of here," Jacob said, pocketing the cards. "Did we get images of the two dead humans to see if we can ID them later?"

"Got it," Taylor said.

"Then let's move."

They made it back down to the street level without any interference from the locals and were a block away from the building when the first aircars began landing on the roof. Jacob could see the smoke roiling out of the window they'd broken as Zadra's belongings continued to smolder after being peppered with hundreds of plasma bolts. Jacob didn't know what sort of public surveillance the planet might have, but given the reputation of the Reaches, he had to assume that even if the city put up cameras, the locals would likely destroy them before too long.

"Split now," Jacob said. "Head back to the *Corsair*."

As they'd planned before even landing on Niceen-3, they peeled off one at a time and took separate routes back to different mag-lev platforms to catch a ride to the starport. There had been some argument during the initial mission planning about the risk of moving individually through the city when one of the team members was as green as a new sapling, but Jacob overrode their objections. Eventually, they'd learn about his...gifts...but for now, he'd let them think he was just another pain in the ass second lieutenant who needed constant supervision.

Jacob was tempted to run to his designated platform so he could get back to the *Corsair* sooner, but since he was carrying the data cards, he decided that trying to blend in was the wisest course of action. It wasn't as if Captain Mosler could leave before the slowest of them made it back anyway.

Maybe it was the perspective gained from just having been in a firefight in the last building, but the city streets didn't seem nearly as threatening to Jacob as they had on the way in.

Niceen-3's immigration control only cared about tracking who was coming in, not who was leaving. Jacob was able to simply flash his credentials that showed him as a member of the *Corsair's* crew, and they let him through. He jumped on one of the automated trams that ran along the perimeter of the active ramp. The ship was parked nearly four kilometers away since Mosler didn't want to be too close to the terminal building itself in case they had to make a hasty retreat.

The open-air tram was only moving at around twenty kilometers per hour, so Jacob didn't bother pressing the button to get it to slow down, instead leaping off and hitting the ground at a brisk run. The *Corsair* was sitting just as he'd left it, but there was a tickling at the back of his mind that something was...off. He resisted the urge to break com silence and call ahead, shaking off the feeling and jogging up the ramp and dropping off his gear in the armory. When he made it to the bridge, however, he wished he'd listened to that nagging feeling and had at least kept one of his sidearms.

"Look, Brown, I know how this looks, but I—"

"You mother fucker!" Jacob raged. "I *knew* it! I knew it when I caught you messing around in that box!"

Murph had beaten him back to the ship. The tall Marine was standing over Mosler's lifeless body, his sidearm still in his hand. Jacob could see that Sully was slumped over in the seat but couldn't tell if the pilot was still breathing or not.

"Damnit, Jacob, you have to listen to me!" Murph had started to raise his sidearm into a defensive posture when Jacob acted. Murph was good, but he wasn't ready for how fast Jacob could launch himself across the bridge. He'd barely brought the pistol halfway up when Jacob slammed into him, knocking the gun away along with his breath. The lieutenant was able to easily slam Murph onto the deck and climb over him, immobilizing his arms.

"You murdering, traitorous piece of shit!" Jacob snarled before driving his fist down into Murph's face, the sergeant still wearing the same astonished expression he had when Jacob had crossed the bridge in the blink of an eye.

13

"So... what'd we miss?"

Mettler and Taylor arrived at the same time, leaving MG as the only member of Obsidian still not aboard the *Corsair*. Jacob had been able to rein in his rage and, rather than kill Murph, had secured him to a seat with restraints he'd found in the armory. Mosler was indeed dead as he'd feared, the loss of his CO hitting him harder than he would have thought given he'd just met the man. Sully was alive, but unconscious. Jacob had carried the lanky pilot to the infirmary and had the automated systems working on him.

"I walked up onto the bridge and saw Murph standing over the captain's body, sidearm still drawn," Jacob said, watching the newcomers carefully. He'd rearmed himself after the fight and was now trusting nobody.

"Wait, what?! Murph fucking killed the captain?" Mettler asked. "Why?"

"I haven't been able to question him," Jacob said. "I knocked him out and he hasn't woken up yet."

"*You* knocked out Murph?" Taylor sounded skeptical. "You, a squeaky new lieutenant who's never even been through BRC or AdSOC training managed to take down an *armed* Sergeant Murphy without getting a scratch on you?"

"I surprised him," Jacob deadpanned.

"Wasn't... me."

"Looks like he's coming around," Mettler said, walking over to Murph. "What?"

"It wasn't...me," Murph struggled to get out.

"It wasn't him." Everyone spun to see who the new voice belonged to, and they saw Sully leaning against the hatchway, holding a cold pack to the side of his head. "It was Scarponi."

"What? Scarponi?" Jacob asked, realizing he hadn't seen the engineer since he'd been back. "What happened, Sully?"

"I gotta sit down before I puke again," Sully said, stumbling over to one of the sensor station seats and collapsing into it. "The med bay computer says I have a mild concussion. Doesn't feel all that mild."

"You saw what happened here?" Jacob pressed.

"Yeah. We were monitoring the inbound traffic when we saw a *Clipper*-class dropship coming down," Sully said. "Those haven't been used in years, so we knew it wasn't one of the other Scout Fleet teams. We tracked where it landed, and Mosler was about to walk over and check it out himself when all the displays began flashing warnings and the lights started to flicker.

"Next thing I know, Scarponi is standing on the bridge with an old pistol—like an actual fucking pistol, an old semi-auto that shoots bullets—and shoots the captain right in the head." Sully stopped and looked over where Mosler's body was still on the deck, covered with a sheet, and broke down for a moment, tears rolling freely down his cheeks.

"How did you get injured?" Jacob asked gently.

"I was sitting down in the pit." Sully gestured to the pilot's station that was sunken into the deck. "His gun must have jammed, or he didn't want to waste the bullets, because when I turned to get out of my seat, he kicked me in the side of the head with those fuckin' safety-toe boots he wears. That was lights out for me."

"And then I came in after Scarponi was already gone, and about five minutes before you arrived," Murph said. "I knew something was up because the ship was locked up tight when I got here and the codes were scrambled. I had to use an override code I'd gotten from Mosler a while back." Jacob pulled the key for the restraints from his pocket and walked over, releasing Murph by touching the coded key to the mechanism and pushing the button.

"Do you need medical attention, Sergeant?" he asked.

"I'll be okay," Murph said, rubbing his wrists. "You pack a hell of a wallop, LT. Don't worry, no hard feelings. I'd have reacted the same way in your shoes. I'm just glad you had the restraint to not kill me."

"Me too," Jacob said, now feeling guilty for reacting without all the facts. "So, humans on the team that tried to hit us, an obsolete human dropship comes in on top of us after an obsolete class of human starship happens to stumble across the wreckage of the *Endurance*. I guess we know where they were getting their information from."

"Scarponi was a replacement crew member who had been with us for less than a month before you arrived," Sully said. "We assumed he was NAVSOC, but I'd never seen him before and it's a pretty small community."

"Let's kill the speculation for now," Jacob said. "Murph, I need you to come with me and make a report to Captain Webb. Taylor and Mettler, get the captain into a body bag and in stasis for the ride back home. Sully, if you're up to it, could you start checking over all the *Corsair's* flight systems?"

"I'll manage," Sully said and waved off Taylor when he tried to help the pilot up.

"Lieutenant, you better have a damn good reason for breaking protocol and contacting me during a mission." Webb's face was a thundercloud on the ultra-high-resolution video link they had via the slip-com node. The faster-than-light communication method wasn't quite instantaneous, but it was close enough that the lag was barely perceptible.

"Commander Mosler is dead, sir," Jacob said without preamble. "He was murdered by Chief Petty Officer Michael Scarponi while my team was on-mission. Our pilot was also injured but will recover. Scarponi is missing, and we believe he may have been working with the Ull and their human collaborators."

"Why is Sergeant Murphy there with you?" Webb asked, seeming to process the news that one of his Scout Fleet captains—and a personal friend—was murdered by one of their own with aplomb.

"Captain, my name *is* Alonzo Murphy, but it isn't sergeant...it's agent," Murph said. "Special Agent Alonzo Murphy, Naval Intelligence Section. Confirmation code is bravo, zulu, zulu, seven, two."

"Standby while I call this in, *Agent* Murphy," Webb said and the screen went dark.

"What the fuck, Murph?" Jacob asked.

"Don't worry about it," Murph said. "I was embedded into Scout Fleet long before you came along. I'm an assimilated O-3, but I won't pull rank on you."

"NIS confirms your identity, Agent Murphy," Captain Webb's likeness came back up on the SCIF's massive wall monitor. "They wouldn't divulge your mission, but the ensign who answered the desk said you could tell me at your own discretion."

"Sir, I was assigned with tracking down any potential security threats within Scout Fleet," Murph said. "There have been a number of breaches and, unfortunately, more than one incident like the *Endurance* attack. Your teams are given a lot of freedom and operate well beyond anywhere the normal Navy does."

"So, NIS has it in their mind that Scout Fleet personnel would have the most opportunity to collaborate with known traitors given they're on such a long leash."

"Correct, sir." Murph bowed his head for a moment before going on. "Captain, I'm sorry about Commander Mosler. I had cleared Scarponi when he was assigned to Obsidian, but it looks like he may have been working with Margaret Jansen's faction. They have been tracking us since we left Terranovus, and I believe he had modified the *Corsair's* avionics to make it possible to board her without us detecting it."

Jacob had no idea who Margaret Jansen was, so he kept his mouth shut and let the people who knew a lot more than he did to keep talking around him.

"I have his service record right here and... Well, this is troubling," Webb said.

"Yes, sir," Murph said. "Scarponi joined the military well after Jansen's group left and he had no known associations with anybody in the original Terranovus fleet. This confirms NIS's fear that a sympathetic element that still exists within the UEAS is actively recruiting within the ranks."

"And here I thought you telling me one of my best friends being murdered was the worse news I'd get today," Webb deadpanned. "What about the rest of Obsidian? Are they clear?"

"I have some...questions...about the lieutenant here, but nothing that concerns him being a security risk," Murph said. "The others are all solid."

"And you have Zadra with you?"

"Negative, sir," Jacob spoke up. "She wasn't at the designated location. She contacted us remotely and explained that the ConFed had been sending in teams to get her, so she gave us a way to find her and left the planet. We were able to recover the data cards with her presumed location even after being ambushed by a group of Ull and humans."

"I see," Webb said. "Agent Murphy, would you excuse yourself and allow Lieutenant Brown and I a moment alone. I don't think there's anything more we need from you."

"Yes, sir." Murph climbed out of the seat, squeezed Jacob's shoulder, and exited the SCIF.

"Jacob, we need this Veran brought back alive." Webb leaned forward. "Normally under these circumstances, I'd tell you to sit tight and wait while we send in a recovery team, but I don't think we have that sort of time. There are a lot of interested parties trying to find

Zadra, and whoever gets to her first will get the keys to the castle. That might not mean much to some, but for Earth, it's enormous to get access to her information network."

"And since we still have a pilot and my ground team is intact, you want me to take command of this mission and press on," Jacob guessed. "Sir, I feel I have to tell you that I'm really not comfortable with this in light of my completely lack of proper training and experience for this."

"I can't turn this mission over to an NIS agent no matter what his assimilated rank is," Webb said. "Sullivan is an officer, but he's never commanded. That leaves you, the only Scout Fleet officer there with mission command experience, even if it was just one stroll into town where you led your entire team into an obvious ambush."

"Thanks for the vote of confidence, sir," Jacob said, keeping the disrespect out of his voice with effort. "There's really nobody else who can do this?"

"There are only two Scout Fleet teams deployed right now, and the other won't be able to disengage and reposition in time," Webb said. "I *could* bring in outside contractors, but Zadra is too critical to trust to anybody I might reach out to given the instability within the ConFed right now. They may turn her over to curry favor."

"What if—"

"How about I sweeten the deal?" Webb said. "I hate that I'm being forced to negotiate with a second lieutenant, but you could turn down this mission and there's no way a tribunal would find you at fault for doing so. How about I give you what you want in exchange for you getting me what I need?"

"Sir?"

"This is how important Zadra is," Webb went on. "As unique as you are, I'd trade a hundred of you for just one of her. If you take the *Corsair* and go recover her, I'll call in some favors and we'll see about getting you a commission into the regular Navy and out of the Marine Corps."

"That sounds too good to be true, sir, no offense." Jacob didn't want to come right out and say the captain was lying.

"It does, but I can make it happen nonetheless." Webbed leaned forward, his eyes intent. "I still have some pull with the policy makers who oversee the UEAS. This wouldn't be an especially difficult task to have you pulled from Scout Fleet and put back on your original career track. It's more or less a personnel issue nobody will even blink at.

"If my generous offer isn't enough for you, perhaps I can appeal to your sense of patriotism...or survival. Earth is a tiny, new power scurrying around the feet of giants that are about to go to war with each other. Access to Zadra's network would allow us to know where and when to dodge once those giants really start stomping around."

"I'll do it if you promise to stop with the mangled metaphors, sir," Jacob sighed. He could protest more, but in the end, he knew he'd wind up doing exactly what Webb wanted, but he'd rather it was on his own terms, not because of being manipulated. "I'll have Sully look at the data cards and once we have our destination, we'll get underway."

"I knew I could count on you." Webb smiled. "Contact me at this node once you have her and not before. Keep off the net until she's secure and the *Corsair* is heading back to Terranovus. Webb out."

"Fuck me." Jacob reached up and rubbed his eyes, almost not hearing the SCIF hatch open behind him. When he turned, he saw Murph and Sully looking like they had some bad news. "What?"

"The *Corsair* is dead in the water," Sully said. "Scarponi sabotaged the grav-drive beyond my ability to repair it here in the field. We'd need an engineering team to come out and do a full recalibration on the emitter drivers before she could safely take off again."

"Of course," Jacob groaned. "We're still being tasked with recovering the Veran. What are our options for getting out of here within the next twelve hours?"

"Steal another ship," Sully laughed. He kept laughing until he saw that the other two weren't. "That's a joke, guys."

"Is it?" Jacob asked. "Tell me, Sully, you think you could pilot one of these alien ships?"

"Of course, I can, but that's not the point."

"Oh, but it is," Murph said, now also smiling. "And this is the perfect world to try something like that on."

"Shit," Sully muttered. "I really hope I don't end up dead on this mission."

"Ready?"

"Ready for what?" Jacob was becoming weary of being treated like a burden. If someone asked him if he was *ready* one more time he was going to snap.

He and Murph had been walking around the perimeter of the landing pad complex adjacent to the one the *Corsair* was parked on. Sully was continuing to recover from the blow to the head as well as prepping the *Corsair* to be abandoned and, possibly, never recovered. They were purging all her navigational records, classified data, and physically destroying some of the ship's more sensitive components.

"Let me cut the bullshit here for a minute. I read your psych profile when you were first identified as a potential recruit for Scout Fleet," Murph said. "While you definitely had the moral flexibility they seem to want, you also have hang-ups when it comes to doing something bad for the greater good."

"You mean I have no problem killing as long as I'm killing for a justifiable reason? Like in the apartment?" Jacob asked.

"In a grossly simplified way, yes, that's what I'm asking. Because what we're about to do now? We're just going to walk up on someone else's ship and take it. If they happen to be there? They'll have to be dealt with, and out here, it isn't wise to leave witnesses or enemies behind."

"So, the question to me is am I willing to commit what would normally be seen as a heinous crime in the service of something more noble, like recovering a vital intelligence asset for my homeworld?" Jacob thought his own question over for a moment. He'd been about to tell *Agent* Murphy to only worry about himself, but the man did have a point. "I won't freeze up again."

"That's not the same as being comfortable with the violence we're possibly about to inflict on someone just so we can take their shit," Murph pressed.

"Whether I'm good with it or not deep down in my soul is irrelevant," Jacob said. "I'll do my job. How about that one?" He pointed to a sleek, graceful ship with beautiful lines, though it looked like it had seen better days.

"Nah, that's an old Jepsen Aero piece of shit," Murph said when he saw the ship Jacob had gestured to. "The company hasn't even existed for the last thirty years or so, and that one looks in pretty bad shape. A good general rule of thumb: the blockier they look, the newer they probably are. For some reason, a lot of the aerospace firms are getting away from the sleek, swoopy designs like the Jepsens."

"Is knowledge of alien spacecraft design trends part of your NIS training?" Jacob asked.

"Not particularly. I just know a few of the bigger names flying around. For example, that bigger ship near the edge of the ramp is a newish Eshquarian design." Murph pointed with his nose to try and not appear so obvious. "Sully will have definitely been trained on that type of ship, and it has a slip-drive capable of getting us the hell away from the Reaches in a hurry."

Jacob looked at the ship he was talking about and saw it was about a third of the size of the *Corsair*. It had a smooth fuselage and the grav-drive emitter nacelles hung off each side of the ship by two pylons each. He couldn't tell if anyone was aboard it or not.

"Looks like it'll be a cramped flight out of here," Jacob said. "Are we sure this is the one?"

"I think so," Murph said, looking around. "The rest of these junkers are either pieced together from other ships or way past their prime. Either way, not something I'd like to trust my life to. We *could* look at the landing pads closer to the starport terminal where the newer, bigger ships are, but then we're dealing with local security as well as a crew that probably has left their own security behind."

"Sounds like our choices have been narrowed down for us," Jacob said. He wasn't entirely comfortable with the fact that Murph seemed to be steering the ship right now despite Webb clearly stating that Jacob was still in command. Given his inexperience and lack of proper training, however, his hands were tied for the moment. All he knew for certain was that it was difficult to know who he could trust and who was actually who they claimed to be in this outfit.

14

"Eshquarian, that's good. Real good. Their control layout is one of the most widely used, so unless that ship belongs to some amorphous blob that had the flightdeck reconfigured, I'll be able to fly it without any problem." Sully was looking over the specs of the model type for the ship Murph wanted to steal.

"Did we find out what was on the data cards yet?" Jacob asked. "Seems pointless to risk stealing a ship without a destination in mind."

"It's decrypting now," Sully said. "Taylor has it running on a portable system we can take with us. He says within the next six hours it should be done."

Jacob had no real idea how encryptions worked past the very basics, so he couldn't say if his tech specialist was being modest, wildly optimistic, or just talking out his ass and they'd never have a destination. He had to assume Zadra would make it tough to get into, but not impossible. She'd also called on them specifically so leaving them information they could never access wouldn't do her much good. The decision he had to make was whether to trust that his tech specialist was able to get through Zadra's security or sit and wait to be sure and risk losing the one ship in the immediate area that fit their needs.

"Tell him to get it packed up and let's be ready to hit it within the hour," Jacob said. "Murph, you're going to be running point on the boarding mission. Sully, feed him any additional information you have on that Eshquarian ship that might be useful to us. Where are we on sanitizing the *Corsair*?"

"SCIF servers are purged. Charges on all the critical avionics boxes are primed. We also put charges on all of the command and control systems for the powerplant and main drive," Murph said. "We'll shut down the main reactor and purge the fuel load as the last thing we do. If our grand theft spaceship plan goes off without a hitch, we'll already have meshed-out by the time the charges detonate in here."

"You think Captain Webb is going to be pissed that we're scuttling the ship?" Jacob asked. "In theory, I agree with why we're doing in. In reality, I think that, as the mission commander, you've all set me up for a court martial."

"That's part of the fun of Scout Fleet, LT," MG said from the hatchway. "You never know if your teammates are trying to help you or fuck you over."

Jacob just rolled his eyes and went back to his quarters to get the rest of his gear. Mosler had been adamant that he not over-pack or bring anything he wasn't willing to never see again and now he understood why. Whatever he put into the small pack he pulled out of the wall locker would be all he took with him from the *Corsair*. Everything else would remain until starport officials dragged her away to be scrapped or another human ship came back to reclaim her. The latter was highly unlikely given the risks associated with flying into the Reaches. The Fleet wouldn't risk it for one small runabout flown by a forward recon unit.

"You got a minute, LT?"

"Barely," Jacob said, looking over his shoulder at Murph. "What's on your mind?"

"How much do you think that desk weighed that you threw at that Ull with the shield generator?"

"Couldn't tell you, Murph." Jacob already knew where this was going. "The adrenaline was really pumping."

"When MG and I tried to move it, we could barely get it to scoot across the floor. You *threw* it hard enough to send a relatively strong species to the floor."

"I'm not hearing a question in there," Jacob said.

"I was being honest when I said I'd vetted you," Murph said, moving around so he could look Jacob in the eye. "Our check into where you came from was a lot more thorough than most, and we found a lot of odd little discrepancies. When we tried to dig a little deeper, the hammer came down from on high and we were locked out of all records concerning Jacob Brown. So, Lieutenant, who are you? Or should I say...*what* are you?"

"You're admitting that my background was classified over your paygrade and now, after lying to all of us about who *you* really were, you're going to make demands of me?" Jacob laughed. "Who says I'm even allowed to tell you? Or that's there anything to tell other than I go to the gym a lot?"

"I'm not going to apologize for doing my job, Brown," Murph said. "And I'm asking because I think it's relevant. Our lives are at risk if you're not who you say you are." Jacob was a bit confused by that.

"What do you think I am?" he asked.

"Given the display of strength, your forged background, the unusual way you were recruited into Scout Fleet, I'm guessing maybe alien or human-alien hybrid," Murph said, trying to gauge Jacob's reaction at the accusation. When Jacob only laughed uproariously, showing no signs of defensiveness or anger, it was Murph's turn to look confused.

"I can promise you I am one hundred percent human," Jacob said. "There's some...irregularities...in my parentage that has given me some genetic gifts, but I've been assured by people who know there isn't a speck of spliced alien DNA in me."

"Your parentage..." Murph trailed off, then his eyes widened. "Holy shit! You're—"

"Don't say it." Jacob held a hand up. "Please. Just...don't."

"There had been rumors about you in the intelligence community," Murph said. "Those involved in covering up what really happened during the second alien attack on Earth speculated that...*he*...might have had a family back home we didn't know about. There were some that seemed to know quite a bit about him but would never say one way or another."

"From what I understand, there are two stories about the man." Jacob shrugged. "He's either a hero the likes of which is rarely seen, or a criminal and a traitor that should be shot on site. I've only met him once so I'm leaning towards the latter. If you don't mind, I'd really rather not talk about it past this once. I didn't know him, but I inherited some of his speed and strength. Let's just leave it at that."

"Fair enough," Murph said, still speaking softly.

"What's all the whispering in here?" MG said from the doorway. "Were you two talking about me?"

"No, we—"

"Just kidding. I don't give a shit what you were talking about," MG laughed. "We're ready when you are, LT."

"Let's do it," Jacob said, shouldering his pack.

"This thing isn't in quite the pristine condition I had originally thought," Murph admitted.

"What gave it away? The patchwork hull or the puddle of *something* collecting under the port engine nacelle?" Jacob asked.

"Look, we need something quick and available. This is as good as it gets right now."

"Let's just get this done so we can get the hell out of here," Jacob said. "MG, Mettler! You're up."

The two Marines dropped their packs where the team was hiding near a small intra-atmospheric runabout and began walking casually towards the Eshquarian gunboat. They'd decided that the direct approach would be best since petty crime and assaults were mostly overlooked on Niceen-3, even at the main starport. MG and Mettler would recon the ship up close and give the team a go, no-go signal for the actual assault. Once they confirmed the ship was either lightly guarded—or, preferably, unguarded—they'd rush up the open loading ramp and subdue the crew.

They'd taken the time to familiarize themselves with the internal layout of the small ship, and Taylor was confident he could circumvent any automated security they might have, as well as bypass all the lockouts so they could actually fly it out of there. Jacob had no choice but to take the cocky young Marine at his word that he was actually that good at working on the alien technology.

"This ship will blend in better than the *Corsair* because the Eshquarians sell so damn much military hardware in the quadrant, including to private firms, that it'll be completely forgettable. The only issue I see is that this is a well-known class of combat ship whereas the *Corsair* was more subtle, designed to look like a high-speed courier," Taylor said.

"Is this something we really needed to know right now?" Murph asked.

"Well *I* thought it was interesting," Taylor grumbled.

"*The ship is wide open*," MG's voice came over the team channel. "*We saw two Impans standing around in the cargo hold, both armed with only sidearms and not paying attention to anything going on outside the ship.*" Murph looked at Jacob expectantly. For his own part, Jacob realized he was about to authorize the killing of beings that were simply in the wrong place at the wrong time. They had nothing to do with Earth, his mission to retrieve Weef Zadra, or posed any threat other than being a mild inconvenience. This is what Webb must have meant by needing Scout Fleet crews to have a certain *moral flexibility*.

"Execute," he said. "Make it quick, and make it quiet. We need that ship."

At his words, he saw MG and Mettler wheel and sprint up the loading ramp. He could just make out the surprised yelps from the

Impans before they were silenced by his Marines, the cough of their weapons on low-power mode barely audible over the ambient racket of the starport's active ramp.

"We're up," Jacob said. "Let's move."

He and Murph grabbed the two spare packs MG and Mettler left and ran towards the ship. Taylor and Sully were both mission critical to gaining control of the gunboat and flying it afterwards so they brought up the rear, shielded by the other two.

"There's one more inside," MG whispered when they stormed up the ramp. "I can't tell if it knows something has happened to its friends yet."

"Take it out, clear the ship," Jacob said. "I'll escort Sully to the bridge, Murph will take Taylor to Engineering." He went over and found the controls for the rear ramp, the alien script giving him a slight sensation of vertigo as his neural implant translated it. It was an odd sensation because it didn't overlay English words he could readily understand, it just *injected* the proper meaning into his mind in a way that was disorienting. The others said he'd get accustomed to it the more he used it.

The team moved quickly through the ship. Jacob heard two more shots fired near the galley as he led Sully up to the bridge. When he walked through the round hatchway, a startled Impan leapt from where it had been lounging in its seat.

"Who are you? What do you think you're—" A single shot from Jacob's carbine ended the conversation, the low-power plasma shot hitting the alien right in the neck. It went down with a soft gurgling and was still.

"Get started," Jacob said to Sully, struggling to get the words out from the bile rising in his throat. He had killed the Ull and their human collaborators without *much* hesitation because they'd been trying to kill him first. This was different. The Impans that ran this ship had done nothing wrong other than to have something in their possession that Jacob and his team needed. Now they were dead.

"The bridge controls aren't even locked out," Sully said, seemingly oblivious to the dead alien a couple meters away. "As soon as Taylor gets us access to the main computer, we'll be ready to pull navigation data and get the hell out of here."

"I'll go check on him," Jacob said, passing Mettler as he did. "You and MG police the bodies and get them into an airlock. We'll jettison them into space once we're underway, I don't want to risk leaving them outside on the tarmac."

"Will do."

Jacob jogged through the ship and climbed down the ladder well —this one an actual ladder, not just steep stairs—into the guts of the ship's engineering section. Murph and Taylor were huddled around a terminal where they had what looked like an oversized tablet computer with cables snaked into an open panel.

"LT," Murph greeted him. "We'll be good to go in a few minutes."

"What's that?" Jacob asked.

"It's a tricky little intrusion AI the folks at NIS gave us," Taylor said. "It makes me seem a lot smarter than I am. You just plug it into any available data port and it goes to work. The computer aboard this ship is both outdated and not very secure to begin with. It should have complete access in about"—there were two beeps from the device and all the screens in Engineering flashed once and then began displaying data—"now. That should do it. Sully will be able to control all shipboard functions from here, and I'll start making sure all the individual terminals that aren't networked into the main computer are unlocked." Jacob blinked at a panel by the door that was labeled as the shipwide intercom and pressed one of the buttons.

"Sully, start getting her prepped for flight," he said. "Murph and I are going back to the *Corsair* for the last load, and then we're out of here. MG and Mettler, post up security in the cargo bay."

"One more load?" Murph frowned.

"I'd like to get as much out of the armory as we can," Jacob explained. "I piled everything up onto one of Scarponi's motorized carts so we should be able to do this quickly."

"We should have just brought it with us in the first place," Murph said. "I'd prefer we make a clean break while we have the opportunity and leave now...sir."

"We had no idea how much resistance we were going to meet here at the ship," Jacob explained. "Carting along a wagon full of munitions while getting shot at didn't seem that smart at the time. If we're heading into any more danger, I'd prefer we have more than just the few weapons we brought with us. There's a lot of weaponry I don't think we're going to be able to just purchase off the street wherever we're heading." He didn't like Murph questioning him so openly like he had, but he was unsure how the chain of command really worked now that Murph was outed as a NIS agent and Commander Mosler was dead.

"Sound reasoning," Murph relented with obvious reluctance. "We'll need to hurry."

"Probably want to make it fast, LT," Taylor spoke up. "My decryption routine just unpacked Zadra's data cards and compiled the data. There's a lot there, but the location we're heading to is in the Concordian Cluster."

"Fuck me," Murph swore. "That's the heart of the Eshquarian Empire."

"The same Eshquarian Empire that has just been invaded and occupied by a ConFed battle fleet?" Jacob asked.

"The same," Murph said.

15

"Lieutenant, we have a big problem."

"Go ahead," Jacob said over the com. Sully had sounded relaxed when he had called, but even from their short time together, Jacob knew the pilot wasn't prone to hyperbole or needless hysterics.

"Group of six Impans are heading towards us, all heavily armed and leading one of those automated cargo sleds," Sully said.

"Impans aren't *that* common in this region of space that there would be two crews of them. They're likely the hard cases that were on Niceen doing a job when we went and wiped out the crew of their ship," Murph said, also transmitting on the open channel.

"Agreed," Jacob said. "Options?"

"Mettler and I can't hold them off," MG said. "Too many of them."

"And Niceen isn't *that* lax that they'll look the other way if we engage them with the ship's weaponry," Sully added. "Are you still at the *Corsair*?"

"Negative," Jacob said. "We're only halfway to the ship."

"Stay there, I'm coming to you," Sully said. "I'm calling for clearance to taxi for a cargo transfer, and then I'll relocate to where you are. I'll drop the ramp, you hop in, and we'll be out of here while these guys think that their own crew just jacked the ship." Murph and Jacob just looked at each other and shrugged.

"Do it," Jacob ordered his pilot. "We're ready as soon as you touch down."

It was another five minutes before they could begin to detect the subsonic thrum of repulsors as Sully moved the gunboat along the taxiway at an altitude of two meters. He swung it around so that the loading was facing them and settled into a low hover, not even dropping the struts down so he could land.

"Let's go! We have to move, *NOW!*" MG was waving frantically as Jacob and Murph ran into the waiting ship. Mettler hit the controls to close the ramp while they were still on it, and once the inner pressure doors slid shut and locked, Jacob could feel that they were accelerating away quickly despite the artificial gravity nullifying their inertia.

"What's happening?" he asked, running onto the bridge.

"The Impans weren't as indecisive as I figured they'd be," Sully said. "They already declared the ship stolen and offered a reward for anyone who can bring us down intact."

"They've been calling on the com," Taylor added. "We were right in that they're assuming the crew was stealing the ship for themselves."

"The call came after we'd already been cleared for orbit," Sully said. "Once we're up top, we'll switch over to the second set of transponders they have on this tub and try to blend in with the rest of the traffic."

"Just do what you have to do and don't bother asking me for permission first," Jacob said, feeling hopelessly out of his depth as they were about to be chased by mercs and pirates looking for a payday.

"Don't worry, LT, we're almost home free." Sully smiled as the sky outside the canopy turned black and the ship shrugged off the last tendrils of Niceen-3's atmosphere clinging to it.

"Mesh-out point is locked in, slip-drive is...ready," Taylor said. "The rest is up to you, Sully."

"This thing is actually a *lot* faster than you'd expect it to be," Sully commented. "Handles like shit, but damn she's got some legs. LT, you want to cycle that airlock and get rid of our passengers?"

"Cycling starboard airlock," Jacob said, watching the display as the Impan corpses were blown out into space once the static barrier was dropped.

For the next four hours, the rest of the crew watched while their pilot skillfully used the sensor shadows of the bigger ships in orbit to hide the small gunboat, switch over to a different set of transponder codes, and then casually meander out of their final transfer orbit, and make a mad dash for the mesh-out point. When they were well past the orbit of the fifth planet, they were spotted, but by then, it was far too late for their pursuers. As three other small ships tried to converge on them, Sully opened up the drive to full power, the vibrations and alarms from the souped-up main drive causing Jacob some distress while they shot ahead. As they closed in on their target, blast shields automatically deployed up and over the transparent canopy to protect the occupants from the brilliant slip-energies released by the drive as well as the increased radiation.

"Mesh-out in three...two...one...and we're out of here!" The ship shuddered for a moment, and then everything was nearly silent, the racket from the main drive gone as the slip-drive took over and all the proximity alarms on the tactical displays were silent in the absence of any enemy ships. Sully checked over the instruments at the pilot's station one last time before climbing out of the seat and stretching, almost looking bored. "I need someone to sit here and babysit the controls while I go back down to Engineering and do one more check on things. I'd feel better before I hit the rack knowing that the reactor and drive are operating within normal limits."

"You actually wouldn't *feel* anything," Murph said. "If the slip-drive screws up while it's engaged, we'll either just pop back out into real-space or, more likely, be extruded back into real-space as a single chain of molecules."

"Cheery thought," Jacob said. "And on that note, why don't you take first watch? I'll take Mettler and begin taking stock of what's on this ship, and Taylor will begin checking all of the non-flight systems. If we need air, food, or water, it's probably better if we find out now."

"Already on it, LT," Taylor said. "I'll have a report for you within the hour."

"Let's go, everyone." Jacob clapped his hands. "The sooner we're done, the sooner we can start a normal watch schedule and people can get some sleep."

It took the better part of three days to completely inventory the gunboat and inspect all of her systems. They found out that the ship was carrying a surprising amount of valuable cargo that they'd try to offload at their next stop, and Taylor's snoopers had ferreted out a handful of discreet trackers and booby-traps left by the previous owners that could have let them track the ship once it re-emerged into real-space. While not as roomy as the *Corsair*, the small ship had a decent size berthing bay, a tiny captain's quarters, and had been fully replenished with consumables while it had been on the ground at Niceen-3.

Taylor spent most of the second day adjusting the gravity and atmospheric systems to more comfortable human norms, as well as programming the food synthesizer for rations that wouldn't make them sick. The unit was fairly standard and worked similarly to the ones on Terran ships. It was loaded with base digestibles and could create a reasonable facsimile of real food when programmed. It wasn't the same as the real thing, but it was pretty damn close. Thankfully, the Impans had the same requirement for pure water as humans so there was nothing to do there except inspect the tanks.

"Here's the target: Formenos Prime," Murph said. "It's one of the Eshquarian-claimed planets that's just outside of the Concordian Cluster, but isn't considered part of the Empire."

"In other words, they pay taxes and are subject to Eshquarian law, they just don't have any representation within the government," MG snorted.

"More or less, but for our purposes, this is actually beneficial. Formenos had no useful exports other than semi-skilled labor, so it's probably still being ignored by the ConFed taskforce overseeing the Empire's...absorption, I guess. One more outdated Eshquarian gunboat that's been beat to hell and back won't even get a second look coming in to land on this planet."

"We'll still need to be careful," Sully said. "When all this shit went down, most of the Eshquarian fleet went into hiding and—"

"Most?" MG asked skeptically.

"Ok, *some* of the fleet is hiding. Rumor has it that they fled into the Cluster at the order of their fleet commanders because the ConFed brought such overwhelming force and caught them by surprise there was no way the ships that weren't destroyed within the Eshquaria System would have been able to do anything."

"What's the part we need to be careful about?" Jacob asked.

"There will be patrols out looking for those fleet remnants," Murph said. "The ConFed Starfleet isn't known for incompetence *or* mercy. They won't leave an enemy force that large behind when they pull out the bulk of their battlefleet. I think Sully's point is that we'll still be flying into contested space in a military-type vessel and we'll need to take precautions. A ConFed cruiser may just blow us out of the sky rather than waste the time seeing if we're really a civilian-owned ship or part of the Imperial Fleet."

"How do we find Zadra once we're there?" Jacob asked.

"The data card had a list of dead-drop message services we're supposed to contact once we land," Taylor said. "There are specific phrases within the information she provided that will let her know we're the ones who found the data card and are there to retrieve her. After that, we'll be contacted with further instructions."

"Doesn't sound very specific," Jacob grumbled. "This has been a hell of a costly wild goose chase so far."

"We're coming out to get one of the most notorious information brokers in this part of the quadrant," Murph said. "She's not going to make it easy for someone to sneak up on her when she knows they're already after her."

"Makes sense, I guess," Jacob said. "I'd still like to have a better idea what the hell we're flying into before taking a stolen, unregistered military vessel into contested space."

"Welcome to Scout Fleet." MG shrugged.

Once the intel session broke, and the crew went back to their assigned duties, Murph came up to Jacob in the corridor leading up to the bridge. "Here," he said and thrust a tablet into Jacob's hands.

"What's this?"

"It's the crew log for this ship," Murph said. "Taylor found it on a computer hidden in the captain's quarters. They kept surprisingly good records for a bunch of pirates."

"Why do you think I should have this?" Jacob asked.

"I think it might...help...with an internal struggle you seem to be having."

Murph walked away before Jacob could ask what the hell he was talking about. He looked at the tablet and shrugged, grabbing something to drink and heading back into the captain's quarters. Out of curiosity, he began reading the logs Taylor had downloaded and, helpfully, translated into English.

The more he read, the more horrified he became. The crew that owned this ship before them had been monsters. Detailed within the logs of the ship's captain were a laundry list of crimes and atrocities that made Jacob's blood run cold. The crew had been trafficking in kidnapped beings, buying them on one planet, transporting them like cattle, and selling them on another. They were part of an elaborate network of smugglers that would target and abduct specific species for tasks ranging from dangerous labor, reconditioning as shock troops—or cannon fodder—and the usual gladiatorial fighters and sex slaves.

When they were between runs, the crew would amuse themselves by running narcotics or weapons for money onto worlds where such things were strictly prohibited. At first glance, the log disgusted him and burned away any guilt he felt for killing the crew and stealing the ship. He lay in his rack, incensed that the injustices found on Earth seemed to be a universal trait among other evolved, intelligent species. After he'd calmed and had time to reflect, however, he pulled the complete log back up and began digging down into the minutia of the former captain's records. Once he moved past the natural revulsion of the crew's actions, he found that it was a treasure trove of details about the quadrant's underworld.

Hours went by, and he began making detailed notes about locations of safe harbors, contacts, hazards to avoid at all costs, and even found more than a few passages of how a merc crew that called themselves "Omega Force" had disrupted their operation by taking out suppliers and buyers. He read these log entries with some bemusement, as if his feelings regarding his father could be more confused. Of all the things he assumed, one of them wasn't that the old man was out here blowing up slavers and drug smugglers.

16

Formenos Prime was a typical secondary world, far from the polish and money of the Core Worlds, but also not a sparsely inhabited hell hole. At least that's what Jacob's crew told him about it. Since Formenos was only the second alien planet he'd ever seen, he couldn't really form his own opinion. They called it a secondary world because Formenos had no indigenous species, or at least an indigenous *intelligent* species, though he had trouble figuring out where the demarcation line was for determining if a species was sentient enough to qualify for protections under ConFed law and which were fair game for displacement by colonization.

The nine-day flight to the Concordian Cluster from the Kaspian Reaches had been hard on the small gunboat. They'd flogged her as hard as they dared while Sully and Taylor did their best to keep it running. Once they landed at a starport with engineering services, however, they'd have to dip into the ship's treasury and get the slip-drive re-aligned and the main reactor looked at. The power surges they'd experienced while in slip-space had been enough to keep Jacob awake for most of the flight.

"This set of transponders is still reading as clean," Sully reported. "The original set is still flagging as 'of interest,' and any ship that sees it is instructed to report the position and heading to Formenos Orbital Authority."

"Running multiple transponders is highly illegal," Murph said. "They can't really claim a ship is stolen and give out four sets of ident codes with it. The crew we took it from probably didn't actually own it, so they're making some show of trying to find it without incriminating themselves."

"They also probably want their cargo back," MG said. "Lots of platinum, loaded credit chits, and those buzz balls the LT made us dump out into space."

"I still can't believe we dumped over seventeen million credits worth of drugs out the airlock," Taylor griped.

"We're not drug runners," Jacob said firmly. "Even in a pinch like this, we're not going to start selling narcotics to fund the mission. Besides, the chits we found will more than cover our repairs and provisioning."

The credit chits were almost like cash, but more akin to bearer bonds back on Earth. They were small, onyx discs that, when pinched, displayed the value that had been loaded onto them by the ConFed Centralized Banking System. They were one of the few forms of untraceable currency still in use in the quadrant and far more useful than the precious metal ingots sitting in the crates next to them. Exchanging or bartering with platinum or gold could make them memorable in some places, but cashing in a few chits to pay for services was normal for spacer crews that traveled between star systems and didn't feel like messing around with individual local currencies.

"LT, a word?" Murph said, nodding towards the hatchway. Jacob nodded and followed him off the bridge.

"What's up?"

"I think we should take some time here and...establish...ourselves while given the opportunity," Murph said.

"I have no idea what you're talking about."

"This ship has a fortune sitting in its cargo hold right now. Just handing it in to Command once this mission is over seems wasteful,"

Murph said. "That money could be used as a sort of covert slush fund for future missions."

"Go on," Jacob said, skeptical that what the NIS agent was about to propose was at all aboveboard.

"Formenos Prime is developed enough to be tied into the Central Banking System," Murph continued. "I think that while the ship is being repaired and we try to make contact with Zadra, it would be prudent to take the chits and the platinum to an Exchange and open up an account that only Team Obsidian knows about. You never know when we'll find ourselves up a creek again without Fleet support."

"Can't Command just send us currency through the same system?" Jacob asked. He didn't want to point out the obvious that Murph wasn't actually assigned to the Scout Corps and was, in fact, an NIS spook whose mission was just busted when Scarponi escaped. There was also the fact that he himself was planning on taking Webb's offer of a Naval commission and leaving the Corps altogether.

"Scout Fleet operates autonomously, for obvious reasons." Murph shook his head. "If we get caught doing something fucked up, it can't be tied back to Earth's government in any way. I still think it'd be nice if we had an independent source of funding for when shit went south." Jacob still wasn't sure what to make of Murph's idea, but he also had no idea what the hell he was going to do with all the valuables in his cargo hold if he didn't go along with it.

"Okay," he said finally. "We'll set that up while Sully and Taylor supervise prepping the ship. MG and Mettler will remain here to guard everything and then, once we retrieve Zadra, we'll be the hell out of here and on the way back home."

"Agreed," Murph said.

Landing on Formenos Prime was a little more complicated than on Niceen-3 because the planet had a rigidly structured orbital control system and a well-organized landing authority you had to petition before even coming out of your holding orbit. Thankfully the *clean* codes they'd switched to didn't pop up as anything of interest on the controller's terminal, and the gunboat was cleared for landing at a starport outside of a city called Sarapis.

The city was the fifth largest on the planet and the ship's database said it was an average urban center that seemed to exist only to support the larger cities. The planet's main export was a type of grain that was broken down into its base chemical components for use in cheap, bulk food stuffs that were then sold to overpopulated worlds like Ver. All things considered, it was an odd choice for someone like Zadra to hide out on, but maybe that's why she chose it.

"Cycling gear," Sully called. "Standby for touch—" *Boom!* Everyone was thrown off their feet as the deck bucked violently.

"What the fuck, Sully?" MG said from where he'd landed by the tactical station.

"Huh," Sully said, completely unruffled. "I think I was reading the altitude wrong on this panel. I thought we had another meter and half to go."

"Did we break anything?" Jacob asked.

"Just my pride," Sully answered. "No alarms on the panel. "You want me to go ahead and call for engineering services now?"

"Yes," Jacob said. "Also for fuel and consumables. Taylor, you make contact with Zadra and hang back here helping with the ship until she replies."

"Sully, call for a cargo van large enough for all the shit that was left in the hold," Murph said.

"I don't think they call them—"

"Just get a fucking vehicle so we don't have to carry it by hand, will ya?"

Jacob left them to argue and went back to his quarters—he took the only private stateroom on the ship since he was still technically in command—and grabbed a sidearm and his credentials. The ship's computer said that Formenos Prime was fairly tolerant about personal armament, especially around the starports, but open carrying anything larger than a pistol was generally frowned upon.

After he was done there, he went down to the hold and began pulling off the straps and cargo nets securing everything to the deck.

The cases containing the platinum were all labeled and weighed, each containing nearly three hundred kilograms of the precious metal. With forty-six crates total spread over three loading pallets, he hoped whatever vehicle Sully secured had a loader.

The chits were all secured in generic looking cases and didn't take up nearly as much room as the platinum. During the flight out to the Cluster, he and Murph had gone through everything to make sure there were no trackers or identifying marks of any kind that would hinder their ability to transfer them into currency. All told, there was nearly four hundred and fifty million credits worth of goods stashed on a ship that was only worth about a quarter of that. On Earth, that would have been roughly eight hundred million US dollars.

"What the hell were these assholes doing with this much scratch?" Jacob pondered aloud.

"Muling it for their superiors," Murph answered from the hatchway above. The cargo hold was as tall as two decks so the entrance to the main part of the ship was up a narrow staircase attached to the forward bulkhead. "I found this in the captain's quarters when we were clearing the ship initially." He tossed Jacob something that looked like an oversized amusement park coin. On one side there was an embossed emblem that looked like a stylized star with twelve streaming points coming off of it. The reverse side had a number in Jenovian Standard, the semi-accepted universal language in the quadrant.

"What is it?"

"A marker. The code on the back is trackable and can be called in to make sure some bit player doesn't jack the wrong crew." Murph skipped down the stairs and walked over. "The sun logo on the back is the symbol of a massive criminal organization led by someone called Saditava Mok. He's a *major* player in this area and not someone you want cross."

"And we just stole a ship full of his money," Jacob groaned.

"Honestly? Mok won't give a shit about this pittance." Murph smiled. "We're talking about a person who has his own private fleet with capital warships. This amount was likely being passed among the lower ranks within his syndicate to launder or as payment for something. It's likely the surviving dipshits that left this unsecured on a planet like Niceen-3 will have to answer for their failure, but nobody is going to burn the resources to track down a few hundred mil across the entire quadrant."

"If you say so," Jacob said, now anxious to get the hardware off their ship.

"Relax, LT." Murph clapped him on the back. "This will be over before you know it." Jacob noticed that when in front of the other members of Obsidian, Murph kept up the ruse of being an ex-Force Recon jarhead, but once he was alone with Jacob, the tough guy veneer dropped and he could see just how intelligent and confident the man was.

Once the heavy hauler showed up, and Jacob paid the fee for it, they were all delighted to see that it came with its own trio of service bots that would load and secure the cargo. The non-sentient, bipedal machines went about their task as the Marines breathed a sigh of relief that they wouldn't actually be required to do any manual labor. The precious metals and cases full of loaded chits were carefully piled onto the vehicles flatbed, and then a slick automated system both secured the load and covered the entire thing with a canopy to keep nosy onlookers from seeing what they were hauling.

"We'll be back as soon as we can," Jacob told MG as the three bots walked over to the hauler, crawled under the chassis, and folded themselves back up into their storage compartments. Despite knowing that they were just programmed machines and not Synths, it was still a creepy spectacle for Jacob.

"We'll hold down the fort," MG said. "Taylor has already pinged the three addresses that Veran chick gave us so, hopefully by the time you're back, we'll be almost ready to grab and get."

"Hopefully," Jacob agreed. As he followed Murph to the hauler's passenger compartment, he realized their group dynamic had been changing subtly. He was no longer called *sir* by his men, but neither was he eyed with suspicion or barely concealed contempt as he was when first assuming this post. Small-unit dynamics are a tricky thing, and he found himself feeling a little proud that his Marines thought highly enough of him to treat him as one of them instead of one of *them:* an officer they just had to tolerate and babysit.

The Exchange was a madhouse. As soon as they walked through the arching entryway, Jacob was assaulted by a cacophony of alien voices and accompanying smells. He closed his eyes for a moment to settle his nerves, and then walked up to the front desk.

"My client needs to open a full-access citizen's account. Our world is a member of the Cridal Cooperative," Murph said to an alien with a plumed crest. Jacob tried to hide his surprised reaction as his partner spoke to the alien in fluent Jenovian. "We'll be activating it using a mix of precious metals and ConFed chits."

"When did you learn Jenovian Standard?" Jacob asked under his breath. Murph just winked at him and continued negotiating with the gatekeepers of the front desk so they could get to someone who could actually help them.

Once past the front desk, the process was well-organized and amazingly quick. There was a bit of administrative work, during which Jacob was able to open the account and set up Murph and Sully as secondary officers on it. Once that was done, they were asked to take the rented hauler around to another building behind the main Exchange where a pair of bored looking Synths—and for machines they did an admirable job of looking bored—directed the service bots there to unload the hauler, whereupon they quickly inventoried the cases and gave the Exchange officer the total amount.

Once the chits were added up, and given the current rate for platinum on the open market, Jacob walked out just shy of two hours later with the access codes for an account containing five hundred and eighty-six million ConFed credits. For all intents and purposes, Jacob was an extremely wealthy man now and, like most lottery winners, he felt the burden of instantaneous wealth. Now that he had so much to lose, he felt like he should be more careful with his life even though the account was meant to be an operational buffer fund for Obsidian. He also kept waiting for the authorities to show up and question just who he was to be depositing so much at one time, but nobody seemed to look at it oddly until the administrator handing him his account credentials asked what business he was in. Murph told him that they were in salvage, and that seemed to satisfy his curiosity.

"I gotta say, this has been one of the more entertaining missions we've had yet," Murph said once they were back in the hauler and heading for the ship.

"I think Ezra Mosler would disagree," Jacob deadpanned and watched as Murph blanched.

"Yeah, I didn't really think that through very well, did I?"

"You think we'll be able to track down Scarponi?" Jacob asked, changing the subject. "Or if not us, someone else?"

"Hunter-killer missions aren't really Scout Fleet's thing," Murph said. "We're the eyes and ears of the Fleet, but we're supposed to try to remain invisible. There are specialized strike teams that handle things like finding Scarponi. To be honest, I'm a little surprised you weren't recruited into one of those considering your unique abilities.

"To answer your question, yes, Scarponi and the rest of his traitor buddies will need to be dealt with soon enough. NAVSOC has to be careful how it executes that mission because a clumsy attempt at rooting them out could end up with Earth being at war with Ull. If it comes out that we started the fight, the Cooperative may not see the need to support us with ships or material."

"So, we just bide our time," Jacob said. "But can we afford to? This group has already shown they're still actively recruiting within the UEAS. Just letting a cancer metastasize and slowly kill the body isn't really much of a strategy."

"Look at you with your big college words," Murph said. "I don't know. I'm a lowly agent—a *junior* agent—that's been assigned to 3rd Scout Corps as a Marine for so long that I'm almost thinking like one now. Maybe they will let a Scout Fleet team take a crack at Scarponi if for no other reason than to send a message to Margaret Jansen and her inner circle."

Jacob fell silent, considering the implications of a well-equipped, and apparently growing, faction of humans that were conspiring with an alien power against their own home world and species. It was mildly depressing to think that after all they'd learned about the universe around them that humans could still be so shortsighted as to risk it all for short-term gains like political power. Jansen's lifespan was finite and short. Whatever she accomplished in that little spit of time could have lasting ramifications for generations, but she seemed to not care.

"Looks like the fueler is just now pulling away," Murph pointed at the cryogenic tanker that had fueled their ship as it lumbered away, hovering a meter above the tarmac on its repulsor drive. Like most other interstellar vehicles in the quadrant, the ship they'd stolen used liquid hydrogen to power its antimatter reactor. The system was able to create its own stream of antihydrogen for the process, but it required a substantial power source to get it running before the reactor produced enough power on its own to be self-sustaining. Most ships also had a fusion backup reactor in case they had to shut their main reactor down. This ship did not. If they had to perform an emergency shut down in space, there would be no way to get it going again without assistance from another ship. The thought had been disquieting for Jacob when Taylor had first told him about it.

"I wonder if we've heard from Zadra yet," Jacob mused as the hauler pulled smoothly to a stop and let them out.

"What's the good word?" Murph shouted up to MG, the latter of whom was lounging on another transit case and cradling his plasma carbine.

"I'll let Taylor tell you," MG said. "We heard back from our target. I think we're being played."

17

"That's all she sent?" Jacob asked.

"That's it," Taylor said.

"Play it again," Murph said. He was the only one who didn't seem agitated at the turn of events. Taylor just shrugged and hit the control to play the video message again.

"Greetings," Zadra's likeness said. "I applaud how quickly you've managed to get to Formenos Prime. It speaks volumes about your commitment to seeing me safely away from my pursuers. Unfortunately, I could not risk staying on Formenos any longer than it took to setup this automated response. This system is secure, my location was not. Please send a text-only reply to this message with the word, 'proceed,' in any language you wish. My pre-programmed responses will then provide you with where you need to go next in order to safely pick me up."

"You have to be fucking *kidding* me!" Sully fumed. "Is she just playing games with us at this point?"

"Perhaps, but she's still the mission," Jacob said. "Taylor, send the reply she requested and wait for our next location. Sully, is the ship ready to fly?"

"Huh? Oh...yeah." The pilot waved him off. "Fuel is topped off and the variance between the slip-drive emitters has been corrected so it'll be a smoother flight out of here. While they were here, I also had them service the reactor cooling system and give the potable water a complete flush and fill."

"Excellent. Go ahead and get your preflight done and, hopefully, we'll be out of here before anyone starts asking too many questions about the pair of humans who just dropped off millions of credits worth of chits and platinum," Jacob said.

"That's true," Murph agreed. "There are informants everywhere. If the ConFed doesn't come asking, we might end up getting a visit from one of Mok's people."

Sully paled noticeable at the mention of the notorious crime boss and hurriedly left the cramped com room. Murph, MG, and Mettler all left to keep watch leaving only Taylor and Jacob to wait on Zadra's return message. As it turned out, they didn't have long to wait.

"Colton Hub?" Taylor asked as the new location popped onto a display along with navigational data. "Where the hell is that? It doesn't even sound like a planet name."

"Hang on," Jacob said, running to his quarters. The name was tantalizingly familiar for some reason, and the only place he could have seen it was the former captain's logs. He grabbed the tablet off the shelf in his quarters and ran back to the com room, running a search for the name on the device.

"Here it is," he said triumphantly. "Colton Hub shows up quite a bit in this asshole's diary. It looks like it is...not a nice place."

"Oh yeah?"

"Yeah." Jacob flipped through multiple entries containing the name. "Apparently, it is a massive, privately owned deep-space platform that falls outside all of the normal jurisdictions. The ConFed leaves it alone, and no local government wants to burn the resources to clean it up, so it's a hotbed for the type of shit our pirate crew here was into. From what I'm seeing, they would actually pick up loads of slaves there and transport them to the buyers."

"That's fairly revolting," Taylor said. "And this Weef Zadra is such a badass that she picked that as a hideout?"

"If you're connected, it's probably a smart place to be," Jacob said. "Any governmental types sniffing around for her would stick out. Send the nav data to the bridge. I'll tell Sully to light the fires and get us in the air."

"We're six days away from the Hub," Sully said after the final course correction had been done and the gunboat was cranked up to her full slip-space velocity. It had been three days already since they'd left Formenos Prime. "Given how often you're saying the previous crew has been there, is it at all wise to take this ship back?"

"That's a fair point, LT," MG said. "What happens if someone recognizes it and starts asking too many questions?"

"The obvious answer would be to not go there," an unfamiliar voice said from the hatchway. All four men on the bridge spun around, two of them drawing sidearms. "Now, boys, that's no way to greet a guest. Any chance you have something to drink on this flying deathtrap besides water?"

"Weef Zadra, I presume," Jacob said, holstering his weapon once he recognized the Veran's face from her video messages.

"Jacob *Brown*," Zadra greeted him with a mischievous, knowing smile. "Please just call me Zadra. *Weef* is a little too formal and sounds like it could be a bodily function in most languages." MG snickered, earning him a playful glare from the Zadra.

Jacob had met a Veran once before, and he knew they were a small, diminutive species, but Zadra took it to the extreme. Her delicate frame and short stature made her seem like an animated doll when compared to the bulk of the Marines around her. Their skin was a light, mottled green and, most distinctly, they had four arms. The two, smaller arms were normally tucked in close and used for more delicate tasks. They were one of the few spacefaring species in the known galaxy that had evolved to keep more than two arms.

"So, the message game on Formenos Prime was just to give you an opportunity to stowaway," Jacob said. "Clever."

"Thank you, kind sir." Zadra bowed. "Now, in addition to that aforementioned drink, could someone explain why I'm talking to a human pup that barely looks old enough to be weaned from his mom instead of Commander Mosler? He is still in charge of Team Obsidian, is he not?"

"Commander Mosler was killed on Niceen-3, ma'am," Taylor spoke up first.

"No!" Zadra looked genuinely stricken, something that surprised Jacob. Had she actually known his former CO? "How? Please say it wasn't because of someone coming for me."

"No, ma'am," Jacob said. "He was killed by a traitor on our crew. We were attacked by the Ull in your office, and when we got back to the ship, our engineer had shot Mosler and escaped."

"And you aren't hunting him down right now?!" The vehemence in her voice made all the battle-hardened Marines take an involuntary step back. "What kind of warriors are you to let something like that go without punishment?" Now it was Jacob's turn to push back, his temper rising.

"Our mission—*his* mission—was to safely retrieve you and take you back to Terran space," he snapped. "We haven't even had time to mourn the death of our captain because of the wild fucking goose chase you've led us on, much less avenge him. Do I want the traitor dead? You fucking bet I do! But I honor Commander Mosler by carrying on and doing my job as he'd want me to, as he would do if one of us fell." Everyone was silent for a moment while Jacob and Zadra stared each other down.

"So, the pup has inherited some of the bite after all," she said finally. "Lieutenant, is there a place I can lay down and rest? I've spent some days stuffed in the ship's hydraulic service bay, and I think I'd like to sleep on something a little softer than starship hull plating. We can talk afterward."

"Please take my quarters," Jacob said. "It's the only luxury available on this ship, I'm afraid."

"It will be more than adequate," she said. "Thank you. Oh, and you might want to drop your slip-space velocity to forty percent or so. We don't actually need to go to Colton Hub, but we should probably talk about a few things before heading back to Terranovus or before you call in for a rendezvous from one of your capital ships." Jacob didn't like the fact that Zadra had barged in and was now presuming to call the shots, but he wasn't so prideful that he'd put his crew at risk just to defy her or prove he was in charge.

"Sully," he said.

"Slip-drive power coming back to our lowest stable speed," Sully reported. "Just under forty-four percent."

"I look forward to hearing what you have to say," Jacob said.

"Oh, I doubt that," Zadra said, turning to leave. "None of it is good news for the Cridal Cooperative or Earth."

After Zadra had closed herself in his quarters, Jacob told the rest of the that the mission objective had actually come to them. Murph had argued against her wishes and leaned hard on Jacob to turn the ship back for Terranovus so they could meet up with a Fleet ship and hand her over. Mettler seemed to not give a shit either way and just apologized for not noticing a stowaway after they'd left Formenos. Jacob strongly considered Murph's request, but in the end decided it wouldn't do any harm to wait until Zadra woke up and passed on the information she had.

18

Terranovus, Naval Intelligence Section HQ

"What can I do for NAVSOC, Captain?"

"You can start by telling me why you embedded one of your agents into Team Obsidian without telling me about it," Captain Marcus Webb strode into the inner office belonging to the Director of Naval Intelligence. While Earth was still figuring out how it wanted to structure its spaceborne military, NIS had stepped in to fill a void left when the civilian oversight couldn't agree on whether their new intelligence apparatus should answer to the military or directly to the civilian government. That made the director the most informed human on Earth or Terranovus, privy to all the secrets that filtered in from beyond Terran space.

The current director, an unimposing man named Michael Welford, was a CIA alumnus that had been part of the Terranovus project since the early days when it was little more than a military compound and top-secret shipyard. He and Webb had known each other since then, back when they were both low-ranking cogs in a wheel, and both were adjusting to their new roles as kings of their respective castles.

"Sure, Marcus," Welford said. "I'll tell you why Murphy is there just as soon as you tell me what in the holy hell you were thinking recruiting Jason Burke's kid into a NAVSOC unit, much less a Scout Corps team. I read about how you railroaded him into a Marine Corps commission. God help us both if *he* finds out what you've done. He asked us to protect Jacob, not put him beyond the front lines. You know what he'll do to us if something happens to his one and only son?"

"Kill us. Painfully." Webb shrugged. "I needed Jacob. Our own cybernetics program is decades away from being able to even scratch the surface of what that boy is capable of by random chance. So far, the Cooperative is being cagey about giving us access to their troop enhancement technology so we've been exploring other options through contacts made via Scout Fleet teams, but so far it's been slow going."

"It still seems risky."

"You've seen the same reports I have," Webb scoffed. "It's all about survivability. There are some tough, mean species out there, and my forward observers and special operators can't always rely on modern weaponry in the places we're forced to send them. Jacob Brown could be a bit of a stopgap. We get real-world operational data on how enhanced humans operate within a team of normals while he's with Obsidian while our scientists continue to pursue a technological answer to the problem in parallel."

"Jacob is not his father," Welford warned. "He's young, green, and he isn't as impervious to injury, nor does he heal as quickly as Burke. You're taking an awful risk using him in an operational role right now. Why not pull him back and utilize him in a training capacity until our own enhancement program comes up to speed?"

"Time is not on our side," Webb said. "The ConFed move against the Eshquarian Empire has the entire quadrant spooked. I'm getting word from my sources within the Cooperative that they may be forced to bend to whatever concessions the ConFed demands. I know you've seen the same reports."

"I have," Welford confirmed, "but while I do my best to stay informed of impending threats, I don't waste undue time on things I can't control. Earth is a two-planet, emerging power. If someone wants to come at us in earnest and take what we have, they're going to do it. I try to focus my energy on the things I *can* control, like the leaky boat that NAVSOC has become. I'm sorry, Marcus, but your outfit seems to be a breeding ground for sympathizers of Jansen's One World movement." When Webb just looked confused, Welford went on.

"That's what she's calling her faction now. It's a marketing thing. If she called it 'I want to rule the world,' I don't think she'd have people lining up to fill the ranks. What she's done is take advantage of all Earth's former nation state governmental infighting to sell her insurrection as a revolution. She's promising to put an end to all the needless and wasteful bickering and focus on making sure all deals negotiated with Earth put humans first." Webb just snorted at that.

"She tried to sell us to the Ull as a subservient worker class," he said. "They get free, skilled slave labor, and she gets to be a puppet dictator of a planet that no longer belongs to humanity. Maybe President Hightower made a serious mistake by pinning the Ull attack on Burke and hiding Jansen's involvement."

"Undoubtedly so," Welford said. "Our esteemed former president had many admirable qualities, but she was still a politician at heart. Covering her own ass was instinctual, and if she admitted that the colonial administrator *she* appointed had built a battlefleet with the help of an alien power, then tried to overthrow Earth's governments, there would have been some uncomfortable questions."

"Fair enough, I suppose," Webb said. "That explains it, but doesn't excuse it. Now, are you going to tell me why you're putting spies in my organization without telling me?"

"I thought I just did," Welford said. "NAVSOC is rife with traitors. I'm trying to weed them out. I couldn't come to you directly because there are four people on your staff who have flagged during the initial investigation. I couldn't risk that our meeting would stay a secret and that it would push them underground. Scarponi's attack tells us they're becoming bold and, more importantly, sloppy. I'm sorry, my friend, but I just couldn't think of an easy way to warn you."

"Then why tell me now?"

"You're asking me a direct question, and you already know I have at least one operative within your units." Welford shrugged. "Seems pointless to lie about it now. Scarponi escaped, which means it's only a matter of time before the other sleepers here are informed of his attack on Team Obsidian."

"Fuck me. If they're able to get word back to their operatives here then the assumption will be that we know about the infiltration," Webb said. "They may not go underground, they may attack us here on Terranovus before we can identify them all."

"Do you have any assets in play you can trust to go after Scarponi before he can make it back to Jansen?" Welford asked.

"At this point, the only team I can trust without question is Obsidian, but they're now being commanded by a twenty-three-year-old second lieutenant, and I have no way to get in touch with them," Webb said. "I told Brown to maintain com silence until they were able to get their objective and were already heading back."

"Weef Zadra." Welford nodded. "She was a personal friend of Ezra Mosler's, was she not?"

"Yeah," Webb sighed. "I don't know what he did for her, but that little Veran has a serious soft spot for Mosler. She's not going to take his death very well."

"Many of us won't," Welford said somberly. "He was one of the best."

"Maybe *the* best," Webb agreed.

"We're rolling up on the end now," MG said with undisguised glee, rubbing his hands together. "All we have to do is keep this piece of shit flying and get our VIP back to the Fleet and it's a short trip to Terranovus where we can get back to our interrupted R&R."

"I'm not going to Terranovus," Zadra said, seeming to appear in the room again without warning.

"Goddamnit," MG sighed.

"What do you mean you're not going?" Jacob demanded. "This entire cluster fuck of a mission was to extract you with the express purpose of going to Terranovus? Are you backing out of your deal with Captain Webb?"

"I'm not sure what that expression means, but any clusters fucked during your mission, Young Lieutenant, were likely because of your own actions," Zadra said. "I'm certainly not backing out of my deal with Earth, I'm just modifying it based on new information."

"That being?"

"The lack of security in your own organization, for one." Zadra sniffed. "Just hear me out for a moment before making yet another rash decision that will get people killed." It took Jacob almost half a minute to get his rage under control at her casual comment, choking down his own comeback and forcing himself to breathe slowly. When he saw her studying him with fascination, he knew that it hadn't been such a casual comment after all; she was prodding him and studying his reactions. She'd provoked him on purpose, and he could see the ghost of a smile play across her wide mouth as his emotions were as plain on his face as his nose. She'd been around humans quite a bit and would know what the purple face and throbbing vein in his forehead meant.

"That was foolish," Jacob said once he'd reined in his temper and felt his supercharged adrenal response subside. Both were some of the *gifts* of his unique genetic makeup, both had been a dangerous liability for him most of his life. "Please, go on with your explanation."

"Fascinating," Zadra said, still staring hard at Jacob. "Let me backtrack a bit... When I reached out to Marcus Webb and told him of my desire to get free and clear of the ConFed, it was predicated on the fact that nobody could know where I was going. He and Ezra Mosler both assured me it would be handled by Mosler's own Scout Corps team and I would effectively disappear without a trace. As it turns out, the traitor who killed your captain also puts my life at risk."

"You think that Scarponi is going to turn you in to ConFed Intelligence?" Murph asked skeptically.

"I think he will report his mission to his superiors within Margaret Jansen's organization," Zadra said. "From the communiques I was able to intercept, they were tracking a few UEN ships because they'd learned of a high-value asset Earth had recently obtained, but they didn't know the specifics. We need to get a hold of this Scarponi before he can tell the Ull I'm that asset."

"Seems a little late for that, doesn't it?" Jacob asked. "They'll have already reported in after Niceen-3."

"Jansen's organization is structured in independent cells," Zadra said. "This is partially to keep herself insulated from any sort of organized coup from her own military leaders, and partially because Marcus Webb's campaign to wipe her out has been somewhat successful. Because of their own security issues, it's almost certain the team that hit you on Niceen-3 will not have reported back yet. The cells are all distrustful of each other and, thanks in no small part to me compromising their communication network, are also distrustful of sending sensitive messages even when heavily encrypted."

"So, you think if we intercept Scarponi and the cell he was working with that you'll be able to remain safely hidden?" Jacob asked.

"Hidden for as long as it takes me to get out from under the ConFed's reach," Zadra said. "Despite their dominion in this part of the quadrant, they aren't powerful enough yet to challenge the Avarian Empire." Jacob had heard of the Avarians, but the information on them was scant. Their empire was supposed to be vast but not many had ventured across the Delphine Expanse—the empty, boundless region of empty space that separated the two superpowers —and had returned to tell about it. He still didn't know what sort of deal Zadra could have cooked up with the Avarians to assume she had safe harbor there, but it had to be something good given that the Empire was known to be hostile to outsiders.

"I see where this is going and we have a significant problem, LT," Murph said. "First off, we're not a tactical strike unit. Scout Fleet teams are small and meant to be invisible. We don't carry the personnel or firepower to engage one of Jansen's hit squads, nor do I think we would be given the clearance to do so. I think we need to go ahead and call this in and let NAVSOC send an Alpha Team out here. We sniff out Scarponi, they come in and drop the hammer." Jacob considered Murph's words and admitted he had a point. Scout Fleet's primary mission wasn't hunt and kill. Their equipment and tactics were all geared towards getting in and out of places unseen. NAVSOC had a whole other group of hunter/killer teams that specialized in what Zadra was about to propose.

"You don't have the time to wait for Terranovus to send out a specialized strike team before we lose the trail of the traitor who killed your captain," Zadra said, still working on the raw nerve of Mosler's murder. "I can find them. The element of surprise is on our side. If you call this in for approval from your commanders, and they decide that Agent Murphy is correct, then it's almost certain that we lose the target *and* our deal. I will be forced to make other arrangements to ensure my safety.

"Believe me, gentlemen, this isn't something I want to do. I'm a sneak and a thief, not a mercenary or a soldier, but if word gets back to the wrong people that I've cut a deal with Earth, then we're all in trouble."

"*Agent* Murphy?" MG asked. "Who the fuck is that?"

Jacob couldn't tell if she was being straight or if her performance was heavy on the hyperbole in order to get them moving in the direction she wanted. Was she really so valuable that governments would go to war over her? And if so, what had been keeping her safe up to this point? If the ConFed was willing to invade a neighboring power on a whim, they'd be more than willing to hit the city Zadra lived in with an orbital strike just to eliminate the threat. Something wasn't adding up in his head about her claims.

"Let's do it this way; you tell me where Scarponi is and we'll talk about whether I'm willing to risk any more of my people to get him," Jacob said.

"We're wasting time while we—"

"You've said that already," Jacob cut her off. "This isn't a negotiation. There is no faith between us. If you want me to trust that you're being honest about your claims, you'll have to give me something other than wild, vague stories about Earth being in danger because of the quadrant's only superpower being after a single Veran that lived in the ass crack of the galaxy." Zadra gave him an inscrutable look—or at least one he couldn't recognize with his lack of familiarity with Verans—and then looked away.

"I can find him, but I can't do it on this ship, and certainly not while we're in slip-space," she said finally. "I'll need a strong Nexus connection to reach out and find him."

"I can see you're considering this, *Lieutenant*, and I strongly advise against it," Murph said. "We don't know nearly enough about this alien or the situation to put ourselves at further risk. We should make contact with NAVSOC Command and let them coordinate the hunt for Scarponi with the Fleet."

"There's one major problem with that, Murph," Jacob said. "NAVSOC has been compromised. To what level we don't know, but what we *do* know is that they've been able to stay one step ahead of us the entire time. Are you forgetting the attack on the *Endurance*? I'm not sure how it fits in but it's too coincidental to be unrelated, and there's no way Scarponi could have coordinated that by himself. The location of the rendezvous had to be given by someone within our own command."

"So, your answer to these issues is to go rogue?" Murph asked. "You've recovered the asset as Webb directed you to. Anything more you do will be outside of the parameters, and *protection*, of your orders. Is this really what you want to do on your first mission, Lieutenant?"

Jacob thought for a long, hard moment about Murph's words. Everything he had said was technically right, and Jacob had sworn an oath to follow the orders of those appointed above him, but as an officer and the on-site commander of the mission, he also had a duty to constantly reevaluate the situation in the field as it progressed. His ultimate duty was to Earth and humanity, not to just blindly follow orders that had been given without full knowledge of the situation. He felt that Captain Webb wouldn't want one of his Scout Fleet officers just shrugging their shoulders and saying, "Those were my orders," when asked why they didn't investigate further when given the opportunity.

"We'll find a way to get Zadra the Nexus connection she needs, allow her the chance to find Scarponi, and then make a decision as to whether we pursue or call in the big guns," Jacob said. "I'm not committing us to anything except gathering more information at this time." Murph didn't say anything, but he seemed satisfied with the answer. Zadra gave no indication either way that she was either pleased or displeased with his decision.

"So, is anybody going to tell me who Agent Murphy is?" MG asked again.

19

"What was this place called again?"

"Empyrea Station," Jacob said. Mettler had asked the same question half a dozen times already, seemingly unable to pronounce the name of the dilapidated shipping hub they were now flying towards.

"How close do I need to get?" Sully asked.

"The com equipment on this ship is surprisingly good," Zadra said. "I only need to be within five thousand kilometers to get the bandwidth I need. The closer the better, obviously, but I don't think we'll want to land here unless we have something to sell. We'd be too memorable."

"We could sell MG," Mettler said. "What's the going rate for one high-mileage, worn out, shit bag Marine riddled with STDs?"

"Not sure." MG shrugged. "You'd have to ask your mom."

"Knock it off," Jacob said over his shoulder. He went back to looking at the enlarged and enhanced image of Empyrea Station that was on the main display. The bridge of the small gunboat wasn't nearly as advanced or user-friendly as the *Corsair* had been. The large main display was a curved monitor that sat at an angle from the deck to the bottom of the sectioned windows that made up the canopy. It curved around the front of the bridge and had no holographic projection capability. Despite its shortcomings, however, Jacob found that the location and shape of the display worked well from where he sat in the command chair.

The trading hub, like most of its kind, was a decommissioned military installation that had been long abandoned by a government that no longer even existed. It sat in a trailing heliocentric orbit, following along behind a small rocky planet in a system that had two habitable moons, but no planets that could sustain life on their own. The smaller of the two rocky planets was dotted with domed mining colonies that excavated its surface looking for anything that could be pulled up and sold at a profit.

Zadra had picked the station because it was one of two major Nexus hubs within practical range for the gunboat and was remote enough that they weren't likely to run into any of Mok's people or the ConFed. During the trip out, she'd spent most of her time working with Taylor to make sure there weren't any other trackers or bugs on the ship that he hadn't found in his own sweep. She also managed to unlock a secret partition on the ship's main computer that Taylor hadn't even been able to detect, much less break into. The information on it detailed the plans the former captain had been making with one of Saditava Mok's Twelve Points—apparently, the direct underbosses in his organization—to try and take out the big boss himself. It was fairly involved and the specifics of the plot were provided in full detail in the hidden files.

The Veran information broker had been beyond ecstatic at the find.

"Do you know what this means?" she cried, hopping lightly on the balls of her feet.

"That this Mok character is about to have a real shitty year coming up?" Jacob asked.

"No, my dense young friend," she said, smiling. "This means that out of your two major problems, one of them is solved. I know Mok personally. When he's given this, from you, he will zero out the debt you incurred by stealing one of his smuggling ships."

"How would we even begin to get this to him?" Murph asked.

"Nothing simpler," she assured him. "I'll take care of it while I find your wayward traitor here at Empyrea. I have a direct line to him. It will mean coming clean about the fact that I'm not longer going to be an available source of information for him, but he's never owned me so that won't be an issue. Mok is ruthless but fair and honorable."

"That's an odd way to describe one of the quadrant's biggest criminal kingpins," Jacob said.

"Mok isn't your typical criminal overlord," Zadra said. "He wasn't even always a criminal. Believe me, loyalty and honor within his inner circle are things he values more than anything. When he finds out one of his Points was getting ready to try and topple him, he will come down hard, but he'll also reward those who brought the information to him."

"Reward?" MG perked up. "What sort of reward?"

"He'll allow you to continue to draw breath after stealing a ship full of chits and platinum from one of his crews," Zadra said.

"A crew that was going to betray him," MG pointed out. "I'd think a little more was in order."

"What do you care?" Jacob asked. "You're a Marine serving in the UEAS. You wouldn't be allowed to keep it anyway."

"I've never been rich before, LT," MG complained. "I'd like to try it out once to see how it feels." Jacob just rolled his eyes but didn't answer.

"We're within range, pilot—"

"I have a name," Sully muttered.

"—go ahead and hold here," Zadra said imperiously. "I'm going to be fairly immersed in my own connections so I'll need Taylor to work with me controlling the flow of information coming back through the link. I'll maintain enough awareness outside of the link that if you detect something coming in, let me know."

"Got it." Taylor sat down at the terminal next to the Veran.

As Obsidian's tech specialist, Taylor had a specialized neural implant that allowed him a deeper level of connection and control over alien technology. Weef Zadra, however, had some wetware that put anything humans had to shame. Her neural implant was so extensive that she'd actually had to have her cranium surgically enlarged, adding sections of synthetic skeleton, in order to house it all. Apparently, Veran's had brains that were especially suited to this sort of work and many of their species that ventured off their home world found work as either network security specialists or criminal code slicers.

Zadra also had one more trick up one of her four sleeves: her brain could actually partition itself off as she needed it to in order to run parallel processing chains. It was a biological quirk of her species that become an especially powerful tool when married to a modern neural implant that could harness it. Jacob watched in fascination as her eyes closed and fluttered while she immersed herself into the Nexus connection. Taylor, who needed to plug in a hardline to his own implant to try and keep up, also appeared semi-catatonic while his hands danced over the controls, his eyes staring off into space, unseeing.

"This is some freaky shit," Mettler said, waving his hand in front of Taylor's face.

"Too freaky for me." MG walked off. "I'll be down in the cargo hold getting some PT in."

Jacob kept an eye on his tech specialist for signs of distress as he watched the pair negotiate through the station's security layers and tap directly into one of the Nexus hubs. *Nexus* was actually a colloquial name used for any public data network and, according to Murph, it was a fairly recently added to the lexicon. Apparently, one of the major tech firms used the term in a marketing campaign and it stuck. Jacob had been fascinated by the story simply because if you just changed the names and places, the story could have easily applied to Earth. He still wasn't sure if he found that all the aliens he'd met weren't all that…*alien*…to be a comfort or not.

"This will take some time." Zadra's voice was flat, emotionless. "Hovering around will only distract us."

Jacob assigned shifts to sit in the com room and keep a watch over the pair with specific orders to pull the plug on Taylor if it looked like he was in trouble. He didn't understand how Taylor was able to control the flow of information within the ship's systems with his neural implant when he could barely make his display the right information half the time even when he was consciously trying. When he'd asked the tech specialist, all he'd gotten was a sympathetic smile, which bordered on condescending, that made Jacob think perhaps he was having more trouble than most adapting to the computer that now lived in his head.

"I'll take the first watch. Go get some sleep, LT."

"Thanks, Murph." Jacob had been up for nearly thirty hours, and the strain was beginning to show. On the flight out to Empyrea Station, they'd had to explain to the other three that Sergeant Murphy was actually an NIS spook who had been sent to spy on them. After assuring a frantic MG that the focus of the investigation had nothing to do with underground fight clubs, and telling Mettler his creative import/export business he had going with the shipping contractor was off the radar, Murph was forced to divulge quite a bit of classified information to explain his presence.

The Marines took it in stride, but Jacob could tell the news had created a rift in the team. No matter. Once they ensured that Scarponi was a threat the Fleet could deal with, he'd return to Terranovus with Zadra and collect on the deal that would see him recommissioned into the Navy and put on a mainline starship.

"Not soon enough," he muttered as his shoulder brushed up against something sticky on the bulkhead of the filthy gunboat.

"They should have checked in by now." Webb rubbed his temples with his fingers. "Either something has gone wrong or they're way off the reservation."

He'd sent a ship to Niceen-3, one of the disguised deep-space freighters used by 2nd Scout Corps, and had the *Corsair* collected before someone on that planet decided to either take it for scrap or managed to dig out any secrets Lieutenant Brown and his crew may have left. Thankfully by the time the *Northstar* had arrived, the *Corsair* was still intact and appeared to be unmolested. The hatches were still locked up tight and the security codes Brown had given him still worked.

What he hadn't counted on, however, was how thoroughly Obsidian would scuttle the ship. It took tech teams from the *Northstar* four days to ferry the needed part down from orbit to get the ship just flight-worthy enough to haul herself back up to the freighter's hangar bay. Once they had her aboard, the *Northstar's* captain broke orbit and got the hell out of the Reaches. A bulk freighter of her size would be a tempting target for the pirates and thugs that inhabited that region.

"My teams weren't able to find any clues as to where they might have gone," Captain John Saraceno said over the slip-com link. "But while we were going back and forth to the maintenance terminals to get common parts for the *Corsair*, we did pick up on some gossip I think might have to do with Mosler's team. I didn't pursue it further because—"

"I realize that type of human intelligence isn't something 2nd Corps has the personnel for." Webb waved him off. "You did the right thing by not chasing down every rumor you hear, especially on some backwater shithole like Niceen-3. What did your techs hear the ground crews gossiping about?"

"Apparently, right about the time Obsidian went off-grid, there was an Impan crew that had their Eshquarian gunboat jacked," Saraceno said. "The reason my people were treated to the rumors is because some of the people at the starport swear it was a group of humans who took the ship."

"I hadn't realized exactly what ship they'd taken but their message said they were finding...alternate transportation," Webb said carefully. "Was that all?"

"That was just the shot, here's the chaser: that ship was running a load that was marked for the Blazing Sun Syndicate." Saraceno leaned back in his seat and the camera in his office automatically followed the movement to keep him framed.

"Shit. Mok's organization." Webb blew out between his lips. "Please tell me it was just a load of laundry for his servants."

"The surviving crew members were apparently being tight-lipped about what they were carrying, right up to the point they were collected by a merc crew that had Blazing Sun's logo on their ship," Saraceno said. "Rumor has it that the gunboat was being used to launder hard currency to the tune of hundreds of millions of ConFed credits and that the Impans had made an unscheduled, unauthorized pit stop on Niceen-3 for a little side deal involving narcotics before delivering it."

"So, the Impans are already dead," Webb sighed. "And they'll have likely told their torturers everything they knew about the human crew that swiped Mok's load. Damn, damn, *damn!* There aren't enough humans out in the quadrant yet for this not to have some negative bounce-back on the 3rd Corps teams still deployed."

"That's all I have, sir," Saraceno said. "I'm bringing the *Northstar* back to Terranovus where we'll drop off the *Corsair* and rotate crew for our next assignment."

"It'll be a milk run this next time," Webb assured him. "You'll be shadowing one of the Galvetic Legions and providing them with signal intelligence while they handle a little border dispute that's erupted for one of their clients. Should be a short one."

"Look forward to it. *Northstar*, out." Webb waited until the screen blanked out and was replaced with his background image.

"Brown, you fucking idiot," he groaned as the full implications of what his rogue second lieutenant had done sank in. Blazing Sun controlled nearly all the major criminal activity from the Orion Spur to the Cygnus Outer Arm, damn near a full third of the quadrant. Saditava Mok's empire had grown exponentially during the last two decades, swallowing up smaller syndicates and adding them to his own while he somehow managed to stay out of the ConFed's crosshairs.

Well, maybe it wasn't such a mystery as to why the ConFed mostly left him alone. Mok was a peculiar type of gangster and kept most of his illicit activities from spilling out into the general populace in the systems he operated in. The old ConFed was more than happy to allow the underworld to regulate itself so long as they kept the civilian casualties to a minimum. The new regime, however, might not be so tolerant of such an expansive criminal enterprise skimming money off the top and not giving the ConFed their tribute.

The real issue now is that Brown's recklessness likely put humanity on Mok's radar. He'll almost certainly try and hunt down the crew that jacked his load if for no other reason than to send a message and his other 3rd Corps teams could now be in danger. Webb had no reliable way to try and contact Saditava Mok, nor did he think that would be a particularly wise course of action. He could try and ask his liaison within the Cridal Cooperative's intelligence service for assistance, but that would require admitting they'd been right and Earth wasn't ready to be operating out in the wild on its own.

"Bennet!" he roared to his aide. "Get your ass in here!"

"You bellowed, sir?" the unflappable young woman said, sticking her head in the door.

"Draft up recall orders for all Scout Fleet units, but don't transmit them yet." Webb stood and started pacing. "First, get me a detailed report on the last known position for all of our assets and call over to your contacts in the NIS and see if they'd provide the same information for theirs. I want to know where all of our people and ships are before we start calling them back home. Obsidian may have kicked over a hornet's nest, and we need to be prepared for any of the fallout."

"Aye-aye, sir," Bennet said and disappeared.

20

"Don't give me too much credit. Your species is still ultra-rare in ConFed space so you're easy to track when you actually use identification labeling you as human. The Ull are only slightly less rare so the fact your traitors are working with them made it almost child's play."

"She's being modest," Taylor said. The Marine looked like a wet rag that had been wrung out, and Jacob was worried he'd overextended himself. "I was watching the dataflow and keeping up as best I could. The way she was able to dig into secure immigration records and port authority computers like it was nothing...amazing."

"Go to berthing and get some rest, Taylor," Jacob said. "You look like you're barely able to stand. Mettler, you go with him and check him over."

"I'm fine," Taylor insisted but trudged off towards his rack anyway.

"I'll keep an eye on him, LT," Mettler said. Jacob noticed that Mettler *accidentally* slammed his shoulder into Murph on the way out of the cramped room. Apparently, even when acting under orders, lying to a teammate was a mortal sin within the tight-knit unit. Murph grunted but didn't respond.

"Okay, out with it," Jacob said. "Where are Scarponi and his buddies?"

"A moon called Theta Suden," Zadra said.

"I've heard of it," Murph said. "It was a half-assed terraforming project that ran out of money. It has *barely* breathable air, but the biosphere is stable."

"Correct," Zadra said. "It was being set up to handle the population overflow on the system's second planet, but there was a geological event that made it unnecessary."

"I don't get it," Jacob admitted.

"Every living thing on the planet died," Zadra said without a hint of emotion. "Oh, don't look at me like that. It happened hundreds of years before either of us were born. Anyway, the moon project was obviously abandoned and started being used as a waypoint for deep-space haulers back when ships couldn't make it across the quadrant without refueling and replenishing. As happens often in this part of space, a waypoint became a trading post, a trading post attracted permanent residents, and the permanent residents formed a government. It's still technically listed as independent since it has no resources any of the bigger powers want, but it is protected by one of the more powerful drug cartels."

"Mok's again?" Jacob asked.

"No," Murph answered before Zadra could open her mouth. "Mok doesn't directly control any of the narco-gangs, likely in an effort to stay on the ConFed's good side. Of all the criminals in the galaxy, few are more willing to hurt civilians than the drug runners."

"This seems like a pretty obscure little rock. Why do you know about it?"

"Classified." Murph shrugged. Jacob gave him a flat stare at that. "What? Just because we're sharing *some* secrets doesn't mean I'm going to divulge everything I know to some Marine second lieutenant. Infiltrating Scout Fleet wasn't my first assignment."

"I don't suppose you were able to dig up an image of Scarponi while you were hacking into their immigration computers?" Jacob asked.

"Hacking?" Zadra spluttered. "What an insulting term."

"Slicing, whatever you want to call it," Murph said. "Just show us."

"Two for the price of one, boys," Zadra said and pulled up a series of images showing two human males, one Scarponi, the other unknown...at least to Jacob. "Not sure who his little buddy is."

"It's a ghost," Murph said, his teeth clenched together.

"Come again?" Jacob asked.

"His name is Elton Hollick. He's officially listed as KIA," Murph said. "He was—*is*—one of ours. It looks like NIS isn't immune to having traitors and sympathizers in the ranks, and now we know why Scarponi fled to Theta Suden."

"*We* don't know shit. *You* seem to have all the answers right now," Jacob said. Murph seemed to be genuinely conflicted, the emotions warring within him plain on his face as he struggled with his need to inform his team what he knew and the instinct of a highly trained intelligence officer to keep classified information a secret.

"Hollick is an OG intel spook since back before the NIS even officially existed," Murph said. "He was a CIA asset that had been put on Terranovus to keep an eye on the pop-up colony that was, in fact, nothing more than a military outpost. He was one of a handful of agents the US government had embedded to try and keep a handle on something they were hiding from the general public back on Earth."

"Makes sense," Jacob said. "Nobody in Washington DC would have been willing to just hand over an operation like that to an administrator without at least putting in a few watchdogs."

"Right," Murph said. "Hollick was actually aboard the Terranovus fleet that had come back to Earth during Jansen's ill-fated coup attempt. The ship he was on escaped with her, and he continued to send us intel, right up until he was discovered and killed. He was one of the first operational assets of the new military's intelligence service."

"How did you know he was killed?" Zadra asked. "Was it an assumption just because the stream of information cut off?"

"He was in the middle of a report when two Ull broke into where he was and shot him," Murph said. "The video is showed to all incoming agents during training. The man is a legend for staying at his post and doing his job despite no chance of being rescued."

"Wait, wait, wait," Zadra cut him off, waving her two smaller arms in front of her. "He was broadcasting *video* back to you? Full bandwidth video of just himself talking?"

"Yeah, so?" Murph's posture was defensive and he glared down at the smaller Veran.

"Come on, Murph," Jacob sighed. "The proof is right in front of you. He was a double agent. Needlessly transmitting so much information when simple text would do just as well should have been a red flag. He used the two-way slip-com channel to pull useable intel from our side to give to Jansen and faked his death once the charade had been played out as long as it could."

"Points for the young pup," Zadra said. "They either discovered him after the fact and turned him or he'd been working with them the whole time. Either way, your Agent Hollick is obviously with the enemy right now since he and Scarponi are hugging each other like long lost friends in this image."

"Damn." Murph looked away, his jaw clenched.

"Does this tub have the legs to make it out to Theta Suden?" Jacob asked.

"Lieutenant, we need to call this in," Murph said. "I indulged your whims as far as allowing Zadra to track Scarponi and see if she could find out where he rabbited to, but this has blown up into something well beyond just tracking down a single traitor. Fleet Ops and NIS need to be informed of this *immediately.*"

"And how long after that do you think it will be before one of the many leaks within either organization sends word to Hollick that they've been compromised?" Jacob countered. "By the time Fleet got around to sending a ship out to this moon, they'll be long gone *and* well aware we know Hollick is still alive and Scarponi is working with them."

"So, what do you want to do, Lieutenant Badass?" Murph scoffed. "Swoop in, guns blazing, and try to take on the entire One World faction with five Marines and one Navy pilot? They'll kill us all before we make it off the back ramp."

"It's *four* Marines and one lying ass NIS agent," Jacob countered, squaring off to the taller man. "Why do you assume that we're going to run this like an infantry operation? They have no idea we've found them, no clue as to what ship we're flying... We have *every* advantage to try and do this right now."

"Once were there, I'll be able to much more accurately track them," Zadra said. "We have the range to make it with the current fuel load aboard."

"Don't encourage him," Murph snapped. "If you don't want to report it through official channels, why not talk to Captain Webb directly? Let him dispatch a—"

"It's still the same problem." Jacob shook his head. "I *might* get a message to Captain Webb that isn't intercepted, but then he'll have to spin up a mission, hand it off to his operations and logistics people, they'll have to call up to Fleet Ops and request a ship, and since we don't know what parts of NAVSOC could be compromised, we have to assume they all are. The real question here is do you accept my authority over this mission?" Murph visibly deflated at that. The crew had an odd mishmash of ranks between a Navy officer pilot, an assimilated rank officer NIS agent, and a freshly minted Marine Corps second lieutenant who had been given overall command of the mission by the NAVSOC Chief of Operations. It made for a tangled web when trying to determine who had the final say according to UEAS regulations.

"While I haven't looked up the specific reg, I'm going to assume that my NIS rank means zilch in this situation," Murph finally said. "I'm not sure what Naval regulations say, but I can already tell that Sully isn't going to buck Captain Webb and take over unless you ask."

"That's not the same as saying you're willing to still take orders from me," Jacob pointed out. Murph took another long break before answering, staring hard at Jacob.

"*Why* are you pushing for this? Are you trying to prove something? Want to make a name for yourself right away? I know for a fact you don't want to be a Marine and you damn sure don't want to be stuck in Scout Fleet. Now, all of the sudden you want to play spec ops and assassinate someone? Why accept so much risk to go so far outside the boundaries of your mission? Just go home and turn the Veran over to NAVSOC and be done with it!"

"I think you're forgetting that I've still not agreed to willingly assist Earth yet," Zadra interrupted. "At least not until we neutralize the risk this Scarponi poses."

"Bullshit," Murph scoffed. "Scarponi has already made contact with his leadership and you know it. What's the *real* reason you're leading Brown down this path?"

"Ezra Mosler was a friend," Zadra said after a long pause. "One of the few real friends I have...had. I take it personally when some halfwit traitor kills him for convenience. If I'm about to leave this part of the galaxy forever, I'd like one my last actions to mean something."

"And you're adamant you won't honor your agreement with Earth unless we do this?" Murph asked.

"My agreement was actually with Webb. He's the one who set all of this up," Zadra corrected. "He's also the one who arranged for my passage across the expanse and for my immigration into Avarian space. If you help me do this, I'll still consider the contract I have with him valid and turn over my entire information network as promised."

"We can let you ride along, but I can't risk putting you in the middle of the action if we find him," Jacob said, wanting to reassert control over the situation. "If you're caught in the crossfire, this whole thing is for naught, and Commander Mosler will have died for nothing." That last line seemed to hit home and any argument Zadra was about to offer died on her lips.

"Agreed," she said.

"Can I talk to you a minute?" Murph asked. "Alone?"

Jacob followed the NIS agent out of the cramped galley and into the cargo hold, closing the hatch behind him. He watched as Murph disabled the hold's intercom and security surveillance at a control panel on the far bulkhead.

"What?" Jacob asked when the other man didn't say anything.

"Assuming we find Scarponi, and assuming we're in a position to get near him, what are your plans?"

"I don't follow," Jacob admitted.

"We're not assassins, Jacob," Murph said. "We're not a strike team with orders, nor are we law enforcement pursuing a fugitive. We're glorified forward observers, and we're way, *way* outside of our mandate with this. If you track and kill Scarponi, it's likely you'll be brought up on charges...probably the rest of us too."

"You're suggesting we capture him?"

"I'm suggesting we abandon this absurd idea and go home, but yes, barring that, I think we have to consider the fact that capturing Scarponi and dragging him back to Terran space is our only viable option," Murph said. "You're so far off the reservation right now that I think bringing him back still breathing will be the only thing keeping you out of the brig."

Jacob carefully considered what he was being told and had to concede that Murph made a solid argument against just blasting Scarponi on sight. No matter how unique Scout Fleet's mission was, they still operated within the confines of the UEAS charter and its laws. He was not given carte blanche to terminate anyone, and even being this far off-mission would likely have serious consequences no matter what the outcome was.

"You're right," he said. "This is getting complicated. I felt like Zadra's refusal to cooperate unless we get Scarponi would put him within our mission parameters of securing her, but Command likely won't see it that way."

"Not a chance," Murph agreed. "Listen, I know you're trying to do the right thing. I want Scarponi dead for what he did, too, but is it worth your career and the risk that we get someone else on your team hurt or killed?

"Ezra Mosler was a highly skilled and respected commander

within Scout Fleet. It's why he was given a mission as important as trying to discreetly pull Weef Zadra out of the Reaches and bring her to Terranovus. You're not him. You're so fresh out of the Academy you squeak when you turn too fast *and* you've skipped a hell of a lot of training. Mosler saw some potential in you and opted to put you in the field early, but that doesn't change the fact that your inexperience could end up getting more people killed."

"Let's compromise," Jacob said, unable to refute any of Murph's points no matter how much he'd have liked to. His training at the Academy aside, he had no real-world experience for the situation he found himself in.

"I'm listening."

"We put eyes on Scarponi, determine what he's doing on Theta Suden and what strength the enemy might have there, and then we call it in. That keeps us still on the right side of that fuzzy gray line but gives Captain Webb the option of either ordering us off or to engage."

"Now you're thinking with a clear head," Murph said, grabbing Jacob's shoulder and shaking him. "I like it. Now, how do you want to deal with Zadra? Assuming she's not overridden the intercom and isn't listening right now, of course."

"We keep her in the dark for now." Jacob shrugged. "She seems a tad irrational about this, and I don't think we need another argument. In the end, if she wants to get away from whatever is chasing her and into the Avarian Empire, she's going to have to play ball one way or another."

"Agreed," Murph said. "I'd suggest that you go brief the others so they at least know we're heading to Theta Suden and we'll be infiltrating the area looking for Scarponi."

Jacob led the way out of the cargo hold, smiling at Zadra as he passed on his way to the bridge. He'd tell Sully to get them moving in the right direction and brief his team on what they'd be doing. The trick would be to hide the fact he wasn't planning on executing Scarponi from their VIP who would almost certainly be listening in.

21

Captain Marcus Webb paced the reception area of his office like a caged animal.

A Jumper had just landed at the base's airfield, and he had been given a heads-up from an old friend in Fleet Ops that the VIP it carried was coming his way. The small craft had been given clearance right from the top to come directly to Taurus Station.

"Sir, we've just been alerted that—"

"I already know, Ensign." Webb waved off one of his aides. "Just have the admiral escorted directly to my office, please."

"Aye-aye, sir."

Webb settled in his chair, collecting his thoughts before his visitor arrived. He didn't have long to wait.

"Take your seat, Captain." Rear Admiral Kelly Remey stormed into the office, his aide barely able to get the door open for her. Webb hadn't actually been getting out of his seat so, instead, he leaned back and assumed an even more relaxed posture.

"What a pleasant surprise to see you all the way out here at Taurus Base, Admiral. I hope that—"

"Shut up, Webb," Remey said with disgust, her reputation for abruptness apparently well-earned. "I didn't fly all the way out here from Earth to waste time on small talk. I want to know how you've managed to screw up a simple contact and retrieve mission so completely that the Chief of Staff himself is asking—and I quote —'Just what the fuck is Scout Fleet doing out there anyway?'"

"I assume you're referring to the mission to transport a citizen of Ver back to Terranovus?" Webb asked.

"If that's the mission where an untrained, untested Marine second lieutenant was sent to fetch an ultra-critical intelligence asset that was to be the cornerstone of our Phase III expansion plans, then yes, that would be the one, Captain." Remey's tone was neutral, but her eyes bore into Webb with an intensity that let him know the next few minutes would likely decide the course of his career. He thought very carefully how to respond to the notoriously short-fused flag officer and, in the end, decided the direct approach was best.

"Is this a request to be briefed on the mission, Admiral? Or is this someone from UEAS Command coming out to make me dance for my dinner before I'm relieved of duty anyway?" he asked. Remey's expression was neutral so Webb couldn't tell how his answer was taken. He made a mental note to never play poker with the admiral.

"Fine," she said after a moment. "Yes, there were some decisions made back on Earth regarding your fate before I was dispatched, but I have the authority to supersede those should I deem it necessary. So, convince me why you should remain in command of NAVSOC, and keep in mind this isn't the first debacle your Scout Fleet crews have caused."

Over the span of the next ninety minutes, Webb briefed Admiral Remey on the Weef Zadra mission without bothering to try and paint himself, or his organization, in a favorable light. If he was going down, it would be for the truth. He started by showing her some redacted footage of Lieutenant Brown during combat training at the Academy to explain why Commander Mosler had agreed to take him on before he'd finished his follow-on training. From there, it was a simple matter of laying out the mission failures beginning with a One

World traitor murdering a highly respected Scout Fleet commander and his decision to allow Jacob Brown to complete the mission to bring Zadra back to Terran space. Along with Brown's unique parentage, he also left out the fact that Sergeant Murphy was actually an embedded NIS agent.

"Margret Jansen!" Remey spat the name once he had finished his brief. She stood up so fast that her chair tipped over, startling Webb, and began to pace in front of the enormous window that overlooked the base.

"Did you know that I served under her? I was one of the first commanders assigned a *Columbia*-class starship. That was back when alien crews were still flying them for us and Jansen was ignoring her mandate to prep Terranovus for civilian settlers and was building a battle fleet to take back to Earth and anoint herself empress."

"I...didn't know that, ma'am," Webb said carefully. The *Columbia* Program ships were *very* early in the Terranovus colonization project. Remey must have been in Jansen's inner circle to be given one of the few starships humanity possessed at that time. Did she harbor sympathies for her old boss? "I served aboard the *Coronado* for a short time."

"Yes, I read all about that mission," she said. "In hindsight, I suppose it's a good thing you failed."

"Yes, ma'am."

"Relax, Captain." Remey seemed to read his thoughts. "I was one of the first to turn on her once we realized what was happening. She apparently never trusted me enough to confide in me her plans for Earth, and by the time we figured it out, the fleet had already made it back to the Solar System."

"Of course, ma'am."

"So, what do we do about our current mess?" Remey picked her chair back up and sat down. Webb idly thought about how imposing she was despite barely being five foot four.

"I take it I'm not being relieved of command just yet?" Webb asked.

"Not yet," Remey said. "The story we've gotten back on Earth about this mission isn't quite what you've told me, mostly due to the nature of information coming out of NAVSOC and Scout Fleet in particular. When I was sent, we didn't actually know that it was Mosler and Team Obsidian that had been dispatched, only that some kid fresh from the Academy had been entrusted with such a vital mission and that it had gone tits up."

Webb contemplated that. His department sent regular updates that were filtered through the communications office on Vanguard Station, the main active military installation on Terranovus, before they were forwarded on to Earth. From what Admiral Remey was telling him, he either had a leak in his own office or someone was creatively editing his reports before they were passed on. Neither prospect was particularly comforting. Before he answered Remey's question, he realized there was a third option: NIS had infiltrated NAVSOC much more thoroughly than Director Welford had admitted and they were passing along supplemental information to the civilian oversight.

"Currently, the only thing we can do is wait for Lieutenant Brown to check in and verify that he has the package and is on the way back," he said. "We've recovered the *Corsair* but have had no direct contact with Obsidian since they...borrowed...a ship from Niceen-3 and went after the objective. I had expected them to check in well before now, however, so something may have gone wrong."

"Are you still even sure that Team Obsidian is viable? After being attacked on Niceen-3, I feel we must assume Jansen's people are tracking them somehow."

"My hope was that the change to a different, random ship, and the fact Scarponi fled, would mean they'd be able to slip away undetected," Webb said. "I've put Team Diamond on standby, but they're keeping an eye on the Eshquarian situation for us. That's critical intel we need so I'm not pulling them off unless there are no other options left."

"This is...not optimal," Remey said finally. "I hate to do this, Captain, but it looks like I'll be staying here on Taurus Station until this situation is resolved. The Navy Chief of Staff himself has asked that I be kept plugged in so that I can report to him directly."

"Understood," Webb said, unable to keep the weary sigh from his voice. "I'll see that you and your people are given office space and assigned quarters. You'll have free run of the base, of course, but I'm afraid that my duties will—"

"Yes, yes, I'm not here to interfere with you, Captain. I'm merely an observer. Thank you for not making an issue of this," Ramey said, standing and smoothing out her uniform. She nodded to him and walked to the door, pausing just before she opened it. "Just so you're not surprised when it happens, if this mission ends in failure and we lose the asset, someone will have to burn for it."

"And that person will be me," Webb finished for her. "Trust me, Admiral, I'm well aware of that."

"Nothing personal," she said before leaving the office and closing the door behind her.

Webb turned and looked out the window, his calm demeanor belying the storm churning in his gut. How had this gotten so out of control? He'd picked Mosler's unit so that it would be a discreet and precise execution of what was a fairly simple mission despite how important it was. Now, it was an all-out cluster fuck that would likely drag down most of NAVSOC's leadership before it was over, and if he'd managed to get Jacob Brown killed, he could look forward to a slow, agonizing death at Jason Burke's hands on top of being drummed out of the Navy. It was days like this that made him miss the simplicity of being an operator just following orders. His more immediate concerns, however, were how to manage NAVSOC's myriad clandestine ops with some pencil pusher from Earth looking over his shoulder the entire time.

"At least *that's* something I can control." He jabbed a button on his desk to summon his aide.

"Yes, Captain?"

"Have the *Kentucky* prepped for immediate departure. Tell Commander Duncan I want to be breaking orbit the moment my shuttle lands in the hangar bay," Webb said, referring to the command and control ship that was reserved for his personal use. "Make sure Orbital Control knows that this is not to be a logged departure, classified on my authority."

"Aye, sir," his aide said smartly before disappearing.

While the admiral would no doubt pester his staff and poke around his offices trying to look for a way to pin Team Obsidian's probable mission failure on him, he would be aboard one of NAVSOC's C&C ships, able to manage his deployed crews while avoiding any direct interference from Earth's two-star lackey.

Theta Suden was a shithole.

The others had tried to prepare Jacob for what he'd encounter on the surface of the dingy, dim moon, but the reality was so much worse once the gunboat had touched down on the landing pad. As the boarding ramp lowered from the side of the ship, the smell rushed in and assaulted his nose like nothing he'd ever experienced. He now knew each place had its own unique ambient smell, but this was so persistent and strong he found it almost unbearable, so much worse than Niceen-3.

"I swear you'll get used to it," MG laughed. "The first few places you land it seems like the smell is going to drive you insane, but after a few missions you barely even notice it. Pretty soon, your nose will be so tough that you'll be able to walk into the head after Mettler and barely gag."

"I doubt that," Taylor said.

"Fuck you both," Mettler grumbled.

"Alright, alright, let's get focused," Jacob said, still feeling a bit overwhelmed by the pungent odor that was the pervading smell of Theta Suden's atmosphere. They'd landed the gunboat at an auxiliary pad that was half a kilometer away from the city's main starport and, after bribing the customs inspector to ignore all the weaponry the crew carried, had managed to secure a vehicle large enough for all of them.

There were many logical holes in Weef Zadra's story about wanting to nail Scarponi because he was a security risk to her personally, but Jacob had been unable to pull any more details out of her during the flight to the smelly moon. She remained adamant that she had to eliminate the loose ends before she would be able to make a clean break from ConFed space. Jacob knew Murph had been right and that it was virtually impossible that Scarponi hadn't already checked in with his One World handlers and told them she was the mission objective. Even that assumed they hadn't already known all along. The strike team they took out at her office may have been there for her, not them. He also had reservations about her insistence that she and Mosler were such close friends.

"Are you sure you want to bring her along?" Murph nodded at Zadra as the automated ground vehicle rolled to a stop behind the ship.

"We don't know whether or not the enemy knows about this ship," Jacob said. "For the time being, I think she's safer with us...unless there's something you aren't telling me about where we're going."

"It's a disused NIS safe house," Murph said. "We still maintain it, but I can't guarantee its integrity given all the fucking leaks in both organizations we work for."

"I still can't believe you're some NIS douche bag sent to spy on us, Murph," MG said.

"Stow it." Jacob waved him off. "We'll hit the safe house first and see if it's still viable. After that, we have thirty-six hours to track down Scarponi before I'll have no choice but to call in our location and status to Command."

The tension between his Marines and *Agent* Murphy had been simmering since Niceen-3 and had just recently begun to boil over. MG and Mettler in particular seemed to view it as a complete betrayal by someone they had trusted, never mind that Murph had just been following orders like the rest of them. Given Jacob's newness to the team and his status as an untested, green officer, they had roundly ignored him when he tried to settle things between them. By the time they reached Theta Suden, he'd given up on any sort of unity and had settled on just keeping them from physically assaulting one another.

"I assume you want me staying with the ship?" Sully asked as they loaded up the vehicle with equipment. The pilot had kept to himself most of the flight and seemed content to just fly the ship and not make an issue of the fact he technically outranked the Marine lieutenant walking around barking orders.

"That's probably best," Jacob said. "Keep her ready to fly in a moment's notice since I can't guarantee we won't be running for our lives soon."

"Comforting," Sully said and trudged back up the ramp.

Jacob had Murph program their destination into the semi-autonomous ground vehicle that had pulled up to their landing pad while he and the others began stuffing gear into the back. He'd commented to Mettler that he was half-expecting to see the skies blanketed with flying cars given the level of technology available on most planets rather than so many mundane wheeled vehicles. The Marine had explained that grav-lev and repulsor drive vehicles were used extensively only on the wealthiest of ConFed planets. Everywhere else, it was considered a vulgar waste of resources and was eschewed in favor of the efficiency of wheeled vehicles and mag-lev mass transit. It made sense to Jacob after he stopped to really think about it. While the technology was certainly available, it still required a lot of energy to safely levitate a few tons of vehicle and cargo. In fact, once you got out away from the major port cities, most planets didn't look all that much more advanced than Earth had been before the first alien attack that had changed the course of their history.

Once they'd all piled in, Murph executed his pre-programmed route, and the boxy vehicle made a few warbling sounds as it performed its safety checks, and then smoothly pulled away from the landing pad. Jacob looked back to see Sully standing in the dilapidated gunboat's cargo bay while the ramp jerked upward and closed. He was ruminating as to how they were going to track down one wayward human on an entire world when Taylor began shouting from one of the front seats.

"That was him! Holy fuck, he was just standing right there!"

"I didn't see shit."

"You're imagining—"

"Shut up!" Jacob barked. "What did you see, Taylor?"

"Scarponi! He was just standing there between two buildings we passed two blocks back now!" Taylor was looking around trying to figure out how to open the side door when Mettler grabbed him.

"Taylor!" Jacob yelled again. "Calm down and listen to me. You're *certain* it was him?"

"Yes, goddamnit! I know what the mother fucker looks like! He was leaning against a building just inside the ally between the two," Taylor said.

"He was just standing there?" Murph sounded skeptical. "If you saw him, did he see you?"

"He...I...he might have," Taylor said. "He was looking out at the road, but he didn't show any reaction. He may have turned his head to follow as we went by, though."

"LT? I can tell this thing to hop off at the next side street and circle around," Murph said. The vehicle was in a center lane and traveling though decently heavy traffic. If Taylor had hopped out as it looked like he'd intended, he would have been flattened by the vehicles behind them.

"No," Jacob said. "We stick to the plan. If he's in this city, then Zadra will be able to track him down again, and then we'll move on him when we're ready and have a proper plan of attack. Just driving around looking for him after a single sighting is too inefficient and a good way for them to spot us, if they haven't already."

"For what it's worth, I agree with Lieutenant Brown," Zadra spoke up. "I can more quickly narrow my search by assuming Corporal Taylor actually did see Scarponi and limit my scope to this city. If he's here and walking about in public, then I'll have his location within a matter of hours."

"So, you believe me that I saw him?" Taylor asked.

"I trust your eyes, Taylor," Jacob said. "If you say you saw him, we'll adjust our planning and assume we'll be intercepting him within this city. Our timetable is still in effect, however. If we don't have his location within thirty-six hours, Sully has been ordered to make contact with Command and call in our location and status."

"Understood," Zadra said.

The rest of the ride passed without any further sightings of a human or their Ull handlers. Per Murph's program, the vehicle passed by the entrance to the safe house three different times, and then rolled to a stop at the rear of the building next door. They'd detected no sign that the building was compromised, and the NIS agent was able to ping the security system through his com unit and verify it was still secure.

"Taylor, Mettler, you're staying behind to protect Zadra," Jacob said. "Murph and MG are coming with me to check the safe house. I'll come back out to get you once we clear it."

"You know the place is already clear, right?" Murph asked once they were out of the vehicle. "I was able to ping the security systems with my implant when we were within half a klick."

"I assumed as much," Jacob said. "I wanted to talk to the two of you alone."

"Hang on." Murph keyed in a lengthy code into the door's discreet security panel while the other two watched in both directions of the sparsely traveled street. With a final *ding*, the panel light flashed green and the locks disengaged on the door. "So, what didn't you want to say in front of the others?"

"Damn! I should have taken that offer to go into the NIS instead of staying in the Corps," MG said as they took in the semi-luxurious appointment of the house. "The spooks get plush couches and a full-service food processor while the Scout Fleet slobs get a ship that may or may not hold together while in slip-space."

"Why don't you put that processor to good use and get some coffee started?" Jacob asked. "I actually wanted to make sure I could talk to you about Zadra without her being within earshot. Leaving the others to guard her gives me that chance."

"I'm listening," Murph said as MG rummaged around in the kitchen area.

"Assuming that Taylor actually *did* see Scarponi, does anybody else feel like it's just a bit too convenient we set down right by where he's at?" Jacob asked. "I know she's supposed to be some hot shit data broker who can slice into secure networks like it's nothing, but this seems like a real stretch for me."

"I've been thinking something along those lines myself," MG said loudly. "The only coffee they have is the nasty canned shit from Earth or the Rocky Mountain Coffee, which says it's from a planet called… S'Tora. Is it pronounced Sa-Tora?"

"That's gotta be a mistake," Jacob said. "Unless that name is pretty common for mountain ranges around the quadrant."

"No, it's legit," Murph said. "Apparently, there are some enterprising humans that are already out here in the wilds of the quadrant and finding ways to make money. Whoever is running that company has managed to get millions of aliens addicted to Earth coffee a few years before the Fleet even officially pushed out of Terran space."

"Back on topic," Jacob said. "What were you saying, MG?"

"I've been running with Obsidian for the better part of two years," MG said. "This job is mostly hours and hours of boring observation and plodding in the *Corsair* to one place or another and just watching the sensors ahead of a Fleet movement. On the few times we've been sent as a tactical asset to secure an objective, it's never been loaded with so many inexplicable coincidences. I can't really explain it past that. Just a gut feeling that we're either chasing the wrong thing or we're missing something significant in the big picture."

"I've been with Obsidian for over a year, and MG's gut feelings shouldn't be ignored," Murph said, ignoring the middle finger from the Marine who was still salty about the NIS Agent's double-identity.

"Recommendations?"

"Let it play out." MG shrugged. "We've already flown all the way out here because our reluctant mission objective won't play ball unless we grab Scarponi. We have visual confirmation that he's here. Stick to the agreement, and once Zadra and Taylor track him down again, go ahead and call it in to Command and let them tell us how to handle it. Odds are good we'll be given our usual mission to observe from a distance and wait for an Alpha Team to come in and turn him into a little pile of ash."

"Murph?" Jacob asked.

"I agree with MG. We're safe here and have a chance to grab Scarponi and Hollick without putting ourselves or our package at risk."

"And in the Corps, you *never* want to put your package at risk," MG added.

Jacob was less confident about his decided course after the discussion than he was when they were flying out to Theta Suden, but he was now committed to at least seeing it through to the point that they had a location for their wayward traitor. A nagging feeling had begun to intrude upon his thoughts that, despite Webb's charge to complete their mission, he had screwed things up spectacularly and would be paying the price for that as soon as he called in their location and made contact with Command.

He just hoped when the dust settled, Captain Webb didn't leave his ass flapping in the breeze and honored his deal to pull him out of the Marine Corps and give him a commission into the Navy.

"Okay," he said. "Let's go get the others and get this search started."

22

The *Kentucky* would never be mistaken for a luxury liner, but she was also much more comfortable than the average frigate. She carried a smaller crew compliment than normal and, despite being designed to resemble an aged bulk freighter, was packed with all the latest and greatest from Naval R&D. From advanced tactical AI computers to deployable plasma cannons capable of limited surface bombardment, the *Kentucky's* offensive capability stretched the definition of a control and command platform.

Marcus Webb had been heavily involved in the outfitting of NAVSOC's *Theia*-class frigates, of which only the *Kentucky* and *Oregon* had been built and deployed. A friend of his had a philosophy when it came to armament: a lot is enough, but too much is better. It was a mantra he'd repeated often when the engineers complained that all the gear he was stuffing into the hull required they upgrade the powerplant and support systems.

"Incoming slip-com request for you, Captain. It's not coming in through the main com relay station."

"Route it into the captain's office." Webb gestured towards the hatchway that led to the ship commander's office right off the main bridge.

"Aye-aye, sir."

Once Webb had closed the hatch and activated the office's anti-intrusion countermeasures, it took another few minutes to authenticate himself on Commander Duncan's terminal. When the image on the other end of the slip-com channel finally resolved, he was unsurprised who it was that was calling given that he had left Taurus Station in secret.

"Director Welford," he greeted the head of the NIS with a nod. "How can I help you?"

"This is more along the lines of how I can help you," Michael Welford said. "We've had a safe house activated on a world where we have no active operations running. The codes used to get past the security perimeter belonged to Agent Murphy."

"That world would be?"

"It's a moon called Theta Suden," Welford said. "It's in our main navigational database. I'm forwarding the information on the safe house to you. I haven't attempted to make contact with Murphy, nor has he made an official call-in. Just thought I'd pass on Obsidian's probable location as of ten hours ago."

"Thanks," Webb said. "Anything else I should know about?"

"NIS access codes are two-part authentication. The first set of digits is the unique identifier while the second part is a status. Murphy coded in with an *all clear* status. If they were in trouble, or he was being forced into the safe house under duress, he would be able to discreetly let me know by using a different code instead."

"Clever," Webb approved. "But it doesn't tell me much about what my wayward lieutenant is doing halfway across the damn sector."

"This is an older safe house and isn't set up for surveillance so I couldn't tell you either way." Welford shrugged an apology. "I don't know if they chased Weef Zadra all the way to that moon or if your lieutenant has made some poor choices along the way and is now chasing the rabbit trying to salvage the mission."

"I appreciate the intel either way, Welford. I suppose I owe you one."

"I may hold you to that...soon," Welford said tightly. "We'll talk when you get back. Welford out."

The screen blanked out, and Webb backtracked out of the terminal and re-logged on with a different set of credentials. This new level of access allowed him to view the last known location and status of all NAVSOC ships and personnel deployed outside of Terran space. Theta Suden was well away from any current Fleet operations, and his own personnel tended to mirror the regular Navy's movements closely. Team Cobalt from 4th Scout Corps was available, but he wasn't sure another Scout Fleet team would be any more helpful than the Quick Response Force he already had aboard the *Kentucky* should Lieutenant Brown have really gotten himself in deep.

He logged out and flicked off the terminal, annoyed at his lack of options. Earth's fledgling space military was already mighty by most measures, but it was still small, and once they covered their obligation to their Cridal Cooperative partners and saw to the defense of their own planets, there wasn't a lot left to go around.

"Commander Duncan to the bridge," Webb said into the intercom. The computer would automatically find the *Kentucky's* CO and pass along the message in near-real time.

"*On my way, sir,*" Duncan's voice came back. Looking at the star charts, Webb could see a friendly system they could park the ship in and loiter that would put them within striking distance of Theta Suden should it become necessary.

Oh, how he missed the days of just being a cog in the wheel. Even when he'd been a US Navy SEAL, and had been approached about detached duty to the colony on Terranovus, it had been a simple mission: track down and kill threats to Earth. Now, as the officer in charge of all NAVSOC operations, his stomach lining was all but gone. He was worried about Team Obsidian, worried he may have gotten Jacob Brown killed when he'd promised his father he'd protect him, and worried that the intelligence asset he'd promised Central Command was either dead or had gone underground because of Scout Fleet's blundering.

"Never a dull moment," he groaned, pushing himself up out of the chair and heading back to the bridge.

"We're tracking two Ull," Taylor told Jacob when the lieutenant walked back into the main room after grabbing a quick nap.

"Already?" Jacob knelt down by one of the monitors and looked at the high-res image of the spindly alien walking around through a crowd. "Source?"

"Public safety net," Taylor said. "Zadra was able to exploit a maintenance access backdoor into the system almost immediately, and then we've had our own computers sifting through the incoming data trying to get an image match on any of our targets."

"The Ull are easy to spot. We've had a seventy-six percent hit on Scarponi and an eighty-two percent hit on Hollick."

"You're not pulling too much bandwidth through that maintenance connection, are you?" Jacob asked. "I'd rather the locals not backtrack us, but we also have to assume the enemy has access to the same tricks."

"We're good, LT," Taylor assured him. "We're only pulling a targeted sampling. The amount of data we're streaming would hardly be detectable."

"Hollick wasn't a tech specialist," Murph said. "If he has access to the Theta Suden public systems it'll be because the Ull have given it to him, and they're not known for being that savvy. Not like our Veran friends."

"Two hits on our human targets, both over sixty percent," Jacob said. "We're in the right place. I'm going to call it in."

"That was the plan," Murph agreed. Jacob paused, looking at the other's pinched expression.

"What?"

"It's just...we don't actually know where they are yet," Murph said. "If we call it in too early, we'll be told to sit tight and the leaks within NAVSOC will have time to warn Scarponi and Hollick before Webb can get anybody here to capture or kill them."

"What exactly are you suggesting?" Jacob asked.

"We wait until we've narrowed it down through Taylor's search, and then we go out and put eyes on the target," Murph said. "Once we've got that level of confirmation about where they are, we can then sit on them until an Alpha Team can be brought in."

"Suggestion noted," Jacob said. "I'll give you this concession: I'll contact Captain Webb directly and not go through the Fleet Ops Com Center. I can patch directly to the slip-com node in his office and bypass any potential OPSEC risks."

OPSEC—short for operational security—was a set of protocols that members of the UEAS had drilled into their heads from the time they signed the papers in the recruitment stations and it never ended, even after retirement. Although OPSEC was a real concern given the sheer volume of security leaks the UEN was fighting, Jacob was beginning to suspect that had little to do with Murph's recommendations.

Murph had been stuck playing Recon Marine within Scout Fleet for over a year. As a young NIS agent, there were likely dozens of better assignments he could have other than sitting on a small ship for months on end, counting ships in orbital traffic around a planet someone at Fleet had interest in. If he grabbed Scarponi *and* Elton Hollick, then he would be able to write his own ticket. Any cushy or choice assignment he wanted would be his, and likely a promotion to go along with it. Jacob now had to be concerned that his embedded agent may be losing focus of the main goal and concentrating on his own ambitions.

"You have Captain Webb's personal node address?" Murph asked.

"You don't?" Jacob countered, already firing up the safe house's slip-com station. Since the machine had been completely powered down when the last person had cleared out of the building, it would take at least fifteen minutes for it to warm up and for the slip-space fields to stabilize. "In the meantime, begin narrowing down potential locations for the target based on when and where they've been spotted on the public surveillance system."

Jacob punched in the com node address he wanted from memory and waited while the terminal attempted to make the connection. At this distance from Earth, the lag in the slip-com signal would begin to be barely perceptible. When the signal finally resolved, he wasn't looking at Captain Webb but at a woman with a stern expression and a star on each collar point.

"This is Admiral Remey," she declared. "To whom am I speaking?"

"My apologies, Admiral," Jacob said. "I must have entered the address incorrectly. I was trying to reach a Captain Marcus Webb."

"You have the correct address. I am currently monitoring all personal inbound com traffic to this office," she said. "I ask again, who are you? From the clothes can I presume you're one of Webb's Scout Fleet operators? Please identify your—" Jacob killed the signal and powered down the terminal without thinking. Why was a Fleet admiral intercepting incoming com traffic to Webb's office? Had he been relieved of duty? Did anyone even know that Obsidian was still deployed and on-mission?

"What'd he say?" Taylor asked over his shoulder.

"We might have a— Ah, he wasn't in," Jacob quickly amended his answer as Zadra walked into the room escorted by Mettler.

"Who wasn't in what?" she asked.

"I tried contacting Captain Webb to let him know where we were and that Scarponi was on this world, but he wasn't in his office," Jacob said, not lying but certainly withholding the entire truth from her. He didn't distrust her specifically, but she was still a foreign national with no clearance for sensitive information.

"What's our next move, LT?" MG asked. He was stuffing his face again, taking advantage of the better food after the slim pickings they had on the Eshquarian gunboat on the flight out to Theta Suden.

"As soon as we've narrowed our search area to a few blocks, we'll need to get live intel," Jacob said. "For right now, I just want to confirm identity and observe. Scarponi is with another human collaborator, and we don't know the strength of the Ull contingent here."

"What if I happen to be observing that piece of shit and he walks close enough that I can pop him without being exposed?" Mettler asked. "Like, it's the perfect shot. Scarponi would just be standing there with no civilians in the area or Ull near him and I would just send a single shot to put him out of our misery?"

"Identify and observe," Jacob said firmly. "If you run across something you think changes the mission complexion, call it in. Murph, I assume this safe house is fully stocked with weapons and com gear?"

"All that plus local clothing, Nexus access points, and currency," Murph said. "There are even a couple decent disguises in there that will mask our species."

"Start kitting up the gear with MG," Jacob said. "Zadra and Taylor will get us a location and we'll get started. It's early morning local time right now. I want to be outfitted and moving out of here by late afternoon. Get to it."

"Wow, you NIS slugs really know how to plan for a party. Why is this place here in the first place?"

"Classified," Murph said, brushing by MG and turning on the rest of the lights. The room they were in was a hidden vault under the subbasement that served as both a fortified panic room and a well-stocked armory.

"You ever been out this way before?" Mettler asked. He'd not been given a specific assignment, so he'd tagged along with the other two. He said that when Zadra would work with all four of her arms it gave him the creeps.

"This is only my second assignment," Murph said. "I completed my training about the same time you guys made it through NAVSOC prelims."

"I was grandfathered in," Mettler said. "I'm ex-Force Recon so they let me skip all the indoc bullshit. I did two months on Restaria training with the Galvetic Legions, two weeks in the infirmary recovering from that, and then it was mostly classroom work prepping for what we'd run into out here."

"I'm one of the few who wasn't prior U.S. or British military in this outfit," MG said. "I enlisted thinking I was going into the Navy, but after my physical fitness test, they pressured me into joining the Corps. I was almost all the way through Basic when I was approached by a Navy lieutenant about volunteering for a new composite force that was being propped up. I signed the paper once he said it came with an automatic step promotion and bonus pay."

"My story isn't too far off from yours," Murph said. "I was in my second year at Ohio State when the money ran out. It was either saddle up with crippling student loans or see what this new space military could offer. I took all the aptitude tests and was contacted by someone in Washington DC asking if I was interested in serving my planet in *alternative ways*. It turns out they were recruiting for the NIS and skimming off all the recruits that showed certain aptitudes on the tests."

"So, the NIS takes the super smart ones and lets the dipshits through to become officers in the regular Fleet. Sounds about right," MG said.

"Actually, it had little to do with IQ," Murph said. "They look for your ability to pick out patterns, notice obscure details, and mostly just match up psychological compatibility for intelligence work."

"Speaking of bullshit stories and lying-ass punks on our team—"

"I don't think that's what we were talking about," Murph objected.

"—what do we think of our new LT? Are any of you buying that he's some fresh greenhorn right out of the Academy? Is he one of yours?" MG asked.

"Even if he was, I couldn't tell you," Murph said as he began pulling weapons off a wall-rack and handing them to Mettler to check. "But as far as I know, Brown is a legit newbie second lieutenant who got conned into taking a commission into the Marines so he could be a ground team commander in Scout Fleet. Mosler told me he has some special family connection and that's why Webb wanted him."

"I still don't buy it," MG insisted. "Yeah, at first he didn't know his ass from a hole in the ground—remember when he froze up in that apartment and almost got pasted?—but now it's like he's been doing this for years. I mean, shit, I *have* been doing this for years and seeing these aliens still freaks me out sometimes."

"I literally shit myself the first two times I stepped off a ship and had to talk to an alien." Mettler shrugged. "It's not a natural thing to fly away from your home planet and have to interact with all these different species."

"Only the first two?" MG asked. "You have me beat. I pissed myself twice in one day on Restaria. Every time one of those goddamn Galvetic warriors would roar at me, it was all I could do to keep anything in my body. Piss, puke, shit, you name it, it came out of me during that training course. I tried to convince them it was a natural defensive response in humans that would allow me to escape but, apparently, they were well aware of our species by that point."

"Hence the rigorous psych profiling we go through before being tapped for exo-Solar duty," Murph said. "Lieutenant Brown's tests indicated he was especially suited for this type of work unless Commander Mosler was lying to me."

The trio worked in silence for the next hour, pulling equipment and putting together individual kits consisting of local clothing, com gear, weaponry, and some specialized equipment that was designed to work with Taylor's neural implant so they could slice into networks and override security systems. Murph opened another safe within the armory and pulled out a pile of local currency and ConFed credit chits and distributed those among the kits as well, carefully annotating how much he'd taken in the log.

"We've still got a lot of time before we head out," MG said, looking at the mission computer on his wrist. "Let's just go down the line and everyone check everything over one more time."

They each took a turn going to each pile and verifying that all the weaponry and equipment was in working order and ready before hauling it all back up to the main level and locking the armory. The tracker team still hadn't come up with a firm location for either human they were after, so Jacob ordered them to get some rack time and that he'd wake them when it looked like they had something to move on. Murph would have preferred to stay and watch the search but the long day was catching up to him and it didn't look like Taylor or Zadra needed his help.

23

"They're right here."

"What am I looking at?" Jacob asked. The view on the monitor was from an orbital perspective and all he could see were rooftops that all looked the same.

"It's a maintenance overflow facility for the city's public transport fleet," Taylor cut off Zadra before she could offer another sarcastic reply. Over the course of the last week, her casual insults and flippant behavior had been fraying at their nerves.

"It's still owned by the city, but isn't used anymore since the smaller street cars have been replaced by a new mag-lev that runs through the center. This building used to be where they'd store the units that were waiting on parts or to be decommissioned completely."

"Do we think that this group has some relationship with the government on this world or are they just opportunists?" Mettler asked.

"It's likely they paid off some low-level bureaucrat to write up an authorization for them to be there," Murph said. "It's effective, untraceable, and far cheaper than trying to buy or rent a space. I can almost guarantee Hollick set this up for them, it's right out of the NIS field manual."

"I like it for our purposes, too," Jacob said. "Low civilian traffic, multiple observation points all around here, here, and here."

"Or...we could have Sully take that gunboat and fire torpedoes here and here," MG said, pointing to the two main service entrances of the building.

"Out of the question," Jacob said firmly even as Murph opened his mouth to shoot down the idea. "We're not opening fire on a— You know what? That's a stupid suggestion, I'm not saying anything past *no*."

"I wasn't being serious," MG grumbled. "Mostly."

"How do you want the team deployed, LT?" Murph asked. "I assume someone will have to stay behind to keep our VIP company?" Jacob had actually forgotten that Weef Zadra would not accompany the recon team, nor could she be left alone inside of an NIS safe house. He looked around at his team, trying to pick which of them was non-critical for the mission, and came to an uncomfortable realization as to who that person was.

"I'll stay behind," he said. "Murph is in command of the operation."

"You sure about this, LT?" Taylor asked.

"You guys all know what to do...so go do it," Jacob said. "You're all trained and have the needed experience and I can't afford to pull one of you off-mission to sit here so I can be where the action is. I'll be monitoring you over coms, and this is going to be just a simple sneak and peek."

Over the next twenty minutes, the team pored over the available data on the target location and began assigning observations spots to individuals. After the first few minutes, Jacob sat back and watched as his team of pros put aside the bickering and bullshitting while they quickly and efficiently set up a plan of attack that would minimize the risk while making sure the building in question had complete coverage. The young lieutenant tried to not fixate on any single detail and, instead, opened his mind up to absorb the planning session and pick up the methodology and rationale behind his peoples' decisions.

After they'd all agreed on how they would execute the mission, he couldn't help but be impressed. When they were aboard the ship and traveling, the Marines had seemed surly, borderline lazy, and not particularly bright. Now that the ground op was starting, their focus was laser-sharp, and Jacob could begin to see why they were considered elite. The attack on Niceen-3 hadn't been a good opportunity for him to see this side of them because the ambush happened so fast and in such close quarters that it was a survival situation more akin to a melee than a precision planned op.

"Don't take any unnecessary chances out there." Jacob had pulled Murph aside for some last-minute instructions as the others mounted up and moved to the rear exit of the safe house. "I'll have Sully on standby for emergency dust off if we've miscalculated. Just remember that this isn't actually our mission, she is."

"Don't worry, Lieutenant. I'll keep an eye on them." Murph winked at him, and Jacob couldn't help but be jealous of how relaxed and eager they all seemed. Pros.

"Go. Get it done."

"Where is he?!"

Admiral Remey had been terrorizing Captain Webb's staff for the better part of two hours, trying to bully one of his junior aides into divulging where the slippery NAVSOC chief had snuck off to. At first, she'd been discreet with her queries, right up until she figured out he wasn't on Terranovus and tracked his movements to one of NAVSOC's two command and control ships that had departed the system weeks ago.

"As we said, ma'am, he doesn't clear his movements with us," Lieutenant Commander Waterman said. He'd taken it upon himself to be the liaison between Remey and the rest of the office staff, which had quickly turned into him being the admiral's punching bag whenever she got an answer she didn't like.

"Very well," she said calmly, handing him a data card. "I'd hoped to talk to Captain Webb face to face before implementing this, but I feel he's left me no choice. Here are authenticated orders from Earth authorizing me to assume command of the NAVSOC group should I deem it necessary."

"You're kidding," Waterman deadpanned, seeming to forget he was addressing an admiral. He reached out and took the card, pulling out a tablet, and inserting it to read the orders.

"Not at all," Remey said. If she was peeved about his lack of proper customs and courtesies, she didn't show it. "This office has been under observation for some time, and the unaccountability of Scout Fleet operations in particular have greatly concerned the admiralty. There have also been...security concerns...that have only raised further questions. Captain Webb fleeing during an extremely sensitive mission while I've been here observing is beyond suspicious. Given that, he's left me no choice but to step in. Do you understand your orders?"

"Yes, ma'am," Waterman said reluctantly. He'd authenticated the orders with Taurus Station's own network and had quickly read through the pertinent parts, enough to know that Remey was really stretching the scope of her orders, but could still be considered technically correct. What the hell was going on here?

"Are we going to have any problems, Commander?"

"My staff and I are professionals and respect the chain of command, ma'am." Waterman's posture stiffened and his voice took on a brittle edge. "We will do our jobs to the best of our ability."

"Excellent. Then you may start by tracking down the *Kentucky* and two teams out of 3rd Scout Corps," Remey said.

"Which teams, ma'am?"

"Obsidian and Diamond."

"We'll start right away."

Waterman could feel her eyes boring into his back as he retreated. He was loyal to Captain Webb and believed in what they were doing in NAVSOC, but he was also a naval officer that had sworn an oath to obey the chain of command and all legal orders. His personal feelings aside, he had no choice but to do as Admiral Remey had requested and do his damnedest to track down the captain's ship. Finding two Scout Fleet teams that were in the field would be next to impossible. By design, the only way they would find either team was if they checked in or returned to base. Hopefully, he could make Admiral Remey understand that.

"Specialist Williams, please send out a meeting request for the operations staff." Waterman flagged down one of his admin personnel. "Flag it as urgent and set it in Conference Room Three for thirty minutes from now. Attendance is *mandatory* for anyone on the recall list that's currently on base."

"Aye-aye, sir."

Waterman rushed to his own office to prep the brief he would give to his people, explaining that they were tasked with tracking down the boss and that, for the time being, he was no longer in command. Captain Webb had handpicked most of his staff, so Waterman expected a combative, uncooperative group. While it was his job to execute the admiral's orders, he couldn't blame them if they wanted to sandbag in a misguided attempt to help out their CO.

"I need to PT more while on the ship," Murph huffed as he climbed up a maintenance ladder that led to the rooftop. His observation post would allow him to see the main bay doors that had been used to get the automated street cars into the facility.

Once he was up there, he stole a quick glance at the target building before breaking out his recording equipment. The windows had all been blacked out, and there wasn't any sign of anybody on the ground. He put aside the tripod he'd been carrying and set the multispectral imager up on the ledge, as well as the laser microphone, the latter of which he aimed at a window on the second floor where the schematics Zadra had dug up indicated was a cluster of offices.

"Birddog One is up," he whispered after keying his com. "Front of building is clear."

"Birddog Three is up," Mettler's voice came over the channel. "Rear entrance is secured and clear."

"Birddog Four is *not* in position," MG said. "The planned observation point is too exposed…moving up two floors. I see what looks like an unused storage or manufacturing space with a few broken windows I can exploit."

"Two, are you good?" Murph asked. "Two?"

"Birddog Two is not showing up on the net," Mettler said. "No sign of trouble. Maybe he has com issues."

"Press on," Murph said. "We'll deal with that when we can. Birddog Actual, copy that Two has dropped off the net?"

"*Copy, One,*" Jacob's voice came in thin and distorted over the low-power tactical coms. "*Concur with onsite assessment…proceed at your discretion.*"

Murph took a moment to reflect on Brown's surprising level of maturity and lack of ego when it came to stepping aside for the good of the mission. Most lieutenants—*especially* Academy grads—were a bit prickly and defensive when it came to any perceived slight against their authority or abilities. It made most overcompensate and, more often than not, led to poor decisions in the heat of the moment. Murph had been pleased that Lieutenant Brown had come to the conclusion on his own that he would be more of a liability than a help, thus saving the team from having to point it out to him.

The *beep* from his equipment signaling it was ready shook him out of his reverie. He ducked back down behind the retention wall and viewed the building through the small monitor, hit 'record,' and settled in for a long, boring day. Peeking up over the edge and exposing oneself was for amateurs. The observation equipment Scout Fleet ground teams used was designed for stealth and flexibility. If needed, Murph could have the data transmitted to his mission computer, the terminal in the safe house, their ship, or all three.

The problem was that Elton Hollick was quite familiar with Terran equipment and its capabilities and would likely either have countermeasures or detection equipment of his own set up. Murph had mitigated that risk by placing actual observers at each point and having the gear hardwired so it wouldn't transmit a data stream and give itself away. It took the microphone a few minutes to calibrate at this range before anything legible could get through. At first, all he heard was the hum of machinery that one would expect in a large, empty building. The air handlers alone would drown out most conversations if they were running. Soon enough, however, a few snippets of conversation began to get through the noise.

"...have less than fourteen hours to wrap this operation up. If your team can't make it happen by then, we'll be forced to pursue alternate means," a raspy, hissing voice was saying. At first, Murph thought it might be poor audio quality thanks to his equipment, but he soon realized that the speaker was an Ull and that it was speaking English. How odd.

"Your alternate means are doomed to fail," a human male voice said. Murph assumed it was Hollick from the authority it conveyed. "You know it, I know it, and Margaret Jansen has repeatedly warned you and your superiors that a forceful move against Earth right now would be premature without first securing the object."

"We grow impatient, Human," the Ull said. "This was supposed to be a simple operation. Now you've led us halfway across the quadrant, and we're no closer to success than we were in the beginning."

"There have been some...missteps," Hollick admitted. "Our operative aboard the *Endurance* royally screwed up, no claiming otherwise, but this operation is still very much alive. Even now we've—" There was the sounds of furniture moving and muffled conversations that were fading as the party left the office. Murph was unable to make out anything else. Maybe the computer would be able to scrub the audio for something else he could use. As Murph was getting ready to cycle the bit of audio through the post-processors, he heard a sharp grunt over the team channel, and then nothing.

"*Check in,*" Jacob ordered, apparently having heard the same thing.

"One," Murph said.

"*Three*," Mettler said. It was another ten seconds before Murph tried to manually ping MG's com.

"Birddog Four, this is one. Check in."

He was answered with nothing but silence. Just when he was about to ask Jacob what he wanted to do about two of their team members dropping off the net, a shadow moved in his peripheral vision. Before he could turn to focus on the movement, his body was racked by intense bursts of pain. He lost control of his limbs, collapsing onto the roof in a heap. Through the pain, he was able to tell what had happened, the telltale fins of a stun dart sticking out of his right side. The small weapon had penetrated the soft armor meant to absorb and deflect energy weapon fire and unloaded its high-voltage payload into his body.

Murph struggled to remain conscious, but his vision began to tunnel, and he couldn't force his hands to key the com and tell his teammates he was down. The last thing he saw before the darkness overtook him was two Ull rushing at him, weapons drawn.

24

"Anyone still on the net, respond! This is Birddog Actual, key your mic if you can hear me."

"Sorry, Young One, but nobody's going to be answering you."

Jacob spun around and looked at Zadra, confused. He saw that the Veran had backed up to give herself some room and now had a plasma pistol trained on him.

"What the fuck is going on here?" he demanded.

"Quiet now," she said. Her demeanor was calm, and Jacob wasn't entirely sure this wasn't some sort of bizarre joke at an inappropriate time. He watched as she reached over to the terminal at her left and deactivated the safe house's security systems, never taking her eyes off him or wavering with her weapon. Before Jacob could get his wits about him, he heard the front door crash open and what sounded like several heavy beings treading into the room. When they walked in, his heart sank.

Ull.

They'd been set up from the start.

"So, you've been working for the other side the whole time," Jacob said, moving away from the terminal he'd been at when the lead Ull waved at him to move.

"Not the whole time," Zadra said pleasantly. "But about the time I realized that for all the talk about becoming an emerging power in the quadrant, Earth had sent out a squad of bumbling amateurs to come get me. Once Jansen's crew got the jump on you, I figured I'd be smart to explore my options."

"We have his compatriots," the lead Ull hissed. "Do we need him?"

"Inexplicably, he's the ranking member of this team," Zadra said. "So, yes, we'll need to keep him alive for the time being."

"Humans are so pathetically predictable," the Ull said. "Hollick is standing by and wishes to see you."

"Wait a moment," Zadra said, moving to the terminal and keying in a local com address. "If you want the package, I'll need to get things in motion from here."

"Hurry up."

"Yes? Why are you calling me? Where's Lieutenant Brown?" Sully's face appeared on the terminal. Jacob opened his mouth to call out, but the business end of an Ull plasma blaster nudged him in the midsection. He nodded his ascent to remain silent. Now wasn't his moment.

"Because I'm the only one left at the safe house," Zadra said. "The team has located Scarponi, but he's fortified with a large group of Ull defending him and asked that you call in Captain Webb. He's currently aboard a Scout Fleet command and control ship, I'm sending you the slip-com node address now."

"How do you know that?" Sully asked, his voice heavy with suspicion. "Or why don't you just call him yourself?"

"An alien blindly calling a human military ship and asking for aid," Zadra scoffed. "How far do you think I'd get with that? Webb would never even get the message."

"Maybe," Sully said. "I'll punch in this address and call in our location and status to Captain Webb *if* he's actually there, but I'm not requesting support until I hear from someone on the ground team directly."

"Very well," Zadra said. "Call our status in, and in the meantime, I'll ask one of your people to come back and verify Lieutenant Brown's orders."

"I'll be waiting," Sully said and killed the channel. Jacob could have kissed the Navy pilot for being naturally distrustful and playing it by the book.

"Don't worry," Zadra said to the Ull. "Once Webb gets a confirmed location from his people, he'll come in himself. I've already verified his ship is in the area with one of the human assets you provided. This will be over quickly."

"Take her to see Hollick so they can finalize their side of the arrangement," the Ull said to one of his compatriots. "We'll remain here to watch him and monitor their com network. I assume the ship pilot will try to make contact again to confirm the human Webb is coming or not."

"Likely, or he'll try to directly contact the other team members on the short-range tactical com," she said. "I assume you disabled those?"

"Do not question me about strategy, Veran," the Ull hissed. "Your deal is with Hollick, not us. If you can't deliver the package we've been promised, your fate will be no different than that of these humans." Jacob watched the interaction closely, trying to gauge Zadra's reaction given the little bit he knew about Veran mannerisms. For someone who had worked within the seedy underbelly of the quadrant's criminal element and had actually lived by herself in the Kaspian Reaches, she did seem genuinely nervous about the Ull's threat.

"You'll get what you want," she said before turning to Jacob. "Sorry, Young Pup, it's nothing personal."

"Feels personal," Jacob grunted as the closest Ull jabbed him with its blaster rifle again.

"I have to stay ahead of the ConFed and make it out of here." She spread her two smaller arms wide in the Veran equivalent of a shrug. "Mosler may have been able to do it, but he managed to get himself killed by a member of his own crew. You? You I have no faith in. Like I said, nothing personal. It's just good business."

"We'll see," Jacob said. He'd been watching events unfold since she'd pulled a weapon on him with a sort of clinical detachment. His lack of a panic reflex had been one of the things that put him on NAVSOC's radar during first year cadet evaluations. Now that Zadra had given him a little bit more information, however, and he knew she'd been making them dance like puppets to get what she wanted, one of his less savory traits was coming to the surface: a white-hot rage coupled with his body's amped up adrenal response.

The two Ull that remained behind to guard him were watching him closely but didn't bother restraining him. One on one, a normal human wasn't much of a threat to the spindly alien species. They had a dense bone structure and were much stronger than their willowy appearance indicated. Zadra left with the third Ull, and Jacob knew it would be a short time before Hollick sent word to execute him.

"So," he asked. "You guys want to play a game to pass the time or—"

Crack!

"Silence!" the closer Ull barked after slamming the handle of its weapon into Jacob's skull. He slumped against the wall, overplaying the amount of pain he was in and letting his head loll to the side as if the blow had nearly rendered him unconscious. He listened to the pair as they made clicking sounds—apparently what passed for laughter among them—and waited.

It still wasn't his moment.

"It's from an unknown source node, but there's an accompanying clearance code belonging to a...Lieutenant Ryan Sullivan, currently assigned to 3rd Scout Corps, Team Obsidian. Shall I accept the channel request, sir?"

"Negative, ensign," Webb said, frowning.

"Sir?" Commander Duncan asked. They were on the bridge of the *Kentucky* when the unexpected com request had come through.

"Sully doesn't have this slip-com address, none of the operational assets do," Webb said. "This is a closely guarded secret that not even Commander Mosler had been privy to. All communication from the field would be routed through the com center on Taurus Station."

"The computer has run facial and voice recognition on the incoming signal and confirms it's Lieutenant Sullivan with a probability of ninety-two percent," the ensign at the com station said.

"This operation has already been derailed by a One World traitor embedded within my Scout Fleet teams," Webb said. "Now, I'm getting a signal to an address nobody should know about from a team that is *way* off-mission without any explanation. I feel like we need to proceed carefully. Ensign, send the incoming signal to the automated messenger service aboard the ship and be careful not to forward it to Taurus Station."

"Shall we reposition the *Kentucky* closer to Theta Suden, sir?" Commander Duncan asked.

"Stand fast, Captain," Webb said. "We'll remain here until we have a better idea what the hell is happening. Hopefully Sully leaves enough details in the message to put the pieces together."

"Aye, sir."

"Alonzo Murphy! Welcome! It's so good to meet you. I hear Welford thinks quite highly of you."

"Hollick," Murph grunted against his restraints. "We thought you were dead."

"That's sort of the point of faking one's death, isn't it?" Hollick asked. "Who did you piss off to get stuck slumming it with these jarheads, pretending to run around and gather intel with a bunch of knuckle-draggers while keeping an eye one someone for Welford?"

"Where's the rest of my team?"

"Your *team?*" Hollick laughed. "Going native already? This is barely your second assignment and you've already lost objectivity? Not good, Agent, not good at all. To answer your question, the other Marines we so easily captured are bound and gagged in one of the offices in the mezzanine. So now, you're wondering why you're here instead of trussed up with them."

"It crossed my mind." Murph said. He was restrained to a chair that was so tall his feet didn't touch the ground, obviously built for a much bigger species. The main problem with that, besides being uncomfortable, was that it took away any leverage he may have had with his feet flat on the ground.

"Honestly, you're mostly a backup plan right now," Hollick said. "Once our other party gets here, we can— Ah! There she is now!" Murph stretched against his restraints to look over and see one of the Ull, this one dressed in tactical gear, escorting Weef Zadra across the factory floor. She didn't look like she was there against her will.

"The message has been sent by the pilot," Zadra said to Hollick, ignoring Murph completely. "Webb's ship was last reported on its way to this general area with him aboard, so I don't think we'll have long to wait to get a response."

"And the kid? Brown?"

"Being guarded by two of ours," the Ull said. "They're to eliminate him and sanitize the building once we have confirmation from the pilot that Marcus Webb is inbound."

"It'd probably be best if he was brought here with his friends once they're finished up at the safe house," Hollick said, looking suddenly concerned. "We're not here to rack up a high body count."

"Why *are* you here?" Murph asked. "I first assumed after the hit at Niceen-3 that you were after Zadra for the same reason we were: her intel network. But from what I'm seeing, she's been working with you the whole time. So, what's up?"

"Shut up, Murphy," Hollick said. "I'm not going to lay it all out for you just because you can't put the pieces together yourself."

"Did you arrange to have Mosler killed, Zadra?" Murph asked, recognizing a closed door when he saw one with Hollick. The agent was too disciplined to start bragging and divulging secrets when he had the upper hand.

"I had nothing to do with that!" Zadra said hotly. "Ezra Mosler was my friend, but I'm also a realist. If you couldn't even protect your own captain, what was the chance that you'd be able to protect me? I made my deal with Margaret Jansen once your incompetence made it necessary."

"It's not too late to unfuck this," Murph said. "They can't force you to give up your network, and we can still get you out of ConFed space."

"They're not after my network, they want something else...something your people have that—"

"Quiet!" Hollick snapped. "He doesn't need to know any of the details of our arrangement. Agent Murphy, unless you want to spend your final hours with a gag, I'd suggest you keep your mouth shut."

"Anyway, now that the Ull know I'm trying to avoid the ConFed, they have the upper hand." Zadra sounded genuinely apologetic. "By just calling in my general location, there would be no way to avoid their fleet while trying to escape. It was nothing personal."

"Does nobody know what the word *quiet* means?" Hollick asked in exasperation. "What's taking so long? We should have heard back from the pilot by now. Check with the safe house team."

"They are not answering on coms," the Ull that escorted Zadra in said.

Hollick swore and turned to look over at Murphy. The other agent had a ghost of a smile on his face, as if he knew something but didn't want to spoil the surprise for anyone else.

25

"This is taking too long. We should have heard back from the pilot by now."

"We could have that one try again...if you hadn't bashed his head in."

"Let's try anyway."

Jacob had been listening as the pair argued about what to do next. The translation matrix loaded into his neural implant had a few gaps for the Ull language, but he was able to pick up most of what he needed. He knew his team had been captured but didn't know if they'd been killed or not. The other important thing he'd discovered was that the Ull planned to give Zadra to the ConFed once they were done with her anyway so, apparently, they were after something else and not her intel network. What that could be he had on idea, only that it involved Captain Webb somehow.

As one of the Ull clomped its way towards where he was still pretending to be unconscious, he was absolutely certain of only one thing:

This was his moment.

When the alien reached down to grab him Jacob rolled over and trapped the offending arm in a wrist lock, bending it back onto itself. The Ull shrieked in pain and tried to wrench its arm free, but it had never come face-to-face with a human processing this sort of strength before. Jacob took advantage of both the pain and confusion and levered himself up onto his knees, still trapping the arm back. He looked over and saw that the other Ull was reaching for its weapon, and he used the pinned arm to spin his opponent around and act as a shield.

The Ull was unbelievably strong. Now that the shock of the situation was wearing off, the trapped Ull was trying to free itself by pushing against his shoulder with its free hand. Luckily, it still thought it was going to get out of the situation without serious injury and was trying to be somewhat gentle while disengaging the crazed little human. Jacob decided to dispel him of that notion. With a heave, he shoved the hand up with his left arm while pulling down with his right, putting every bit of strength he could muster into it.

When the bone snapped, it did so with a sharp *crack* that made Jacob's ears ring. What the hell were these things made of? Everyone in the room froze at the sound for a split second, and that was all Jacob needed to release his hold and grab the broken arm in both hands, wrenching it back and forth and maximizing the damage. This seemed to break the dam, and the alien shrieked in agony.

"Kill him! Kill him! *KILL HIM!*"

Jacob released his prey and rolled away just as the other Ull opened fire. The shot went wide and blasted through a wall, setting it on fire. The injured Ull tripped on its own blaster, which it dropped when Jacob grabbed it, and went down, landing on its injured arm. Its shrieks went up another few octaves until Jacob almost couldn't even hear them.

Another shot slammed into the floor in front of him, sending burning chunks of tile spinning off in all directions. Jacob ignored the bits that pelted his arms and face as he ran for the only cover in the room: the heavy table that all their gear had been stacked up on. He leapt onto it, catching the edge with his hand and tipping it up as he did so that when he landed it was propped up on its side in an impromptu barricade.

"Fuck!" he snarled. His plan had been to use the table for cover and go through the window that was directly behind it, certain he could easily handle the two-story drop to the pavement below. What he hadn't counted on were the security bars one he was able to look past the heavy privacy curtains.

Another shot blasted into the table and burned a hole straight through it to his right. He'd only meant for the table to be a distraction and maybe slow them down a bit, not actually protect him from incoming energy weapon fire. Now he was trapped, and the fires the plasma shots were igniting were really starting to pick up, setting off the automated suppression system. He slid around and braced himself against the wall, pulling both knees towards his chin, chambering what he hoped would be one hell of a kick. He absently registered the hissing sounds of the directed foaming agent that was being sprayed on individual fires.

Two more plasma blasts hit the table in quick succession, blowing another hole in it to the left of the first and taking one of the corners completely off. The entire sequence had taken less than ten seconds since he grabbed the arm of that Ull, but his adrenaline-soaked perception made it seem like half an hour. He fired both legs out with as much force as he could, his boots slamming into the synthetic surface and sending the table across the room as if shot from a cannon.

When he kicked the table, Jacob felt something pull in his right ankle, but he ignored it and rolled to his left. The table had clipped the Ull with the broken arm in the head as the alien had still been kneeling on the floor. When the table caromed off the probably now-dead Ull, it had flown right into the active com terminal, the equipment exploding in a shower of sparks.

"I will kill you!"

Jacob snapped his head over and saw the second Ull struggling to rise. He had no idea how it had been injured, but he wasted no time thinking about it. He spent a millisecond looking for a weapon and, seeing none available, charged the alien. The Ull's mouth opened wide in shock at the smaller human sprinting across the room at it. Jacob drove his shoulder into the skinny alien, driving it into the floor. His shoulder throbbed as it felt like he'd tried to tackle a telephone pole that was still in the ground.

The Ull swung its weapon, clipping Jacob across the forehead and laying the skin open. He grabbed the barrel and forced the weapon aside as it tried to get the unwieldy plasma rifle turned to fire on him. Jacob was in too close, however, and his unexpected strength seemed to confuse the injured alien. With blood running from his forehead into the Ull's face, Jacob managed to get his left hand on the weapon's foregrip and push it down so it was laying across its neck. The alien seemed determined to bring the weapon to bear on Jacob and kept both its hands locked onto it even as Jacob started to drive it into its throat.

"Please have a fucking larynx or whatever it is you scrawny freaks breathe through," Jacob grunted, arching up onto the balls of his feet and really driving it in. Too late, the Ull realized its error and began to thrash about wildly, but that only compounded the mistake. The movement let Jacob turn the weapon so that the raised sighting rail was now laying directly on the Ull's skin. Within seconds, the panicked thrashing became weaker and weaker as the Ull faded out underneath him. The alien looked him in the eye one last time, seeming to accept the inevitable, and let its hands fall from the weapon.

Jacob held fast for ten more seconds to make sure it wasn't playing possum, and then stood on shaky legs. He couldn't figure out how the Ull weapon fired so he limped over to where his own tactical harness had been flung in the corner of the room, retrieved his own sidearm, and shot both aliens in the head. It'd be his luck that they were able to regenerate or weren't actually dead, so he also gave each of them a few more shots in the torso.

"What a mess," he groaned. The fire suppression system had done its job, and where the plasma shots had set the interior ablaze, there were sputtering piles of foam. He limped over to the control panel on the wall that was mercifully still working and reactivated the building's security system and commanded the air handlers to begin pulling out the smoke. Thankfully since it was a human-operated safe house, the controls were familiar.

The com terminal was a complete loss and his injuries were beginning to make themselves known now that the adrenaline was wearing off. He decided to prioritize his problems and attack them in a row starting with getting himself to the safe house infirmary and patched up. After that, he'd find a way to get a hold of Sully on the ship and see what could be done about tracking down his team.

The infirmary was state of the art, which surprised him a bit given that Murph claimed this was just a remote outpost that hadn't been operational in some time. The computer read his neural implant and recognized that, as an active member of the UEAS, he was authorized to use the infirmary. It then began talking to the device in his brain to see the extent of his injuries to determine treatment. No more, "tell me where it hurts."

"Please sit," a pleasant female voice said and a green holographic halo was projected over one of the reclining chairs. He did so and watched as another hologram was projected in front of him, this one a rotating model of his body with the injuries highlighted and a running tally of the damage.

"Do you authorize me to treat your injuries, Cadet Brown?" the voice asked. Apparently, his rank hadn't been updated by personnel in the database after he'd been commissioned in that bullshit late night ceremony.

"Yes, and hurry damnit! The shock is wearing off."

"Standby...nano-treatment commencing."

Five articulated arms descended down from the ceiling and began applying a viscous suspension fluid loaded with nanobots both topically and injecting them. The specialized microscopic robots would go to work repairing his body at the cellular level and then be filtered out and expelled by his body once they were finished. The miraculous machines were alien tech they'd received as part of the trade agreement with the Cridal Cooperative and, practically overnight, they'd rendered much of human medicine obsolete.

Other than where they were stitching up his forehead, he couldn't really feel what they were doing, but on the hologram of himself he saw that the bulk of them were at work repairing the tendon tear in his ankle and a hairline fracture in his right forearm that he had no idea how he got.

"How long until I can get out of this chair and how long before I'm combat effective?" he asked.

"You will be ambulatory in fifteen minutes. It is recommended that you allow the nano-treatment a full forty-eight hours to address the most serious injuries—"

"That's not what I asked," Jacob interrupted. "Combat effective, not feeling one hundred percent and perky. You're an NIS med computer, I know you have varying degrees of gray that you operate in."

"You will be able to move and fight within the next ninety minutes." The computer almost seemed reluctant to give him that information.

"Thank you," Jacob breathed. Already, he could see the swelling and angry red color leaving the ankle and the sharp pains in his body were ebbing away while the legion of microscopic machines in his body did their work. "Now, is there a backup com suite in this building?"

"The team at your safe house isn't responding."

"And you're sure it's nothing to do with your coms?" Hollick asked, not bothering to look up at the Ull while he worked on his tablet.

"Quite sure."

Hollick knew where the conversation would lead. They would want to hit the safe house in force to make sure their people were okay. Unfortunately, there were only five Ull left there at the factory to run security and after that, it was himself and the three other humans he'd brought with him. Scarponi was less than useless in this situation, so he couldn't count on him for much more than getting in the way.

"Our bargaining chips are all secured and locked away right now," he said. "I'm assuming you want to go check on your people?"

"Yes."

"How many do you need?"

"Three of us will go."

"Three?" Hollick was pleasantly surprised that he didn't have to negotiate down from all of them. "Very well. We can manage here with what's left."

"We will be quick," the Ull promised.

"By the way, where the hell is your ship?" Hollick asked casually. "It's overdue by days and, without it, this operation goes belly up. Webb will not be arriving by himself, and the few of us here are in no way capable of handling one of his security teams."

"It will be available when it is needed, human," the Ull hissed before spinning and walking off.

"Interesting," Hollick murmured. "So, it's already here."

"What's already here?" Scarponi asked. The man had been following him around like a lost puppy since he'd arrived on Theta Suden. Hollick rolled his eyes before answering.

"The Ull ship I was *just* talking about," he said, indulging the new One World recruit. "They were supposed to bring in enough soldiers to overwhelm any force Webb might bring down from the *Kentucky*."

"Ah," Scarponi said. "So, they've been putting you off about where the ship is exactly but you think it's already sitting in the system." Hollick raised an eyebrow, reassessing the Navy engineer he had first assumed to be a bit dense when it came to anything that wasn't a starship engine.

"I suspect as much," he confirmed. "What about you, Scarponi? Any regrets about joining this resistance movement?"

"I'm not proud of killing Mosler, but I'm happy to do my part," Scarponi said carefully.

"Uh huh," Hollick said. The One World movement attracted two types of people: zealots and opportunists. He knew for a fact that Scarponi had been promised an obscene amount of wealth and prestige if he helped deliver Webb to Margret Jansen. "How about you keep doing your part and go keep an eye on the door of the room we stashed your old teammates in?"

"Sure."

26

"Channel open, sir."

"Lieutenant Sullivan, this is Captain Webb. What's your status?"

"I've just been waiting for word from the team, sir," Sully said. "I take it you got my message?"

"I did. Tell me, son, how did you get this node address?"

"Zadra contacted me and told me to call in our position and status to you. She's the one who gave me the address. Is something wrong, sir? I haven't been able to get a hold of Lieutenant Brown or any of the others on the ground team." Sully said.

"What shape is your gunboat in, Lieutenant?" Webb asked.

"It's rickety but functional," Sully said.

"I'm sending you a set of coordinates for a spot outside a system not far from you," Webb said, his mind racing in light of the new information his Scout Fleet pilot was telling him. "I need you to meet me there."

"You want me to abandon the ground team, sir?"

"I need you to help me save what's left of it *and* this mission,"

Webb corrected. "If I'm right, then they've either already walked into a trap or are about to."

"Location received and confirmed," Sully said, looking off-screen. "I'll be there in...four hours, assuming I don't get delayed leaving the surface."

"Make it happen, Lieutenant. Webb, out."

"This is a lot different than what you originally talked about, sir," Commander Duncan said, referring to Webb's plan to try and feel out the pilot and see if Obsidian had been further compromised.

"That little Eshquarian ship they stole isn't a threat to the *Kentucky*, and we'll stand-off at max sensor range to see if someone uninvited shows up with him," Webb assured his ship captain. "If Zadra gave him one of the secure node addresses to this ship, that means that not only has she mapped out most of our secure com system at NAVSOC, she's also likely flipped sides and is working for Jansen's people."

"And what about this other NIS agent Lieutenant Sullivan spoke of in his message?"

"Elton Hollick. If he's indeed alive and working with Jansen and the Ull, we have a real problem on our hands," Webb admitted. "With him assumed dead, a lot of codes and protocols were never rotated as they would if we'd known he was captured or flipped. Hell, for all we know, he's one of the ring leaders. Actually, that would explain a lot about how One World knows so much about our current intel apparatus and stays one step ahead of us."

"And the purpose of bringing Sullivan out here with their stolen ship?" Duncan asked.

"Playing a hunch," Webb said.

"Yes, sir." Duncan's tone wasn't openly disrespectful, but he obviously didn't like being kept in the dark.

"Don't worry, Captain, what I have planned won't put the ship at risk."

"Yes, sir."

Jacob felt immensely better within the span of two hours. The silvery line along his forehead where the nanobots were still repairing the split in the skin itched like hell, and his ankle still was a bit tender, but all things considered, he felt pretty damn good.

He'd availed himself of the house's armory again and fully outfitted himself with fresh clothing, new tactical gear, and new weaponry. The backup com equipment that was down in the subbasement wasn't of human design, looked outdated, but with the help of his neural implant he was able to determine it was functional. Unfortunately, he wasn't able to raise Sully on the gunboat or any of his team members. Jacob tried a few more tricks he knew to see if he could at least get a *ping* off any of the com gear carried by the team but ultimately decided he couldn't afford to waste any more time on it.

"Time to put up or shut up," he muttered to himself. He had no idea what had happened to Murph's recon team other than that they'd been captured by the enemy. Their numbers, armament, and intent were all a mystery to him. Everything he had assumed about the mission—even with Scarponi's betrayal—had been upended when Zadra had sold them out and admitted to manipulating them the whole time in order to get them to Theta Suden.

He felt like he was hanging on to a runaway train and the convoluted machinations of seasoned intelligence operatives trying to get an advantage over one another was something his Academy-fresh instincts and training weren't equipped to handle. But in spite of that, he felt loose and ready with just a touch of anxious energy in his gut that made him want to get started only because the waiting was so unbearable.

"Are there any vehicles on the premises?" Jacob asked the house computer. Murph had taken the boxy cargo vehicle they'd obtained at the starport.

"Affirmative. Two wheeled ground cars and one repulsor-drive air car are available for use," the computer told him.

"How rare are aircars on this world?"

"Aircar traffic accounts for seven-point-two percent of the total vehicular traffic in the metropolitan area and nineteen percent of traffic globally."

"Hmm," Jacob mused. "I think I have a really stupid idea."

The passage of time weighed heavily on his mind as he worked, rushing to the armory to pull the rest of the gear he would need and taking it to the vehicle. The aircar was under a retractable shelter on the roof so it took five trips to lug everything up the narrow staircase. Thankfully, the aircar, which was manufactured on a world he'd never heard of called Sirona-2, had been refitted with a control interface he was familiar with. It took him less than five minutes to program the vehicle to do what he wanted it to do.

On a whim, he pulled another case of munitions out of the armory and went to work on all the ground-level entries. He knew the Ull at that factory his team had been scoping out would eventually come back here to find out why their two guards—which were *really* beginning to stink—weren't answering their coms. Jacob had watched the arrogant, brash Ull in action enough by this point to know they'd likely just kick a door down than try and infiltrate through an upper window or the rooftop. If they did, the anti-personnel mines he was planting on the walls would give them his warmest regards.

"That should just about assure that I get court martialed for destroying an NIS facility," he said, setting the trigger thresholds on the last of his munitions. He set them back enough and rigged them so they wouldn't go off if the Ull used explosives to breach the doors, only when they detected the close proximity of a biological being. He just hoped Murph was right and there weren't any NIS operatives currently using the safe house who might be coming home to a nasty surprise set up by one dumbass Marine.

He grabbed the heavy plasma rifle he'd picked as his primary weapon and ran back up to the roof, his injured ankle now barely throbbing as he pushed off on the steps with all his strength. He'd tried to be smart and methodically plan his next moves like he'd been taught at the Academy, and like he thought Captain Webb would want him to do, but now that he was ready, the only thing on his mind was getting to his men. If they died because he'd wasted time here, he would never forgive himself.

"Slip-space signature is consistent with an Eshquarian Type-S1 gunboat. Looks like she has a bit of a radiation leak coming from the real-space engines."

"That's our ship," Webb said. "Hold here. Maintain EMSEC...*no* emissions of any kind, com or sensor. I want to be a dark spot in space."

"Holding fast, running silent, sir," Commander Duncan said.

"She's lit up like a flare, sir," the com officer said. "Navigational beacon and ident transponder are both squawking, and Sullivan is hailing us over short-range coms."

"Look sharp, people," Duncan said. "We're looking for another ship that should be meshing-in right on top of us within the next... forty-five minutes to an hour."

While they waited, the calls from Sullivan in the gunboat were more and more frequent. Although he maintained his professionalism over the com, Webb thought he could detect a certain resignation in the pilot's voice. Perhaps he realized he was being dangled out in space like a worm on a hook.

It was nearly an hour and fifteen tense minutes later before anything happened. The visible flash of a ship meshing-in lit up their sensors and tripped half a dozen alarms. The *Kentucky's* bridge crew reacted swiftly and, per Webb's orders, began plotting targeting solutions for the newcomer before they'd even positively identified it.

"What's the range to the gunboat?"

"Target ship is six-hundred and forty thousand klicks away from Lieutenant Sullivan's ship, sir. It's come to a full stop and is actively scanning the gunboat."

"That's our cue," Webb said. "If you would, Captain."

"Light it up!" Duncan barked. "Full active sensors. Tactical, keep both XTX missiles updated with new firing solutions. I want them both targeting the enemy amidships. Helm, begin your pursuit. Get us closer and keep our bow on that ship."

The *Kentucky* surged ahead on her gravimetric engines, bearing down on the suspected enemy ship while the tactical officer programmed two of their XTX-2 "ship buster" missiles with the targeting package. The ship may have been disguised to look like an outdated bulk freighter, but her engines and weaponry were some of the best equipment money could buy.

"Profile confirmed, sir," one of the sensor operators called. "That's a known Ull ship."

"Tell Sullivan to get the hell out of the way," Webb said. "Captain Duncan, would you do the honors?"

"With pleasure, sir." Duncan stepped forward. "Confirm targeting data."

"Target package confirmed, Captain."

"Very well. Fire missiles one and two, stagger pattern."

"Missile one, firing!" the tactical officer almost shouted. "Missile two...firing! Both missiles away and tracking to target."

"Two of our XTXs may have been gross overkill, but I believe in being thorough," Webb said quietly to Duncan.

"If one missile is good, two is better, sir."

The XTX line of missiles was equipped with a skip-drive system that made them difficult to intercept or elude. Each had a one-time use slip-drive that would allow it to close the distance with the target virtually instantaneously. The missile would re-appear in real-space close to the target and make any final course corrections it needed before impact. This meant that it had to be fired from extreme distances in order to give the skip-drive enough space to function.

"Confirmed impact! I'm not sure which one hit it, sir, but the enemy ship has been destroyed, broken into three large pieces that are drifting away from each other. No escape pods or shuttles were detected leaving the ship."

"Very good. Please put Lieutenant Sullivan through now."

"What the hell, sir?!" The pilot was visibly shaken and looked pissed. "What just exploded behind me?"

"That was the Ull support ship that you drew away from Theta Suden for us," Webb said. "Good job, Lieutenant."

"What?!"

"Bring your ship aboard, and we'll explain it to you," Webb said. "And be quick about it. Once you're docked, we'll be heading back to that moon to help out the rest of your team."

"Aye, sir!" That last part snapped Sully into action. On the sensor display, Webb could see the gunboat come about and begin accelerating towards the *Kentucky*.

"Please inform the hangar boss that we have an incoming Eshquarian ship," Duncan said. "And then have Lieutenant Sullivan escorted to the bridge."

"Aye, sir."

"That was brilliant, sir, if you don't mind me saying."

"That was mostly luck," Webb admitted. "Once we knew Zadra had flipped on us, it was a safe bet that either she or her Ull buddies had put a tracker on the ship at some point. I've also been dealing with these clowns long enough to know they'd have at least one support ship hidden in a system they were running a major counter-intelligence op in. The lucky part was that when Sullivan ran, they decided to follow him."

"Yes, sir," Duncan said. His face was still flush with the thrill of combat, even if it had been fought entirely on terminal monitors and over a distance of a few million kilometers.

"Go ahead and call this in to Fleet Ops," Webb said. "Have them send a recovery ship out to collect the wreckage for analysis. Once the gunboat is aboard and secure, set your course for Theta Suden and get us there as fast as this thing can go."

"You think the ground team has managed to survive this long without support?"

"I'm hoping against hope that they have, Commander."

27

"The second team is no longer responding on coms."

"What the fuck?! There's no way some greenhorn butter bar just took out over half your troop complement!"

"Local law enforcement is responding to reports of explosions in the area," Zadra said. She'd been pressed into service monitoring the local Nexus now that Hollick's force was being spread so thin. "I pulled up a few images from public cameras, and it looks like the front door to the safe house was blown clear of the frame. There's a lot of smoke coming from the rear of the building. Brown probably rigged both doors with explosives."

"We must assume this *budderbar* you speak of isn't so helpless," the Ull officer hissed in anger. "That's five soldiers dead because you've underestimated your opponent." Hollick was speechless for a moment. Could he have really underestimated some kid who just stepped out of the Academy? Maybe he'd not been curious enough about why Webb would put a complete rookie on one of his Scout Fleet teams. Who was this guy?

"Can you slice into the house's internal systems and see what the hell is going on?" he asked Zadra.

"Not with the access codes you gave me," she said. "It looks like the system is completely offline. I can try to find a workaround, but that will take a bit now that the locals are locking down the area."

"Forget it." He waved her off, turning back to the Ull. The arrogant bastards never gave them names to address them by. He'd be glad when Jansen was able to end her partnership with this insufferable species. "So, do you think *now* is the time to call in reinforcements from the ship?" The Ull just stared at him with its normal, unreadable expression.

"The ship is not responding to hails," it said finally. "It left high-orbit to pursue the ship our captives arrived on. We expected it back some time ago."

"Wait! Sullivan left with that stolen ship? Why isn't anyone telling me these things as they happen?!" Hollick could feel success slipping through his fingers at each new revelation. "Did that piece of shit manage to shoot down your support ship?"

"Of course not," the Ull hissed. "But it was able to elude our ship and make it to slip-space. The last transmission I received stated they had activated the tracker this Veran had attached."

"It's a burst tracker so they'd get regular updates even while the ship is in slip-space," Zadra said.

"Yeah, but if Sullivan and Brown decided to cut their losses and fly back to Terranovus, or were ordered back, how long will your ship chase them before coming back?"

"I am not in command of that ship."

"You people are utterly useless," Hollick said. "Why we're stuck with such a—" he got no further as the Ull grabbed him by the throat and lifted him off the ground.

"Remember your place, Human," it said. "It is we who are stuck in this partnership with your undesirable species, waiting for what you've promised us to be delivered. Without our aid, your own people would have hunted you down and killed you all by now. I'm beginning to think we should let them."

"Put me down...now," Hollick managed to get out. The Ull opened its hand and the ex-NIS agent hit the ground with a thud, his legs buckling.

"It looks like I picked the wrong time to flip sides," Zadra grumbled. "I would have been better off sticking with the young pup."

"Shut up," Hollick snarled. "And you, figure out a way to recall your ship or find another in—"

"Attention assholes and traitors in the building I'm currently hovering over," a voice boomed from outside. "I think it's time we made a deal."

"Who is that?!" another of the Ull asked from where it stood near an exterior door.

"That's the young human who's managed to kill five of your buddies and find our secret hideout," Hollick said. "He's in an aircraft above us. Resourceful little shit, apparently."

"I'm waiting," Brown's voice came again. "Or would you rather I alert the local authorities about this little paramilitary party you have going on in the warehouse district?"

"Inform your human soldiers I have need of them on the roof," the lead Ull said imperiously.

"That's not a good idea. This is obviously a—"

"The time for debate and half-measures is over," the Ull said. "We will eliminate this *slysta* for the lives he took, and then we will figure out how to successfully conclude this mission."

"Fine," Hollick sighed at the inevitable and keyed his com. "Baker, Miklos, leave Meyer there to guard the Marines and meet our Ull friends up on the roof. Keep sharp, the real attack will likely come from the building to the southeast."

"So, let me ask you one question," Zadra said as the two remaining Ull marched off. "Do you have a contingency plan to get out of here?"

"Without Webb there's no deal, Zadra," Hollick reminded her. "Your intel network is a tempting offer, but we both know you're unenthusiastic about handing it over to us and will likely sabotage it in ways we'll not discover until you're long gone."

"You'll still need to be alive for that," Zadra said. "As will I."

"Your survival instincts are keen, it would—"

"*Sir, it looks like this idiot is just sitting in an aircar above the building,*" Miklos's voice broke in over the com. "*If he keeps shouting over that PA, the local LEOs are going to eventually come over to see what the hell the ruckus is about. He's already drawing a crowd below.*"

"Maybe I gave him too much credit if he's actually in that thing." Hollick frowned. It didn't seem right. This kid had the balls and skill to wipe out five Ull soldiers and then sits like an idiot shouting from an aircar. Even if anyone in this district gave a shit, there wouldn't be a law enforcement response if all he was doing was being loud. He looked at Zadra, but her expression gave no hint that she knew what the jarhead lieutenant might be up to.

"Marines...so predictable," he muttered before keying his com again. "Have the Ull take him down. Try to keep out of sight, he may do something stupid like—"

An explosion rocked the building so immense that Hollick was thrown to the floor. Every window in the main factory area was blown out, and the skylights were blown in. The massive pressure wave that followed threw transit cases and equipment around the room like scrap paper in a hurricane. He could only hear a ringing in his left ear, nothing at all in the right, and his vision swam in and out of focus. Surprisingly, he found he could stand and walk, his neural implant doing its best to help his demolished inner ear maintain his balance.

"What in the unholy hell was that?!" he shouted, barely hearing his own voice.

Jacob knew he'd royally screwed up when he triggered the explosives he'd planted in the aircar before one of the Ull could shoot it down. It was supposed to be enough of a focused explosion to create a downward pressure wave that would incapacitate anybody stupid enough to have climbed up on the roof when he was yelling and disorient everyone in the building when the skylights gave and the building over-pressured.

Instead, the blast had launched everyone that wasn't vaporized off the rooftop so quickly that Jacob had barely been able to track them, and he'd seen the walls of the factory bulge in places from the pressure wave directed inside. He must have completely miscalculated how many demo packs he needed for the desired effect. There was no way an explosion that size was going to go unnoticed by the local authorities. Worse than all that, however, was the fact he'd been standing too close to the building when he'd triggered the blast and had been launched into the door of a freight entrance to the building across the street.

Now a little woozy and feeling like he may have cracked a couple ribs, he was running full tilt for a door in the factory wall that had been blown open by his careless application of high explosives. He'd actually rigged a spot on the wall he planned to breach after his... diversion...but thought better of triggering another explosion after the first mishap.

He didn't know where his team might be in the building—assuming he hadn't inadvertently killed them all—so he dialed the aperture on his plasma rifle all the way down for pinpoint fire. They weren't terribly accurate weapons by nature, but at least he wouldn't be saturating the place with wide-area bursts. With any luck, the handful of bodies he'd seen hurling from the rooftop at near-supersonic speeds were the bulk of the defenders.

When he moved into the building, the first thing he saw was Weef Zadra lying prone on the floor. There wasn't anybody else visible but there was a lot inside the factory to hide behind. His boots crunched over the broken glass of the skylights as he made his way cautiously to the downed Veran.

"Zadra, you alive?" He gently nudged her with his toe as he continued to scan the area. "Zadra!"

"Y-yes...I think I'm still alive. Did *you* do that?"

"It was an accident," Jacob said. "Where's everyone else?"

"Hollick ran—I have no idea how, I can't even stand up—and the rest were on the roof," she said, her voice shaky. "Your team is in the last office on the left when you go up those stairs."

"You stay right fucking here," Jacob said, barely controlling his temper. "I should shoot you for what you did."

"You're too smart for that, Pup," she smiled at him, lying flat on her back. "I'm still the mission...at least for you. I think I saw your traitor engineer go up on the roof, so congratulations there."

"Stay here," he repeated. He had restraints but not enough for both sets of arms and her legs.

"I wouldn't go anywhere even if I could feel my legs, which I can't. Thanks for that."

Jacob did another quick scan of the area before sprinting for the stairs to the mezzanine. Since the office complex above the factory floor was essentially a building inside of a building, everything upstairs looked surprisingly undamaged. There was a tipped over chair here and there, but the walls and doors were all still intact.

When he cleared a corner to move where his team was being held, he saw a human standing guard by the door. Without thinking, he raised his weapon and fired. The pinpoint plasma bolt struck the guard in the throat and dropped him before he could raise his own weapon or sound the alarm. Jacob felt little remorse for the kill. The man was one of Hollick's people and therefore a traitor, the same as Scarponi.

The man didn't get back up, so Jacob continued to advance. He made a mental note that his weapon seemed to shoot high since he'd been aiming center-mass on the target. There was no sign of anyone else guarding the office, so he picked up the pace. Maybe it was target fixation on the door his men were behind, maybe it was because he didn't have enough experience to temper his impatience. Whatever the reason, Jacob walked by an open office door without clearing the room.

A shot he never heard took him in the back where his soft-armor was able to absorb and dissipate most of its energy. He instinctually tried to move away from the source of intense heat, at first not realizing he'd been shot with an energy weapon, and his dive to the left likely saved his life. The second shot passed within millimeters of his head, the intense heat of the plasma burning away his hair and peeling away the skin of his scalp. Jacob kicked backwards with his right leg as he fell, his boot making contact with someone's shin and eliciting a grunt of pain.

"Hold still, you little shit!"

A third shot went far wide and burned into the wall, not even close to where Jacob had been. He rolled to his right and looked up. There, still standing in the doorway, was Scarponi. The traitor had a plasma pistol and was waving it at him.

"Hands off the weapon," Scarponi ordered. "Toss it aside, asshole." Jacob popped the quick-disconnect on his sling to detach the plasma rifle and shrugged it aside, keeping his hands up.

"What're you waiting for?" Jacob asked, tasting the hot bitterness of defeat. Not only will Earth not get Weef Zadra's network, his men will still be held hostage and, in the ultimate insult, the man who killed his CO will also be the one who kills him.

"You're going to join your Obsidian buds in that office right after I restrain you," Scarponi said. "I'll let Hollick decide what to do with you. Mosler thought you were hot shit before he brought you aboard, so who knows, maybe Earth will negotiate for your release."

"Not the brains of this operation, I see." Jacob shook his head. "Hollick is gone, dipshit. Everyone else is dead or hasn't landed yet after being blown off the roof, and Earth isn't going to negotiate for the return of one measly ass lieutenant."

"So, you're arguing in favor of my shooting you?" Scarponi asked. "Don't move!" Jacob had rolled to his right slightly to conceal that his sidearm was still holstered on his thigh. The fact the engineer had been so focused on the rifle and not the other weapons Jacob carried told him Scarponi was out of his depth.

"I'm not moving," Jacob said. "Look, there's no reason to— Did you hear that?"

"You can't possibly think I'm that stupid," Scarponi said. "You carrying any restraints? Where are they?"

"Right calf pocket," Jacob said. "I brought them hoping I'd get to ship you and Hollick back to Taurus Station in them. Seriously, though, I heard something. It sounded like maybe the roof getting ready to give."

"Cocky ass lieutenant," Scarponi scoffed and walked over to Jacob's right. "You couldn't even manage to—" the loud groaning of metal reached their ears, and the floor seemed to drop an inch or so. Apparently, the mezzanine hadn't escaped being damaged after all.

Scarponi had been in the process of bending down to check the calf pocket when the tremor hit and was thrown off balance. Jacob acted without thinking, lashing out hard with his left foot and catching the traitor in the stomach and sending him backwards. Scarponi's eyes widened in surprise, but he never let go of his pistol. Jacob drew his own weapon while Scarponi, now realizing how badly he'd screwed up, raised his at the same time. Jacob panicked and fired first without aiming before Scarponi could get his weapon up for a kill shot.

Jacob hit the engineer in the left outer thigh, the close-range shot obliterating the unprotected flesh when it struck. Scarponi howled and fired as he fell to his left, the shot sailing wide and harmlessly hitting the far wall. Jacob fired twice more, his pistol still resting on the floor, and scored two more hits along his target's unprotected left side. Scarponi rolled to his right and curled up into a fetal ball, moaning in agony as the smells of scorched flesh and burned clothing filled the hall.

"Moron," Jacob muttered, rolling to his knees and yanking Scarponi's pistol from his hand. The moaning engineer didn't even react. After retrieving his rifle, Jacob jogged to the door at the end of the hall, pulled the dead guard out of the way, and kicked it in.

His team was all lined up, sitting in chairs that were too big for them and restrained. They looked like they'd been worked over pretty good from the bruising and cuts he saw on their faces, but they were otherwise unharmed.

"Holy shit! LT!? What happened to you? It looks like half your head has been burned off."

"We need to move!" Jacob said, pulling his combat knife and

cutting through the plastic restraints holding Murph to the chair. He then handed the Murph the knife and pointed to the others. "Free them. Mettler, Scarponi is in the hall and needs medical attention. We're taking him with us. I'm going back down to collect Zadra, and then we need to get out of here. Fast!"

"After that first explosion, I figured Webb sent a ship to hit the place with an orbital strike," MG said. "What the hell was that?"

"Later," Jacob said. "Hurry!"

Jacob raced back down the hall, stopping to check that Scarponi was still out of commission, and ran down the stairs to get to the factory floor. He came around the corner of a machine just in time to see Hollick trying to pull Zadra up onto her feet. The Veran looked to be resisting, but she was obviously still in no shape to put up much of a fight.

"Hollick! Drop her!" Jacob shouted, sighting down his rifle at the ex-spook.

"Lieutenant Brown!" Hollick smiled. "So, you survived your own idiocy. Impressive." Before Jacob could say anything else, Hollick looped an arm under Zadra and pulled her around in front of him, using her as a shield and pressing the muzzle of his pistol into her head. "Careful, Lieutenant, you wouldn't want to explain to Captain Webb how you made it all this way and then shot through your mission objective to get to me."

"Great, another standoff," Jacob muttered. He was running on fumes at this point, the constant running, shooting, surviving, and adrenaline dumps having sapped away his energy to the point that he felt like a wet noodle. There was almost a sense of detachment as his neural implant worked to block the pain signals from the worst of his injuries, like he was watching everything happen to someone else instead of him.

"I just want out of here, Brown," Hollick said. "I'll take her to keep everyone honest. We'll all go home, lick our wounds, and then you guys can take another crack at getting her."

"That's not—" the sound of running feet cut Jacob off. Hollick looked to his right and yanked his pistol away from Zadra's head, firing wildly at something Jacob couldn't see from his vantage point. Since nobody was returning fire, he had to assume it was his own people. They must have taken a different route across the factory floor when they came down.

He still couldn't get a clean shot at any of Hollick's vital areas with Zadra in the way, but the idiot was holding his pistol far out and away from his body. Jacob lined up his shot, remembered that the rifle hit a little high, and squeezed off a quick burst. The brilliant blue bolts hit Hollick mid-forearm, severing his hand and sending it, and his pistol, spinning away. Astonishingly, that only seemed to piss him off. He gave Jacob a hate filled glare before shoving Zadra away and sprinting the opposite direction.

Jacob went to give chase but his legs felt like rubber. He was spent. By the time he made it to Zadra, his team was walking into view, Mettler dragging a bandaged up Scarponi, and the others checking the area for any weapons they could use to defend themselves.

"Take a load off, LT, and I'll check you over," Mettler said. "That head injury looks pretty bad."

"It's not great," Jacob agreed, sinking to the floor and resting his back up against a crate. "I'll just be right here if you guys need me."

"Murph's going to find a workable com so we can call in the cavalry," Mettler told him. "Just hang on and we'll get you patched up. You did good, LT."

Jacob's vision blurred and tunneled as he tried to watch his team go about their tasks. Fight it though he tried, he slipped into unconsciousness moments later.

28

"You back among the living, kid?"

Jacob's mind was still a little fuzzy, and he figured he must still be unconscious and dreaming. There was almost no pain throughout his body, and it felt like he was lying in a plush, comfortable bed. When he cracked his eye open, he was assaulted by a bright, white light and a moan escaped his lips.

"Shit, sorry. Is that better?"

When he opened them again the room was much dimmer, but no less confusing. The last thing he remembered was slumping over on a factory floor on Theta Suden, but now it looked like he was in a hospital room of some sort.

"Med bay on the *UES Kentucky*." Captain Webb seemed to read his mind. "Murphy got hold of a com unit on the surface and called in your status. We were already in orbit so we sent a team to retrieve you. It was a race to get there before the locals did, but we were able to extract you without much trouble."

"My men?"

"Safe, sound, and bored." Webb smiled. "You've been sedated for a few days while the doc tended to your injuries. The broken ribs were no big deal, but that plasma bolt that grazed your melon did some real damage. Even with all the slick nano-tech we have now, you're still going to have a hell of a scar."

"Zadra?" Jacob's mind was starting to chug up to full speed and the memory of all that happened on that godforsaken moon was coming back.

"She's in a VIP suite two decks down. You did damn good securing her, Lieutenant...damn good."

"Sir, she sold us out." Jacob tried to sit up. "When we—"

"I know, I know." Webb pushed him back down. "Welcome to the intelligence world...where you can't trust anybody, not even yourself. Murphy and Mettler filled me in on most of the gory details about how she'd been manipulating things since Niceen-3."

"They wanted you," Jacob said, his eyes narrowing. "Hollick didn't give a damn about her intel network, they were trying to get you specifically there."

"Yes," Webb said simply. "The reason for that is classified about a million levels above your paygrade, but I can let you have a peek. You're aware that the new classes of starships being built by humans are far more advanced than our first efforts, right?"

"Sure."

"Well, they're also quite a bit more advanced than most space-faring species in this quadrant can build," Webb said. "We've publicly said we reverse engineered the ships from the first alien attack on Earth, but that's only part of the truth. We've had some...help...along the way. Margaret Jansen has managed to figure that out and who the key players involved were. She thinks that if she captures one of us, we'll be able to lead her to the source."

"Since you're telling me this, I'm assuming that's not the case," Jacob said. "Either that or you're going to kill me."

"She's mistaken in her belief that we'd be able to gain her access," Webb said. "I think she assumes that it's just a... You know what? Never mind. It doesn't matter either way because all of the principle players involved have agreed that none of us will be taken alive to be questioned and we've ensured that with certain steps." Jacob decided he'd rather not know any more. He'd carried so many secrets since finding out about his parentage as a teenager that he didn't need another on top of it.

"What happens now, sir?"

"We're about a week away from Terranovus, where I'll either be commended for successfully retrieving the asset or relieved of command because one of my *covert* recon teams blew up two buildings on one world, shot up an apartment building on another, and during all that, found time to steal an unlicensed warship from a starport because they scuttled their own irreplaceable vessel," Webb said. "Oh, you meant what happens to you?"

"Yes, sir," Jacob said, deciding not to refute the captain's laundry list of fuck-ups he'd been central to on this mission.

"In your own way, you successfully wrapped up your mission and satisfied the terms of our deal," Webb said. "I'll cash in a few favors and you'll be an ensign in the Navy and put back on the career track of serving aboard capital ships, if that's what you still want, of course."

There it was. After that nightmare of a mission Webb was going to honor his deal and Jacob would get what he wanted. So why was he hesitating?

"This job...it's...*important*, isn't it, sir?" Jacob was struggling to put his thoughts into words.

"Sure." Webb shrugged. "You remember what you're taught at the Academy: *all* jobs in the UEAS are important. From the lowly cook to the—"

"You know what I mean, sir," Jacob interrupted. "This mission...we were right in the middle of something huge, something that would have a large impact on Earth as a whole."

"I know what you mean," Webb said. "While I'm tempted to take advantage of your post-op enthusiasm, let me temper it with a dose of reality. Most missions aren't like this one. For the most part, my Scout Fleet teams do a lot of boring recon of systems and planets at the behest of Fleet. It's probable you'd go the rest of your career without getting shot in the head again or having to outwit another ex-spy that faked his own death and is working with our enemies.

"You do seem to have a knack for this work. You also seem to share your father's unbridled passion for destroying large tracts of property to minimally advance your mission goals, but a knack nonetheless. This work is important, but I won't lie to you and say it's always this...exciting."

"Would I get to stay with Obsidian?" Jacob asked.

"Yes, but I can't leave you in overall command of the team as a second lieutenant," Webb said. "This was an oddball situation, but before Obsidian is deployed again, I'll have to move over one of our more experienced team commanders to take Mosler's spot."

"Understood," Jacob said, secretly relieved. And in that sense of relief he had his answer. Somewhere between being pissed off about getting forced into NAVSOC and running a counterintelligence operation on an alien world, the idea of spending the rest of his career trying to climb the political ladder of starship command no longer appealed to him like it once did.

"If it's all the same to you, sir, I think I'll stay where I am."

"Very well, Marine." Webb stood up. "Somehow, I thought that might be your answer."

"Can I still have that political favor you were going to burn and save it for later?"

"Don't push it."

Webb's return to Taurus Station was not that of a conquering hero. In his absence, Admiral Remey had done a lot of damage, likely because she saw an opportunity to edge Webb out and take command of NAVSOC herself. On Earth, she was little more than a glorified errand runner despite the star on her collar. But on Terranovus, she could rule over an entire section that came with its own fleet, fat budget, and a secret base. When Webb had fled aboard the *Kentucky* to salvage the Zadra operation, Remey had quickly gone to work using her contacts in Central Command get her reports to the right people and paint a picture that Captain Webb was a dangerous loose cannon who was only barely in control of his own people.

The result was that by the time Webb's Jumper landed on the pad, his *secret* installation was awash in brass and their staff, all waiting for his return. He'd been given a bit or pre-warning from one of his more loyal aides who had managed to get a message to the *Kentucky* in a clever roundabout way, so when he landed at his base, he was ready for the firing squad Remey had doubtless organized in his honor.

"Captain Webb, your presence is requested in base ops immediately, sir."

"Understood. Please have Commander Waterman called down there to meet me."

"Sorry, sir, but Lieutenant Commander Waterman has been reassigned. He's no longer on Taurus Station."

Now Webb was pissed. They must have found out that Waterman had warned him about Remey's witch hunt and had the officer shipped off where he couldn't cause any more trouble. When he marched into base ops, he was directed to one of the main conference rooms. He couldn't help but notice all the extra security in place around the building, most of them Navy military police and not ones he recognized. He was escorted into the room and offered a seat while Remey and a vice admiral he'd never seen before walked in with their staff in tow.

"Captain Webb, welcome back," Remey said. "This is Vice Admiral Wynne, he's here at my request to discuss some of the…irregularities…I've discovered during your recent disappearance."

"I did not disappear, Admiral," Webb said. "As I clearly stated to you when you arrived, I had active operations in the field that I needed to support."

"And that's where you were?" Wynne asked, not bothering to offer a greeting or proper introduction. "On an active operation?"

"Yes, sir. One that was successfully concluded, I might add."

"What was the mission?" Wynne asked.

"I don't know if you have the clearance to know that, sir," Webb said. "This was a mission for NIS at the request of Director Welford." Wynne's expression was blank, but Webb could see the red creeping up his neck and the flushing of his cheeks. He probably could have handled that better.

The cat and mouse game went back and forth for the better part of an hour. The longer it went, the worse it got for Remey. She'd had to admit more than once in front of her boss that she'd far exceeded her authority as an observer by assuming authority over the base without knowing where Webb had gone or why. Wynne had insisted that a unique, composite force like Scout Fleet made more sense as an NIS managed program until Webb had shown that most of the work they did was directly for Fleet Ops, not NIS.

By the end of the second hour, the tables had been turned and Remey was fighting for her professional life as Wynne grilled her on the content of her reports and her baseless insinuations. Webb felt genuinely bad for her. She probably saw an opportunity, miscalculated when she thought she could push a lowly captain aside to get it, and was then committed to riding it all the way into the ground afterward. It was the sort of political bullshit that infected the command structure of any large military organization.

"One last issue, Captain, and then I'll let you get back to your duties," Wynne said. "We've received some disturbing reports about the actions of one of your Scout Fleet teams...lots of collateral damage and destroyed Fleet equipment in the course of a simple recovery mission. Where is that team now?"

"Unfortunately, that team suffered heavy casualties during that mission, sir," Webb said, now aware that Wynne had already known all the details of the Zadra mission when he'd asked the first time. "The surviving members are recovering in an NIS facility until they're fit to travel back to Terranovus."

In truth, the remaining members of Team Obsidian had loaded back aboard their stolen gunboat and had flown to a planet called Fideon Prime, where they were staying at another NIS safe house. At least Webb had been honest about that last part. When he'd learned about the potential political fallout waiting for them back on Terranovus, he had put Sullivan in command of the team and ordered them someplace outside of Naval jurisdiction and told them to lay low until he sorted things out. He didn't want his low-ranking personnel getting caught up in a dragnet meant for him.

Once he was certain Remey's half-assed attempt to get his job had died out completely, he'd send word and recall the team...maybe. The more he thought about it, the more it made sense to not have 3rd Scout Corps teams based out of Terranovus. Maybe he could work out a deal with Director Welford and have them deployed remotely so they'd be able to more efficiently respond when a tasking came down. His internal musings were interrupted when he realized that Wynne had addressed him.

"Sir?" he asked.

"I said you're dismissed, Captain," Wynne said. "We won't need to take up any more of your time for the rest of this."

"Of course, sir." Webb stood. "Have a safe flight back to Earth, Admirals."

"Like father, like son," Director Michael Welford said, whistling in appreciation at the damage Jacob Brown had done in the course of rescuing his own men. The images on the large wall monitor in his office were from the *Kentucky*, taken when the ship had been in low orbit.

"So it would seem, but don't tell him that," Webb said, swirling the expensive whiskey in his glass. "That kid really hates his old man."

"The best soldiers usually do," Welford said. "They always seem to fight just a little harder with that chip on their shoulder. We do need to be careful, however. If Burke finds out—"

"I know, I know." Webb waved him off. "But Jacob volunteered for this in the end. I gave him the option of getting out and standing around on a fleet cruiser playing grab ass while they fly around following a Cridal ship."

"You're in an odd mood considering the fact we've successfully acquired one of the most extensive intelligence networks in the region," Welford said.

"How is Zadra?"

"Loaded up onto a high-speed transport and on her way to the Avarian Empire to start her new life. Everything she gave us checks out. It won't be cheap to use her network as a strategic asset, but it'll be worth it."

"As to why I'm in a mood, you don't find it just a bit depressing at how many people the One World faction has been able to flip?" Webb asked. "I never saw how deep the poison had gotten, and that lack of sight cost me one of my best people."

"We've got Scarponi in advanced interrogation," Welford said. "But none of this is why I wanted to talk to you in person."

"Oh boy, I can't wait for this," Webb said.

"I've been hearing rumors that Earth is propping up some black programs having to do with genetic manipulation," Welford said.

"The super-soldier shit *again?*" Webb groaned. "Every group of volunteers has gone batshit crazy and homicidal whenever we've messed around with their genetic makeup."

"With all the new nano-tech we've gotten recently, along with the reports from people who've seen Jason Burke in action, someone has decided that it's worth another look," Welford said. "The reason I'm telling you is that I'm worried stories about your new Scout Fleet lieutenant's feats of strength may put him on the wrong person's radar. If you want him to live his life other than as a lab rat, I'd suggest you tell him to keep it reined in."

"Noted," Webb said. "And you've just reminded me of something I wanted to ask you. If we can make my idea work, it'll make it that much harder for some black program to get their hands on him."

"No promises," Welford said. "You still owe me a new safe house on Theta Suden out of your budget."

"You'll love this. Trust me."

EPILOGUE

Team Obsidian had been sitting around doing nothing for the better part of two months now, with no word from Command. Jacob's injuries were fully healed, though he now had a jagged, nasty looking scar down the right side of his head. Murph wasn't sure what his status was since his cover was completely blown, but he hadn't been recalled by his NIS handlers either. For the time being, he was still taking orders as if he was a Marine staff sergeant.

Sully was in overall command of the team now since he was the highest-ranking officer left alive after their last mission. The team didn't need a lot of managing so his job was fairly easy. The world they'd been ordered to was nice, but it was the interminable waiting that was starting to set everyone on edge. Had Command forgot about them? They knew Webb was still in command of NAVSOC, so they assumed he remembered where he'd stashed one of his 3rd Scout Corps teams.

"The proximity alarm on the ship just triggered again," Sully yelled from the kitchen. "Who wants to check it this time?"

"I'll get it," Jacob said. The gunboat was parked at an airfield since the closest starport was over two hundred kilometers away from the safe house. Sully hadn't wanted their only ride off-world being hours away by public transit, so he opted for a local cargo airport instead. The problem was that young Vothans played games along the fence where the ship was parked and would sometimes set off the proximity sensors. For Jacob, each time they did it was a golden opportunity to get out of the house and away from his teammates for an hour or so.

He ran all the way to the airfield, enjoying being able to fully inhale now that his ribs had healed up. As he expected, the ship seemed to be untouched. He boarded and went up to the flightdeck to make sure it had just been one of the security sensors like they assumed. He reset the system, took one last look around, and walked back down onto the main deck where a surprise was waiting for him.

He wasn't alone.

"Please, sit," the voice rumbled out of a powerfully built alien. The being exuded power and confidence, and Jacob found himself obeying without thinking. There were some things that transcended species, and this alien had an aura of danger lingering about him. He was also dressed in a manner that indicated he was quite wealthy.

"A human. Imagine my surprise when my people told me it was a human crew who had stolen my ship and its cargo. Your species is so brazen. I've had many dealings with a few of your kind, and it always costs me money. Do you know who I am?"

"Saditava Mok," Jacob said, the pieces falling in place in his mind.

"You know who I am and still you stole the ship?" Mok asked.

"Like I said...brazen. What's your name?"

"Jacob Brown. We didn't know the ship was yours when we took it. If we had, we'd have probably picked another target."

"That would have been for the best," Mok agreed. "Normally, my people would have just killed you on principle before bringing something so trivial to my attention, but I stepped in when I received an interesting message regarding a possible coup attempt within my organization that you uncovered. So, what am I to do? Look weak by letting you live after stealing my money, or take the dishonorable path and kill you just to save face after you've given me such valuable information?"

Jacob said nothing, convinced he was about to die. Maybe he could turn over the accounts with all the money they'd taken and Mok would let him walk away. Doubtful, but worth a try.

"You're not a smuggler or a ship thief," Mok said after staring at him a moment. "You reek of military, and not ex-military turned mercenary either. You're somebody's operational asset."

"I can't answer that, sir."

"And yet you just did," Mok laughed. "I'm not going to kill you, Jacob Brown."

"No?"

"No." Mok stood and smoothed out his suit. "You're either one of Marcus Webb's or Michael Welford's people. Tell whichever it is to be more careful who they're stealing from in the future."

"That's it? Just the message?"

"Oh, no," Mok laughed again. "In exchange for your life, you now owe me a favor. And let me be clear: *you* owe me a favor, not your chain of command or homeworld...you. Does that sound fair?"

"How big a favor?"

"At least equal to the value you place on your own life, which I have magnanimously allowed you to keep for the time being," Mok said.

"Fair enough," Jacob said, his ass beginning to unclench as it looked like he might survive in the short term. Mok pulled an odd-looking com unit and tossed it on the galley table.

"Keep this," he said. "Make sure to check it often. I already have your slip-com address from the ship's computer so I'll be able to keep tabs on you. Welcome to the game, kid."

"Are you taking the ship back?"

"This piece of refuse is of little value to me without its crew or cargo," Mok said, and then he was gone.

Jacob sat there for a long moment thinking about the implications of what he'd just done. Sure, he got to keep breathing for a while longer, which was good. But now he owed a favor to one of the quadrants most notorious crime bosses, something of equal value to his own life. That didn't sound promising. It was almost certain that his command wouldn't be too thrilled with whatever task Mok set him to.

"Eh," he grunted, standing up. "Maybe he'll forget all about me."

ALSO BY JOSHUA DALZELLE

Thank you for reading *Marine*.

If you enjoyed the story, Lieutenant Brown and the guys will be back in:

Boneshaker

Terran Scout Fleet, Book 2.

For news on upcoming projects and new releases, connect with me on Facebook and Twitter:

www.facebook.com/Joshua.Dalzelle

@JoshuaDalzelle

Check out my Amazon page to see my other works including the #1 bestselling military science fiction series: *The Black Fleet Trilogy* along with the international bestselling *Omega Force Series*.

www.amazon.com/author/joshuadalzelle

(Continue on for a word from the author…)

AFTERWORD

When I first decided to add another series to the Omega Force Universe it was for two reasons: I wanted to do a more traditional military sci-fi within that universe that centered around Earth's new space military, but I also wanted to isolate Jason Burke from that story. A lot of the dynamic that makes Omega Force work is that Jason is (usually) the only human in the story. I felt like if that series became inundated with humans from a slip-space capable Earth that it would begin to lose a big part of what many found appealing about it. (For those that haven't read Omega Force, many of the events alluded to in "Marine" took place in book eight of that series and the timeline of this story starts just at the end of book ten.)

As some of my regular readers correctly guessed when I announced this series, I decided to provide some continuity by using Jason Burke's son as my main character. Jacob Brown seemed to be the most obvious choice for a number of reasons. He was different and unique thanks to his genes, had already been exposed to the outside galaxy, and his low opinion of his father is an interesting dynamic to play with.

This is the type of small-unit focused military sci-fi that I most enjoy writing. I feel like once stories grow in scope to the point that you have entire fleets/planets/species going to war with each other that the individual characters can become lost due to the sheer scale of what you're trying to write. A favorite series of mine, "The Corps" by W.E.B. Griffin was a large influence in how I built this story. In Griffin's series, Ken "Killer" McCoy is just an enlisted Marine that is often tangentially involved in some of the most important events during WWII, but his story is very much about a single Marine doing his job, not singlehandedly saving the world. I wanted to try and emulate that by having Jacob—a fresh second lieutenant—brushing up against monumental events but still be well within his role as a team member in a forward observation unit.

I was careful to avoid the trap of making Team Obsidian just a mirror of Omega Force by including a battlesynth and a Galvetic warrior (which is how the first outline was written) and stick to it being a team of only humans. Hopefully the Omega Force faithful enjoyed the cameo appearances by some of that series' supporting characters.

So, the big question... will the two teams ever cross paths in either series? It's highly likely, but it won't be in the near future. Any potential meeting will be a huge turning point in the lives of both main characters so I need to make sure it's done in such a way that it serves both series.

Thanks again to all the regular readers and to the first timers... it's truly a privilege to be able to share these stories with so many people.

Cheers!

Josh

Printed in Great Britain
by Amazon